NORFOLK BOY

Dennis A Roberts

The Book Guild Ltd

First published in Great Britain in 2024 by
The Book Guild Ltd
Unit E2 Airfield Business Park,
Harrison Road, Market Harborough,
Leicestershire. LE16 7UL
Tel: 0116 2792299
www.bookguild.co.uk
Email: info@bookguild.co.uk
X: @bookguild

Copyright © 2024 Dennis A Roberts

The right of Dennis A Roberts to be identified as the author of this
work has been asserted by them in accordance with the
Copyright, Design and Patents Act 1988.

All rights reserved. No part of this publication may be
reproduced, transmitted, or stored in a retrieval system, in any form or by any means,
without permission in writing from the publisher, nor be otherwise circulated in
any form of binding or cover other than that in which it is published and without
a similar condition being imposed on the subsequent purchaser.

This work is entirely fictitious and bears no resemblance to any persons living or dead.

Typeset in 11pt Minion Pro

Printed and bound by CPI Group (UK) Ltd, Croydon, CR0 4YY

ISBN 978 1835741 023

British Library Cataloguing in Publication Data.
A catalogue record for this book is available from the British Library.

PROLOGUE

June 1839

Filled with dread, Isaac looked around the wood-panelled courtroom searching for a friendly face. If only one of his family were here, or the lads from the yard.

All around him the townsfolk gossiped and argued as they waited to hear the verdict. He had tried to tell the court that it was a mistake, that he was an honest boy, but each time the judge had bellowed at him to be quiet. If only he had remained in the Brecks, never gone to Newmarket, none of this would have happened. He could have been happy at the hall, safe with his family.

Unable to stop his arms trembling, he gripped the rail and looked across the court to where twelve men huddled together, occasionally glancing at him as they talked in hushed voices.

Once they were back in their places, the elderly judge – seated beneath a soaring, carved canopy – furiously banged the desk, the black sleeve of his robe trimmed with white ermine cutting the dusty air as he shouted to make himself heard.

Sure his legs were about to give way, Isaac felt the breath of the constable who stood behind him in the dock brush his neck. His heart racing at the pace of thoroughbreds pounding across the gallops, he listened as the judge put down his gavel and addressed a portly, well-dressed man, who had risen unsteadily to his feet.

'Foreman of the jury. Do you find the defendant, Isaac Bone, guilty or not guilty?'

ONE

March 1835 – Norfolk

The warmth of the straw mattress was refusing to let Isaac go as he stirred at the voice of his older sister, Alice. Still sleepy, he watched fingers of silvery light creep through the slatted window and across the floor, the sparrows and finches outside chirping their welcome to a new day in the Brecks.

Born and raised in the small village of Tottington, yesterday had been his twelfth birthday. The end of days spent trapping rabbits on the warren with his friends, of warm, lazy days by the shallow waters of the pond, of lessons at the small flint schoolhouse. Today, like his father and generations of his family before him, he would enter into a lifetime of service at the hall.

Reluctant to rise, he tugged the patched blanket over his head and tried to shut out his sister's threats to go without him. Unable to ignore her any longer, he slipped from beneath the thin blanket and felt around in the early light for his breeches, careful not to wake his two younger sisters, curled up together on the pallet bed opposite. The floor was cold beneath his feet as he tiptoed across the room, still threading the leather belt around his narrow waist, and pulled back the ragged curtain to find his sister waiting, holding out a pair of worn, scuffed black boots, a look of frustration on her face.

More used to the sand of the Brecks between his toes, he reached out and took the boots. Too big for his young feet, he slipped them on and pulled the laces as tight as he could, throwing his sister a sideways glance.

'I could almost get both feet in one boot,' Isaac grumbled.

'Don't exaggerate,' Alice said. 'Mother had to scrimp and go without to buy you those, so stop complaining.'

Isaac looked across to the stove where his mother stood, her hair now almost white, the constant worry of how to keep them all fed and clothed etched deep into her brow. Wiping her hands on her apron, she walked towards him and planted a kiss lightly on top of his mop of unruly black hair. 'Your father would be so proud of you,' she said. 'All grown up, a proper little man.'

Without taking it out, Isaac felt in his pocket for the small horse brass given to him by his father. As he traced the curves of the precious keepsake, he thought back to the golden summer day when he had sat and watched his father buckle the new harnesses for the plough horses. Once finished, his father had handed him the leftover brass, its polished yellow metal cold to touch. A promise made to keep it safe.

'Now, Isaac,' his mother waved a finger at him, 'it was lucky a position became available when the Parks moved away. Your wages will help make ends meet, so remember your place and don't go speaking out of turn. People like His Lordship don't want to hear what you have to say – we have our place and his type have theirs. Just you remember that, and you'll be fine. Promise me?'

Isaac reached up and pecked his mother on the cheek. 'I promise,' he said before winking at his two sisters, now awake and standing side by side in the doorway.

'Alice, are you ready?' he goaded his sister. 'I can't wait for you. I'll be late.' Ducking a playful swipe, he dashed towards the door and flung it open, the dozen or so chickens pecking lazily at the earth scattered by the sudden commotion.

Their breath hung in the crisp air of the new spring day as Isaac and his sister walked briskly past the village church of St Andrew's. Nearly a year had gone by since his family and friends had stood, tears running down their faces, as they watched his father lowered into the sandy ground. When his father had first fallen ill, he had brushed aside their worries, telling them it would pass. But as the weeks went by, they had watched their father's strength seep away, until he was barely able to rise from his bed. They had spent what little savings they had on doctors and medicines, and when His Lordship had heard, he had sent his own physician, but it was too late. The kindly man who never raised his voice to man nor beast faded away.

Beyond the church, the narrow track was hemmed with stubby gorse, its yellow flowers a welcome shot of colour across the ever-present browns and greens of the sandy breck. They skirted the plantation of soldier-straight pines and headed towards the pond. A sharp gust of wind shrieked across the heath, its icy blast slapping their faces as they closed their eyes tight against the fine sand thrown up in its wake. As the rush died away, Isaac looked down at the unfamiliar black boots. When his mother had told him there was a position at the hall stables for a furrow boy, he had felt relief that he would follow in his father's footsteps, working in the open air and on the land and with the horses, rather than in the rigid, stuffy formality of the hall that Alice was always talking about. When his father had been alive, Isaac had often visited the stables, watching in awe as he calmed the sleek, powerful hunters with a soft word, or coaxed the shaggy-footed punches to move. But now, in the bitter cold of the early morning, he wasn't so certain.

There was a second gush of wind, and the pines shuddered in its breath as he felt his chest tighten and had a strange notion his future would take him away from the Brecks. No one from his family had ever left the Brecks; born, living and dying here, just like his father. Overhead the sky hung grey and unbroken as he tried to push the thought from his mind, telling himself that his life would be spent at the hall. Still uneasy, he shivered and yanked up his collar, tucking his hands deep into his pockets, and prayed it wouldn't rain.

TWO

With Warren Hall in sight, Isaac stooped and rubbed at his already sore heels. The grand two-storey red-brick hall stood defiant against the wide Breckland sky. Owned by the Stanton family since Tudor times, the hall was surrounded by a low wall; an intricate pair of wrought-iron gates guarded the entrance to the hall, with a gilded stag at their centre. Isaac had spent many happy times at the stables with his father, but he had never been inside the hall, and he marvelled at the rows of square glass windows stretching away on each side of the imposing arched doorway. He could hardly count how many rooms there were, but his sister had told him that when the bell in the servant's hall rang, it took five minutes to get to the dayroom or the library at either end of the hall's wings, but only if they hurried.

It was forbidden for servants to walk down the drive, so Isaac and his sister skirted round towards the stables along the towering wall that protected the fruit and vegetable gardens, the gravel path scrunching beneath their feet. Without warning, a sturdy wooden gate in the wall flew open, and an excited brown-and-white terrier raced out, the panting, red-faced gamekeeper close behind.

'Good morning, Alice. Morning, Isaac.' The gamekeeper doffed his cap and wiped his brow. 'Sorry if I startled you. When this one gets a scent, I can't keep up with him.'

Isaac grinned as the impatient terrier scampered in circles around his legs. He had known the gamekeeper since he was old enough to walk, often visiting the small lodge on the far side of the estate with his family. They had spent hours together as he had learnt how to snare rabbits and to track the hoofprints of the red deer that roamed the estate. Each spring he would hold in the palm of his hand the pheasant chicks that would be reared over the summer for the autumn shoots, their feathers downy and warm.

'Look at you. All dressed up in your jacket and black boots. First day?' the gamekeeper asked. 'Suspect there will be plenty to keep you busy, and if you have half the talent your father had, you will have those horses eating out of your hand in no time. Mind, your father was bigger than you.' The gamekeeper playfully cuffed Isaac with his cap.

Impatient to be off, the terrier gave a sharp yap, jumping to snatch the cap from the gamekeeper's hand. 'I'd best be off before she wakes the entire hall. Good day to you both.' The gamekeeper pulled his cap back on and turned to follow the racing terrier, now darting away between the thorny bushes.

Alice and Isaac giggled at the thought of the gamekeeper spending all day trying to keep up with the eager terrier as they hurried down the path to the servants' entrance.

'Remember what Mother said.'

'Yes,' Isaac said.

'Good, I'll see you tonight at home. I may be a little late as one of the maids is off visiting her sick sister in Watton.'

Patches of blue were appearing overhead as Isaac made his way to the stables. Lifting the latch of the small door set into the main gates to the stables, he stepped into the small yard, the cobbles still glistening with dew. The top half of the dozen or so white stable doors already stood open, and the expectant faces of Lord Stanton's hunters nodded and snorted in the soft light. Unseen, the rustle of the heavy Norfolk punches could be heard while the grey face of the yard's hack peered out from her box, chomping noisily.

The grey had been the first horse Isaac had ever ridden. His father had lifted him onto the broad back of the lumbering, gentle-natured old mare, leading them round the yard until one day he had handed the reins to Isaac and stepped away. Progressing to the livelier piebald pony, which Isaac had ridden whenever he could, he had relished the joyous sound of clip-clopping hoofs on the cobbles, the warm feel beneath him as he cantered across the heath. His father had said he was a natural and taught him how to fit the saddles and harnesses to the horses. Never one to raise his voice, his father had shown him how to approach the hunters, keeping his voice low and never approaching from behind.

'Horses know a person,' his father had told him. 'They have an instinct, know who's good and bad. Treat them well and they will do almost anything for you, but mistreat them and they'll remember.'

'Morning.' Isaac turned to see Fred, with his usual wide grin, emerge from a door on the far side, next to the steps that led to the hall. A fair-headed lad, lean and a good three hands taller than Isaac, Fred had started work at the stables when he was Isaac's age and had recently become lead stable hand.

'You ready to get started? His Lordship wants the new top field finished, ready for sowing. We need to get the girls ready and up to the ploughman as soon as we can.'

Isaac followed Fred over to the far side of the yard where the pair of broad-faced punches now gazed patiently from their boxes. Sliding back the bolt, Fred rubbed the white blaze on the big chestnut mare as he slipped the bridle over her head and handed the reins to Isaac.

'Lead her out, will you? There's a ring on the wall next to her box, just tether her to that. She is as gentle as a lamb but can be stubborn. Just encourage her like this…' Fred clicked his tongue against the roof of his mouth.

'Come on, girl.' Isaac repeated the noise Fred had made, coaxing the mare forward. Towering over him, the horse stepped forward, her shaggy white hoofs clipping on the cobbles as Isaac led her out of the stable and tethered her to the iron ring.

Once the second mare had been fetched from her stable, Fred showed Isaac how to buckle the harnesses into place, his long fingers pulling the straps through the brasses, then giving a sharp tug to make sure they were tight. Finished, Fred patted Isaac on the shoulder. 'Run and open the gates. The ploughman will already be up at the field and best we don't keep him waiting.'

Each leading one of the plodding mares, Isaac and Fred made their way across the heath, the patches between the gorse dotted with rabbits who scampered back down their holes at the thud of the heavy hoofs.

'Seems you're a natural, just like your father, God rest his soul. The old punches won't budge for just anyone. Took me weeks to get them to move when I started, even with your father's help.'

The sun was peeping through the clouds as Fred introduced him to the waiting ploughman.

'Isaac, this is Bert, he'll show you what to do. I'll be back late afternoon to help you take the girls back.'

Isaac nodded at Bert. 'Good to meet you.'

'And you. Hope you are ready for some hard work. We need to get this done today, so best we get on.'

Isaac watched as Bert fastened the mares to the plough, hooking a long set of reins to the harness and walking round behind the plough.

'Follow alongside and I'll show you what to do. You ready?'

Isaac moved to the side of the plough as Bert cracked the reins, and the mares pulled on the harness as the silver blades cut into the soil. After a few paces, a ding filled the air as the blades hit one of the shiny black flints that were common across the Brecks. Bert pulled the powerful horses to a stop, keen to avoid blunting the blades.

Isaac watched as Bert scraped out the surrounding earth, lifted the stone and pointed to the edge of the field.

'Heap these up over there. The workmen will collect them later and take them off to repair the churches or cottages. That one was easy but you will need a rope to tug out the larger ones.'

It seemed to take an age to reach the marker that indicated the edge of the new field, a freshly turned furrow in their wake. All day Isaac followed the plough up and down the field, with only brief breaks to water and feed the horses, the piles of flints at the side of the field growing until finally the last furrow had been turned.

The sun starting to sink, Fred returned, uncoupling the plough horses ready for the walk back.

'Tired?'

Isaac nodded as he arched his back against a dull ache from the constant bending and lifting. His hands bore a lacy pattern of nicks and red lines from the flint's sharp edges.

Just as the mares were clean of the yellow sand and back in their boxes, the sharp clip of footsteps sounded across the yard. Dressed in black, shiny riding boots, a tailored checked tweed jacket and pristine cream riding breeches, the neat figure of Mr Downs, His Lordship's estate manager, approached.

'Good evening, Fred. Did everything get finished as per His Lordship's instructions?'

'Yes, Mr Downs, although I have to say it is sandy old soil, not sure it will be good for much.'

'Not for us to decide, Fred. How did he do?' Mr Downs looked at Isaac.

'Reckon he did all right. Handled the horses like a natural and did a good job, although I fear we may have worn him out.'

'Maybe we have.' Mr Downs smiled at Isaac. 'Don't worry, you'll get used to it, healthy lad like you. Get off home and we will see you in the morning.' Bidding them both goodnight, Mr Downs headed back to the hall, the tap of his crop against the side of his glossy boot fading.

Once the stables were closed, Isaac stepped through the gate, retracing his steps along the gravel path. Every part of him felt as if it had been trodden on by one of the big mares, and his oversized boots were filled with coarse, sandy soil. Convinced he could never work so hard every day, he slipped off the black boots, wriggling his toes in relief, and started home.

THREE

May 1838

Keen to be at the stables early, Isaac strode across the heath, its yellow gorse blossoming as winter faded, the birds and rabbits renewed with the warm spring sun, his sister struggling to keep up.

'Come on, Alice. I need to be sure everything is ready. Lord Stanton will expect the horses all saddled up and waiting when they come out after breakfast.'

Still only as tall as the shoulders of the sleek hunters he exercised daily across the Breck, Isaac was no longer a child. His boyish body had grown muscular and strong from the strenuous work. A fine shadow of dark hair had appeared above his lip, matching his black locks. His natural ability with the horses had caught the eye of Mr Downs, and when Fred had married and moved away, Isaac was the natural choice to take over, the extra wages more than welcome.

'These house parties cause so much extra work,' Alice puffed. 'There are more fires to light, more fetching and carrying, more ladies to dress. There's one lady, Mrs

Stokes, sharpest tongue I have ever known. Not a please or thank you, just barks orders and watches you with these crow-like eyes. The valet looking after her husband says he is such a nice man, though, doesn't know how he puts up with her. Says he fought alongside Wellington, now trains racehorses down at Newmarket.'

'Don't think I've met her,' Isaac said, 'but she sounds unpleasant. The colonel was round the yard yesterday with Mr Downs, seems a decent enough man. Word is he is an excellent horseman. Thanks for the warning about his wife though – I'll mind myself when she's around.'

Parting as they always did at the side gate, Isaac's mind brimmed with the tasks ahead. Pleased to see the stable boy already hard at work, Isaac heard the whinnies and snorts echo across the yard at the sound of his footsteps. He had gone through the arrangements with Mr Downs the previous day. They would ready His Lordship's horses, each one saddled for a particular guest. He alone would see to the lively hunter that had arrived yesterday afternoon from one of Lord Stanton's neighbours.

Satisfied everything was in hand, Isaac made his way across to the box, keen to get the borrowed horse ready before the party arrived for the ride. As he approached, he could hear the wilful black colt as it kicked and thrashed around, clearly unsettled in the unfamiliar surroundings. Gently, he eased back the bolt, careful not to startle the horse. Keeping his voice low as he edged alongside, he ran his hand down the long, coal-coloured mane as wide fiery eyes flicked from side to side. The task of fitting the bridle was made more difficult by the twisting colt. Isaac lifted the soft leather hunting saddle into place before he led the horse out into the yard and let down the stirrups.

As a final check, Isaac ran his hands through his hair and buttoned up his jacket, winking at the red-liveried footman who had appeared, as the heavy studded door at the rear of the hall swung open and Mr Downs stood at the top of the steps. As he descended into the yard, the familiar figures of Lord and Lady Stanton appeared, followed by Lady Stanton's brother together with Sir Nicholas Flatt, their wives immediately behind, deep in conversation. Next, Colonel Stokes made his way through the doorway, his rigid posture that of a man who had spent many years in the army, his magnificent moustache and mutton-chop sideburns neatly combed. As he began to descend the steps, a woman dressed head to toe in black, her face pinched, set with small unsmiling eyes, jostled him to one side. Ignoring the other guests, she strode across to where the party had gathered, snatching a crystal glass from a tray held aloft by the rigid footman.

Isaac looked at the woman as she stood frowning. She looked so at odds with her husband, who stood grinning and laughing with the other guests. Her cold face sent shivers through him.

'Everything ready as we agreed?' Mr Downs approached, his brow creased, the rapid tap of his crop against his boot giving away that the day was already proving difficult.

'All done, Mr Downs. Have to say I'm worried about the borrowed colt. Gave me a hard time in the box and won't settle properly.'

Mr Downs frowned. 'Well, the colonel is a splendid horseman. After a few miles I expect he will bring the horse to heel.'

When the guests' glasses were empty, Mr Downs turned to Isaac. 'Let's get the ladies mounted up first. Sooner they are out on the heath, the happier I will be. Bring the bay mare round for Mrs Stokes – she's not one to be kept waiting.'

Isaac walked over and untethered the mare. Usually calm, the horse seemed to sense the unpleasantness of the woman, who was now approaching the mounting steps. Avoiding the stare of Mrs Stokes, Isaac ran a hand down the neck of the mare. A few paces away, she stopped and gave a sharp huff, the mare resisting on the reins as he waited.

'I need a decent horse, boy, not some country nag.' Mrs Stokes raised her whip. 'Bring me that black colt.'

Isaac stayed silent, conscious of his instructions from Mr Downs, aware that the rest of the party had fallen quiet and was now watching.

'Madam, if I may suggest,' Mr Downs intervened, 'the mare may be a more suitable mount. He's a bit—'

'Rubbish, man. I've ridden since I was a child. I'm not some country bumpkin who doesn't know one end from the other. I want a decent horse today, not some half-hearted pony.'

Sensing the tension, Colonel Stokes left the party and

crossed the grass. 'Now, dear, the mare looks a decent mount and is all ready to go. I'm sure she will—'

Isaac watched as Mrs Stokes brushed off her husband's hand. 'I'll ride the black colt and let that be an end to it.' She stared at Isaac. 'Well, don't just stand there, bring him round.'

Isaac gulped and gripped the reins tightly to hide his shaking hand. Mr Downs glanced across to where Lord Stanton stood, the barest of nods passing between the two men.

'Take the mare back and fetch the colt,' Mr Downs instructed.

Isaac walked the mare back across the yard, looped her reins to the iron ring and untied the colt. Leading the horse across the yard, Isaac held on tightly as the colt jerked its head up and down, nostrils flared. Isaac led the nervous animal towards Mrs Stokes. With a bad feeling in the pit of his stomach, Isaac recalled his father's words, sensing the colt's reluctance.

'Stop dithering and get the horse across here now.' Mrs Stokes stood waiting impatiently, her black boot firmly placed on the first step of the mounting block.

Isaac edged the horse alongside the steps, leaning firmly against the hard shoulder of the wilful colt as it continued to resist. White streaks of sweat showing on its neck and flanks, the colt pulled at the reins, its hoofs slipping on the cobbles. Shortening the reins, Isaac pushed against the solid flanks and tried to steady the twisting colt. Her foot partway into the stirrup, Mrs Stokes reached out and made to mount. Isaac pushed again as the colt shifted on the cobbles.

'Are you completely useless? Hold the horse still,' Mrs Stokes barked, a hint of panic in her voice.

Isaac gave a sharp tug to dip the colt's head as he fought to control him. Aware of the widening gap between the horse and the step, Isaac looked at the stranded figure of Mrs Stokes, who now hung precariously in mid-air, unable to mount the twisting colt or regain the steps. Isaac pulled again, the battle now to drive the colt back towards Mrs Stokes. He nearly had it under control, when the sharp command of Mrs Stokes to bring the horse closer unnerved the colt once more. Its power magnified by fear, the colt found its footing and dug in. Horrified, Isaac watched Mrs Stokes' black-gloved hand begin to slide from the saddle as the space widened. Concerned Mrs Stokes was about to be trampled on, he could only watch as she lost her grip entirely and tumbled in a cloud of black towards the cobbles. A loud gasp of air expelled from the woman's lungs as she hit the floor.

As Isaac manoeuvred the colt away from where a dazed Mrs Stokes lay, her dress crumpled beneath her, Mr Downs and Colonel Stokes ran forward. Clearly shaken, Mrs Stokes pushed away their offers of help and clambered to her feet.

'Imbecile,' she shouted at Isaac, 'don't you know how to control a horse? You could have killed me.' At the centre of the yard, the other guests stood, a mix of astonishment and embarrassment etched on their faces.

'Now, dear,' Colonel Stokes tried to soothe his enraged wife while she brushed furiously at the dirt on her dress, 'I think maybe—'

'Maybe nothing. I want him dismissed. You hear me? He deliberately pulled that horse away just as I was about to mount! I'm lucky to be alive.' About to continue her barrage, Mrs Stokes looked over at the faces of the rest of the party. Pride dented, she hesitated and announced she could feel one of her heads coming on and that she would be retiring to her room.

Isaac held on to the colt, now so spooked and agitated that he doubted anyone could ride it today. 'His Lordship thinks it best if we leave the colt,' Mr Downs said, 'so change the mare over to a full saddle as quickly as you can.'

Isaac nodded and led the colt away, stopping to allow Mrs Stokes to pass as she headed back to the hall. She looked down at him, her eyes alight with fury.

'Think you can make a fool out of me? I have a long memory and, mark my words, you'll pay, boy.' With a last glance back at him, she continued towards the hall.

Isaac gripped the reins tightly, shaken by the woman's words, as he led the colt back to its stable. Fearful he was in trouble, he beckoned the stable boy over and instructed him to take the side-saddle off the bay mare and put on a hunting saddle, noticing Colonel Stokes deep in conversation with Lord Stanton.

Unable to convince himself that everyone wasn't watching him, he helped the rest of the party mount up, the earlier laughter now gone.

Gates open, the solemn party passed through the arch at a trot, the flat heath stretching away from the hall, green and unbroken, into the distance. A raised crop from His

Lordship saw the party break into a canter, the thud of hoofs on the sandy soil slowly fading as the stable hands ran to close the gates, a welcome relief descending on the now empty yard.

FOUR

With the last of the horses groomed and settled, Isaac was about to leave when he heard Mr Downs call his name from a door at the rear of the hall. 'Lord Stanton wants to see you in the small study before you go.'

Isaac pushed his fingers through his hair and pulled his cap from his pocket. 'Any idea why?'

'Best I leave it to him to explain.' Mr Downs stood aside to let Isaac enter. 'Try not to worry. You did a good job with the colt – things could have turned out much worse than they did.'

Convinced his summons could mean he was about to be dismissed, he entered the passage that led from the kitchen. Not sure where to go, he spotted the footman who had served the hunting party earlier and waved. 'Can you take me to the small study? Lord Stanton wants to see me.'

'You in trouble after that incident with Mrs Stokes this morning? Word is that if she hadn't been so demanding and impatient it never would have happened. She's been putting on her parts since she arrived, trying to blame everyone else. Best hurry. They go in for dinner soon.'

Isaac followed the footman up the stairs and out into a wide hallway. High above, white puffy clouds filled a pale blue sky painted on the ceiling. Beneath his feet a chequered black-and-white marble floor gleamed, while the eyes of Lord Stanton's dead ancestors stared down from ornate gold frames that filled every wall.

'Are your boots clean?'

Isaac kicked up his heels and nodded as the white-gloved hand of the footman knocked twice on the heavy door.

What if he was dismissed? No one would employ a servant without a reference.

Hearing a muffled command from inside the room, the footman pushed the door open, whispering good luck as he ushered Isaac through.

Inside, through a fug of sickly smoke, Isaac saw Lord Stanton and Colonel Stokes standing either side of an ornate marble fireplace, each holding a long brown cigar.

Isaac removed his cap, a trickle of sweat adding to his already soaked shirt. 'Am I in trouble, sir?'

The two men looked at each other before Colonel Stokes marched stiffly across to an enormous desk and placed his still smouldering cigar on a glass ashtray. 'Lord Stanton tells me you have worked for him for a while and, according to Mr Downs, you know your way around horses. The incident in the yard this morning…' Isaac gripped his cap tightly, fearful of what was coming, 'well, you did a good job on holding that colt. He could easily have bolted, and your actions saved Mrs Stokes from being trampled on. Needs more than just strength to bring a beast like that to heel.' Colonel Stokes picked up the smouldering cigar and rolled it in his fingers.

Confused, Isaac waited.

Colonel Stokes returned the cigar to the ashtray. 'I have a proposition for you.' He looked directly at Isaac. 'I'm looking for lads who can handle horses. You are the right build, so I've persuaded Lord Stanton to let me offer you a trial of six months at my racing stables in Newmarket. I'll give you board and lodging and see how you shape up. If you grow too much, or it doesn't work out, Lord Stanton has said you can return to the hall. But if you do as well as I think you will, we might make a jockey out of you.'

Isaac felt a flood of relief. He wasn't being dismissed after all. But what had Colonel Stokes just said? Leave the hall? Go to Newmarket? He must have misheard.

'Bone.' Lord Stanton broke into Isaac's thoughts. 'Did you hear what the colonel said? Do you have any questions?'

His throat dry, Isaac twisted his cap in his hands. 'No, my lord.'

'Well, Colonel Stokes leaves the day after next, so we will need your answer by dinner tomorrow. Tell Downs what you decide, and he will make sure we get the message.'

Colonel Stokes smiled broadly at Isaac. 'This is an excellent opportunity, so consider carefully. I have great hopes for you.'

His head in a spin, Isaac pulled his cap back on and nodded at the two men. The polished brass doorknob slipped in his palm as he grappled to heave the heavy door open. Back in the hallway, he tried to make sense of what had just happened, the gazes of the paintings boring through him as he headed towards the high doors at the front of the house. Just moments ago, he had thought he would be sent away in disgrace, but now he had been given an opportunity to become something, to make a better life for himself and his family. About to turn the handle, he checked himself, turned and cut back across the polished floor and down the stairs to the kitchen.

FIVE

Isaac burst through the door into the cottage, his mother and sisters jumping at the sudden crash.

'There you are. We've been worried sick,' his mother said. 'Alice said there was an incident with a woman and a horse.'

'Lord Stanton – no, Colonel Stokes – wants me to go to Newmarket, work for him in his yard. I'd get proper papers, maybe become a jockey.'

His mother dragged a stool from in front of the fire. 'Come and sit down, Isaac, and begin again, but slowly.'

Isaac sat down, took off his jacket and told his family what had happened.

'I thought they were going to dismiss me when I was summoned, but Colonel Stokes said I had done a good job controlling the colt and that Mrs Stokes could have been trampled on. Then he said I was the right size for a jockey and offered me a chance to move to Newmarket to try out. But it would mean having to leave you all.'

His mother placed her hands on his shoulders. 'Isaac, things are changing. People are moving away from the land, going to the cities to work. Look at the Parks. Generations of families like ours have worked the Breck, tied to whichever lord it might be. But you have a chance, Isaac. Alice is working, and the girls are bigger now and can help with the chores, and if someone else is going to feed you...' His mother forced a smile. 'When do you need to decide?'

'I must give them my answer tomorrow. Colonel Stokes leaves the day after.' Isaac stood up and pulled on his jacket and made for the door. 'I need to think. I'll be back in a while.'

The soft evening light silhouetted the pines of the Brecks against a yellowing sky, as Isaac walked slowly across the heath towards the pond. Sitting on the weathered bough, Isaac's head bounced with questions. This was his home, the only place he knew and loved. The windswept heaths with their stunted gorse and ever-changing colours. What was Newmarket like? The furthest he had ever been was Watton, then only for a few hours. But his mother was right. New ways of working the land meant that machines were replacing men and horses. People were leaving for a better life in the cities, whole families uprooting and heading to work in the factories up north. What did the future hold for him and his family? But the ragged newssheets Alice sometimes brought home from the hall told stories of towns full of danger and disease. What if he got sick, or grew too much? The questions jumbled in his mind. How could he leave these wild heaths, his home, and his friends? He wouldn't know anyone in Newmarket, except Colonel Stokes and his unpleasant wife.

Isaac looked down at his reflection in the tranquil water, wondering what his father would have said. Taking the brass from his pocket, he turned it over in his hands. He was the man of the family. It was his duty to look after them. If he took this chance, he could do that. If things didn't work out, Colonel Stokes had said that he could return after six months.

The dusk cast its shadow over the heath as he leant back on the branch and looked up at the sky. This morning he had been working in the stables of the hall, the years mapped out in front of him. Now he had an opportunity. To make something more of his life, provide for his mother and sisters. With one last look at the familiar pool, Isaac pushed himself up, slid the precious brass back into his pocket, and headed home.

SIX

Tears streaming down their faces, his mother and sisters wished him luck, making him promise to write as soon as he could. Kissing them all goodbye, his own tears mingling with salty cheeks, Isaac picked up his small bag and headed out the door. It had seemed so simple to accept Colonel Stokes' offer. He knew his father would have been proud. But now his mind was filled with doubts. His heart was torn by sadness at the thought of leaving behind his family and the Brecks.

Alone at the crossroads, the rumble of hoofbeats grew louder as the carriage taking Colonel and Mrs Stokes back to Newmarket approached. It was pulled by two black horses, their coats glossy, already breathing hard; the coachman drew them to a halt a few steps away from where he stood.

'You ready, Bone?' Colonel Stokes leant out of the window. 'We've a few miles to cover, and I want to be home before dark. Stow your bag on the rack and jump on, then we can—'

Interrupted by the sharp voice of Mrs Stokes demanding to know why they had stopped, the colonel smiled and pointed to the rear of the carriage. Isaac wedged his bag between two wooden trunks and clambered up onto the narrow wooden seat. He barely had a chance to sit down when the coachman cracked the reins; the horses responded to his order, and the carriage lurched on its way.

The track was filled with ruts and holes, and a continual torrent of complaints coming from Mrs Stokes. Isaac held on tightly to the wooden rail as the familiar landscape began to change: the browns and greens of the open Breck and the spindly pines, replaced by ancient woods of oak and beech, with unfurling ferns and lush green bushes at their feet.

Reaching the inn at Elveden, the coachman pulled the horses to a rest. His arms stiff, Isaac uncurled his fingers from the rail, glad of the break. As he stood stretching, he overheard Colonel Stokes tell the coachman that he and Mrs Stokes would take refreshments at the inn, and to let him know when they were ready to leave. Overcome with hunger, Isaac retrieved his bag, took out the piece of pie his mother had given him that morning and looked for somewhere to sit.

Already unwrapping a large chunk of bread, the coachman waved him over to where he sat on a wooden bench propped against the whitewashed wall of the inn. Isaac sat down next to him and took a bite from the pie, the rabbit rich and soft, and wondered when he would next taste his mother's baking.

'Hear you are going to be trying out for Colonel

Stokes,' the coachman said. 'He runs a good yard, plenty of top horses, and the lads all say he's a fair man. That wife of his, well, she's bitter to the core.'

Isaac took another bite of pie. 'How come?'

'Rumour is that she was the last of four sisters left unwed, that tongue of hers putting off any acceptable suitors. Took up with a right cad, big gambler by all accounts, and when her father found out, he threatened to disinherit her. Forced her to turn on the charm and managed to marry her off to the colonel. Poor old sod.'

'She blamed me for an incident at the hall, but it was her fault. The horse sensed she wasn't a nice person.'

'Keep clear of her, that's my advice.' The coachman stood up, brushing crumbs from his coat. 'Just going to check the wheels on the carriage and make sure the horses are watered and sound, then we'll be off.'

The horses now rested, the Colonel and Mrs Stokes appeared from the inn and climbed back into the carriage. The journey continued in much the same way as the road became busier with carts piled high with wood, hay bales, crates of chickens, and the occasional sheep. Those too poor to afford a cart pushed overloaded barrows, shoulders hunched as they tried to stop the barrow spilling its contents across the road. From within the carriage the constant grumble of Mrs Stokes could be heard, and a torrent of threats when the coachman was too late to avoid a deep rut in the road that almost dislodged Isaac from his seat. After a break to check for damage, the carriage rumbled on, a loud snoring now mixing with the hoofbeats.

His back aching, Isaac sensed the carriage slowing as it entered an avenue of trees; the already dimming daylight was made darker by the lofty boughs that stretched overhead. As the carriage turned, Isaac could just make out a long street, shops and inns flickering with light, people busy about their business. Now at a crawl, the putrid smell of rotting rubbish and human waste churning under the wheels threatened to overcome him. Was this what towns were like? He reached in his pocket for a handkerchief, already missing the fresh air of the Brecks.

Once they had stopped, Isaac jumped down, careful to miss the puddles, as a pair of black gates set in an archway loomed over the carriage. The sound of activity could be heard from within as the gates swung open. With a flick of the reins the carriage rumbled through the arch, Isaac walking behind, into a square yard lit by flickering lanterns. The gates shut behind them. He massaged his stiff limbs, glad the journey was over.

'Good journey, Colonel?' A broad man, white whiskers running down his jaw, his head completely bald, approached.

'Bit bumpy, Mr Hunt. Everything all right here? Horses all well?'

'Yes, Colonel. All good.'

The colonel appeared to be about to continue when a roar came from within the carriage: Mrs Stokes complaining sharply that her husband thought more of his horses than he did of her. The carriage door was opened, a set of steps was pulled down, and Mrs Stokes burst out, thrusting a black bag at her husband, and headed towards a doorway and disappeared.

A visible look of relief on his face, Colonel Stokes beckoned Isaac forward. 'Mr Hunt, this is Isaac. He is going to try out for us. Could you show him to the loft? He can begin work in the morning.'

'Will do,' Mr Hunt said. 'Got a bag?'

Isaac fetched his bag and followed Mr Hunt across the yard and up some wooden stairs. Without knocking, Mr Hunt pushed it open and entered the room beyond.

'Here, lads, got a new one for you. Mind you make him welcome.'

The room was lit by a single lantern. Isaac saw three lads, he thought to be a little older than him, sitting around an upturned crate playing cards.

'Will do,' one of the boys said.

Isaac walked across to where the boys sat, his eyes adjusting to the dim light.

'I'm Frank, and this is Jim, and that's Mac. That's because he is from Scotland, and they are all called Mac in Scotland. Isn't that right?'

Mac rolled his eyes. 'Thinks he's funny. Come over and take a seat. What's your name?'

Isaac edged forward as the other boys made space on the bench.

'Isaac, Isaac Bone.'

'Well, nice to meet you, Isaac. You hungry? There's a bit of bread and cheese here and some water in the flask.'

Isaac took the offered food and sat down on the bench. 'What are you playing?'

'Newmarket, of course,' the lads said in unison. 'Everyone plays it. Can't be in a town called Newmarket and not know how to play. We'll teach you if you like.'

Ready to drop after the long journey, Isaac tried to stifle a yawn.

Frank nudged Jim. 'Well, we can show you another night. There's a mattress in the corner and a spare blanket on the rafter. We get up at first light, break for porridge after a couple of hours, then work till lunch. Me and the lads will just finish this hand, then we are going to call it a night.'

Grateful, Isaac fetched the blanket and made his way across to where Frank had pointed. The loft felt warm and homely; there were three more mattresses tucked under the eaves, a marble-topped washstand and a row of hooks. As he plumped a pillow from his bag, he thought of home, of his younger sisters tucked up, sleeping peacefully, Alice and his mother sitting beside the fire. Exhausted, he lay his head on the lumpy pillow and for a moment heard the rustle of horses in the boxes below before he fell into a deep sleep.

SEVEN

Aware of movement, Isaac sat up and rubbed his arms, stiff from the previous day.

'Time to get up, country boy,' Jim encouraged as he buttoned up his breeches. 'First lot ride out an hour after first light.'

Already fully clothed, too exhausted the previous night to undress, he followed the others out to the top of the stairs. Able to see the stables properly for the first time, Isaac gasped in astonishment. There were at least three dozen boxes hemming a perfect green lawn, a magnificent stone fountain shooting jets of silver water high into the air from its centre. At the far end, the pair of stout wooden gates they had entered by last night barred the way to the street beyond, a heavy beam securing them shut. Over the red-tiled roofs, an expansive green unbroken heath sloped up and away. The crown of the hill was topped with thick green trees, tall and full.

'Come on,' Frank called from the foot of the stairs. 'There's work to be done.'

Isaac dashed down to where Frank stood.

'Mr Hunt said for you to stay close to me for a couple of days, get to know the place. Eventually you'll get some horses of your own to look after, but for now, you can help me. That sound all right?'

'Good for me,' Isaac replied, somewhat flustered at the frenzied pace of the yard, lads scurrying back and forth, the reins and saddles in hand. Most of them were around Isaac's age, wiry and short, except one podgy lad with lank, floppy hair, his face red as he attempted to place a saddle on a horse that twisted and bucked, defying all his attempts.

Isaac nodded in the boy's direction 'Who is that?'

'That's Mrs Stokes' nephew Solomon,' Frank said. 'Came here about two years ago when his mother died. Keeps himself to himself most of the time, but she makes him work around the yard. Not very good with the lively ones. Mind you, he's not overly good with any of them, to be honest,' Frank chuckled. 'Has a room in the house but the mistress doesn't like him much, constantly on at him about something. Think that's why he always looks wretched. Look sharp now, here come the riding lads.'

Isaac watched as a line of boys, all stick-thin, marched into the yard. Dressed in knee-high brown boots, beige riding breeches and white shirts, riding crops in hand, they swiftly mounted up and took the reins. With practised ease the dozen or so horses formed into a string, a handsome chestnut mare in the lead. Isaac saw Mac and Jim head towards the big black gates, pushing up the heavy wooden beam before they dragged them open to reveal a near-deserted street beyond.

The line trotted through the open gates, the horses light of foot, the lads rising and falling in tune with the motion beneath them, and turned towards the heath.

The last of the string gone, Frank glanced at the sky. 'Looks like it will be a dry day. Takes longer to get the string rubbed down and back in their boxes when it's wet. Right, let me show you around the old place so you know where everything is. We call this the top yard. Over there by the gates, the house with the big columns is where the colonel and Mrs Stokes live. Solomon has a room in there as well. The boxes in this yard are for the best horses. Couple of champions in here and a few who will be contenders for next year's classic races. Worth a few guineas. Those stone steps beside the gates lead up to the gatehouse loft.'

Skirting the lawn, Frank pointed to a blue-faced clock with slim black hands, set in a cupola atop the roof. 'That's how we run the yard. There is a clock on each side, so wherever you are, you know the time. Colonel is hot on making sure we do everything to time. Dare say it's the military in him.'

Finished in the top yard, Frank led Isaac to a smaller pair of gates, lifting the latch on a small door set into the corner. Frank stepped through. 'This is the second yard.'

Isaac gawped in amazement. He had thought the first yard was big, but this was enormous. 'New horses and the ones that are still in training get stabled here,' Frank said. 'If they show promise on the gallops, or the owner has money, then they get moved to the top yard. Sometimes the owner of the yard, Lord Beaumont, who lives down the street in King Charles's old palace, comes to look at the top yard but he never comes to this one.'

Isaac raised his eyebrows. 'King Charles's Palace? You mean *the* King Charles? We learnt about him at school.'

'Yep, it was him that really began all this racing lark here at Newmarket. His Lordship lives there now, real grand place.'

'So, Colonel Stokes doesn't own the yard?'

Frank shook his head. 'No, he just runs it for His Lordship. Bit like we do, only he gets a big house and well paid and we get to sleep in the loft. Truth is, old Stokes knows a lot more about horses than His Lordship, although of course it is His Lordship and his friends that have the money. Mrs Stokes finds this all beneath her, makes that plain enough, but for the most part she doesn't interfere in the stables. Now let me show you what makes this yard extra special.' Frank showed Isaac a set of boxes standing separate from the others.

'This is the veterinary hospital. We are the only yard in the town to have one. If a horse gets injured or ill, most places just shoot them. Here, Colonel Stokes and Mr Hunt bring them to the hospital and try to heal or cure them. See there? That little mare came in last week, was having difficulty breathing. They punched a tiny hole in her neck and inserted a little metal tube, and stayed with her day and night, made sure she didn't lie down. Every few hours they gave her this medicine. We were all worried for a bit, but she is well on the mend now. Talk is that they might try her on the heath for a bit of a gallop in the next few days.'

Frank looked up at the clock as it struck the hour. 'The first lot will be back soon. The riders have their breakfast in the long room and go out on the second string at half past. When they have gone, we wash the first string down and get them fed and watered. Then we will wait to see what Mr Hunt wants us to do for the rest of the day.' Frank gave Isaac a friendly punch on his shoulder. 'Got all that? Good. Let's get on.'

EIGHT

April 1839

The damp heath ensured the horses returned from their morning exercise covered in mud, their riders splattered from head to toe. With a full string to scrub down, Isaac and the others set to work. Now used to the frantic pace of the yard, he had formed an easy friendship with Jim, Frank and Mac, learning more each day about how the yard ran and how to handle the tricky thoroughbreds, although he still lost every time they played Newmarket. If all went well he and the other lads would soon get their tryout in a couple of weeks, the chance to become apprenticed to the yard.

Isaac coaxed the mare, while Mac dipped his brush in and out of the bucket as he cleaned the horse's flank, which was caked in the dry mud of the gallops. 'You got a proper hold on her? She can be a bit of a handful. See the bite she gave me last winter? You can still see the teeth marks.'

'You are such a girl,' Jim said, making them all laugh.

A bang from across the yard caused them all to look up. Head back, her expression even more stormy than usual, Mrs Stokes marched across the yard towards them, dressed head to toe in the usual black and a matching hat with the veil pinned back. She waved a piece of paper in the air. 'One of you come here,' she demanded.

'You go, Jim.'

'Why me, Mac? It must be your turn.'

'For goodness' sake,' Mrs Stokes barked. 'I have better things to do than stand here all day. I need an errand running now.' Her eyes settled on Isaac.

'Ah, it's you. That fool of a boy from Norfolk. One of my husband's acts of charity. If I'd had my way, you would have felt the sting of my crop and been out on your ear. I wouldn't trust you with a dog, let alone a horse.'

Isaac felt the awkwardness of his friends as he tried not to show his fear of Mrs Stokes.

'Get down the street to Musk's and give him this order of meats. Tell him it must be delivered by four o'clock today, or I'll move my account.'

Without speaking, Isaac took the list from Mrs Stokes' gloved hand, doffed his cap, and ran for the side gate. Beyond, the street swilled with the dirt and filth churned up by the previous night's rain. Faced with the crowds of a busy market day, Isaac pushed his way through the higgledy-piggledy market stalls, merchants in full cry as they vied to sell their vegetables or brightly coloured ribbons. At the edge of the square a plump woman leant against the wall of one of the public houses, her teeth black and rotten, the hem of her dress soaked with mud.

'Fancy a rumble, little man? Only sixpence. Show you what old Rosie has hidden up here.' The woman hitched her skirt higher and took a step forward. Isaac hesitated. His gaze fixed on the woman's pockmarked face as he turned sharply away, colliding with a red-haired boy who let out a cry as he landed on the slimy floor.

'Oh, I'm so sorry,' Isaac gabbled. 'Are you all right? Here, let me help you up.'

The youth held out a slender hand towards Isaac, the back of it covered in light freckles. Surprised at how light the boy was, Isaac helped him to his feet, taking in the fancy clothes. The once-white breeches were now stained with the grime of the street, the well-tailored mottled waistcoat dripping brown mud down one side.

'My, you are in a hurry,' the youth spoke for the first time with a heavy accent Isaac couldn't place. 'To be sure, you near killed me.'

'I'm sorry, I didn't…'

'What, kill me? It's all right, only a bit of mud and the landlady will get that out.'

Unsure why, Isaac felt strangely ill at ease, the faint hint of sweet scent, the slender hands more like those of his elder sister making him wary.

'I'm Jack, and you are?'

'Isaac, Isaac Bone.'

'Well, Isaac, although I'm covered in muck and that's your fault, I suppose I'm pleased to meet you.' Jack wiped his hand down the clean side of his waistcoat and offered it to Isaac. 'Where are you off to in such a rush?'

Isaac shook the hand, the skin soft in his palm. 'I was just on my way to Musk's the butcher's. With an order from the mistress.'

'And which mistress might that be?' the youth enquired.

'Mrs Stokes; her husband trains for Lord Beaumont.'

'Ah, I know the place. Rumour says there are some excellent horses there. So, Musk's, is it? Well, it happens I'm heading that way. Maybe we could walk together? Make the best sausages in town, they say – secret recipe.' Jack tapped his nose.

Isaac felt conspicuous alongside the dapper figure as they threaded their way through the crowds. 'So how long you worked in the yard?'

'About eleven months, get my first trial soon. Then, if everything works out, I'll get my papers, become an apprentice jockey.'

'You must be good, then. That yard is one of the best in the town. Any tips for a little wager? See you right if they win.'

Isaac hesitated. The unwritten rule was that the lads never spoke about the big hopes in the yard in case it brought bad luck, but what harm could there be? He worked for the best yard in town, that's what the lad had said. Filled with pride, Isaac proudly told Jack how they hoped to run Fever Tree in the Derby, and a couple of fillies in the St Leger in the autumn. All good hopes.

'I must make a note of that,' Jack said. 'They must be worth a few guineas?'

'Suppose so.' Isaac checked himself. He shouldn't have said anything; the lads would be furious if they thought he had cursed their chances.

'Bet you keep that yard well locked up?'

Keen to get away, Isaac kept walking. 'Yes, very, the gate is barred from the inside and you can only get in through the side gate if you have a key.'

'That so?' Jack said. 'Well, here we go. Musk's the butcher's, purveyor of fine sausages to the gentry.' Jack made a sweeping bow.

Isaac looked through the window. Above trays of pink and bloody flesh, brightly coloured pheasants hung from shiny metal hooks. A swarm of flies was waved away by the fat butcher.

'Thanks,' said Isaac. 'I should get on.'

'Sure, see you around, no doubt.' Jack turned half away before turning back. 'Maybe a beer for my trouble one evening?'

'I don't drink really, puts weight on, not good for a jockey.' Isaac made to join the waiting queue.

'Well, I'm sure we will bump into one another again.' Jack grinned. 'No joke intended. Then I'll say goodbye for now.'

Isaac joined the queue, pleased the youth had gone. When his turn came, he handed the butcher the order, passing on the message from Mrs Stokes, receiving a sympathetic smile in acknowledgement.

Back in the street he looked for the red-haired youth. Keen to avoid him, he turned, hurrying down Palace Street. Slackening his pace, he reached the rear of the newly built Rutland Hotel. Standing in a doorway, Mrs Stokes was deep in conversation with a tall man. Dressed in a sharp knee-length coat, the man rested his hand on Mrs Stokes' arm. At least ten years her junior, the man was handsome, his skin smooth and golden, a noble air in his posture. Everything about the man said he was the sort women fall for, his only diminishing feature a thick scar that clipped his right eye, which stared straight ahead.

Having had enough encounters for one day, Isaac crossed the street, eager to be back at the stables. About to turn the corner, he stopped and looked back. The man now pressed against Mrs Stokes, who gazed up at him before she took his hand and stepped through the door into the hotel.

NINE

Clear blue sky stretched for miles. The distinctive shape of Ely Cathedral perched far away on the horizon. Behind them, the dense wood of oak and sweet chestnut trees had sprung into leaf; in front, the hill sloped gently down towards the town; the spires of St Mary's Church and the rooftops and smoking black chimneys of the Rookery were visible in the dip.

The sun burning through the fine early mist, Isaac led the horse round at the top of the gallops. He was nervous at the prospect of his first proper ride, a chance to gain his papers, become an apprentice. It seemed so long ago when his father had lifted him onto the old hack, his first rides on the hall's pony, then the spirited hunters from Lord Stanton's stables. The exhilaration of being astride such a powerful creature, as it galloped out, had always given Isaac a thrill, and while the hunters could be temperamental, these hot-blooded thoroughbreds, descended from Arabian stallions, had a will and spirit it would take all his strength and courage to race over the course in front of them.

Now just over five feet tall, his frame lean and muscular, with strong, slim limbs, he was the ideal build for a jockey. He knew the horse, September Rain, could be a bit of a handful, needing a strong rider to keep her on a straight course. So each day since being told she would be his mount for the tryout, he had visited her, a carrot always in hand as he stroked her white muzzle. Used to being ridden, the mare would sense a novice; a novice who was a stranger would likely find themselves thrown from the saddle, risking broken bones or worse. Day by day, Isaac and the bay mare had built trust in each other as she became familiar with his scent and touch, his firm but friendly chatter building a partnership.

'Mount up,' called Mr Hunt.

Jim took the reins from Isaac, careful not to jerk or startle the horse. 'You ready?'

'As I'll ever be.' Isaac tried to disguise the slight tremble in his voice.

Isaac rubbed the brass in his pocket before he stepped into the cupped hands of Mr Hunt. His stomach churning, Isaac glanced down the hill to where the colonel and others had gathered, tiny figures next to the white post that marked the finish.

'Let's just drop the stirrup a little, lad, so you can lengthen your legs,' Mr Hunt said. 'Remember, let her do the work. Little digs with your heels, not too hard. Just keep a firm grip on the bit but take care not to pull it too hard. Just let her find her pace. Remember, you are not a jockey yet.'

'Yes, Mr Hunt.'

'Good. Now, Jim, you lead her round and set her off on my word.'

Isaac leant forward and whispered into the mare's ear. 'Remember all those carrots? Plenty more where they came from if you get me down there with no funny business.'

The horse was keen to race and Isaac pulled back, waiting for the command.

'Release!'

Isaac loosened his hold, digging his heels into the belly of the mare, feeling the powerful rear legs thrust the horse forward. Knees tight in her sides, he dropped his hands, letting her find her stride. The wind rushed at his face, the grass on either side of the track now a sheet of green velvet as the horse found its speed. Gently, he dug his heels into the horse's sides again, the strong, agile force beneath surging, eating up the six-furlong straight. Their breathing was now one. Isaac pushed himself up from the saddle slightly, the sheer rush of the animal's rhythm beneath him leaving him breathless.

He had wanted and waited for this moment since he arrived in Newmarket. He had envied the apprentices as they went out every morning. The chatter when they returned, their faces flushed as they talked about how the ride had gone, how one horse seemed off that day, teasing each other with gentle rivalry. Now he was racing down the straight, soft track, the animal beneath him fifty times his weight.

The thud of the four shod hoofs merged into one as the solid mare, nostrils flared, galloped at full pace towards the finish marker. Once past the post, Isaac instinctively pulled back on the bit to slow the mare, first to a canter, then to a walk.

The sweat from his forehead dripped down onto the mare, mingling with the white foam that spread across her neck. His whole body trembled as he gasped to fill his lungs, empty from the thrill of the ride. Still panting, Isaac rode the mare in large circles and waited expectantly as the colonel walked over.

'Good work, Bone. She's a tricky ride, but well done. Mr Hunt and I need to discuss things, so take her back to the stables and get her rubbed down. We will talk later.'

TEN

'You ready?' Jim asked. 'I'll be another year older by the time we get to the Wagon and Horses, and I want to see if that little serving girl is there. Get me a nice big kiss.'

Frank pursed his lips and blew. 'Mac will give you a kiss, big sloppy one just like he does his horses,' he said, making everyone laugh. 'Or like Mrs Stokes did her fancy man, hey, Isaac.'

'Be quiet, Frank. She has it in for me as it is without thinking I'm gossiping. You promised not to say anything.'

The rain beginning to fall threatened to add to the puddles and slimy mess that wound its way down the street as they made their way to the Wagon and Horses. Inside they were met with a thin fog of tobacco mixed with smoke from the blazing log fires, the mix of spilt ale and damp punters making their eyes smart.

'Over there.' Mac threaded his way through the crowd to an empty table flanked by two low benches.

Seated, Frank looked around. 'Now all we need is some ale.' Frank beckoned one of the serving girls over and ordered a jug of beer.

When their tankards were full, Frank stood up. 'A toast, to us, the four apprentices.'

With a solid clink, the friends cheered and drank to their good fortune. The four of them had waited nervously for two days until Mr Hunt had told them that the colonel had decided they were all to be apprenticed to the yard.

Not used to drinking, the boys bantered back and forth as the ale took effect. Their voices rising, they boasted about who would have the best horses next season, the races they would win when they were jockeys, which of them would be the most famous.

They felt emboldened as the evening wore on, their shyness with the serving girls faded, and Jim tried to impress.

'How about a kiss?' Jim pointed to his cheek. 'Then when I'm famous you can tell everyone you kissed a famous jockey!'

The serving girl grinned as she swiped at Jim. 'I don't have time to go kissing you. Anyway, what if the landlord saw me? He doesn't keep that kind of house.'

'Just a little peck? He won't see.'

'He sees everything. Tell you what, though, I get off soon, and I said I'd meet my sister and her friends along the street in the Bull. Maybe you and your pals could buy us all a gin?'

'See, boys, irresistible, didn't I tell you?' Jim punched the air.

As they drained their tankards, Isaac felt his head spin.

'You all right?' He felt Frank's arm around his shoulders.

'Think I've had too much ale. I'm going to head back to the yard.'

'You can't go yet. Hey, Mac, Jim, Isaac says he's going back.'

His friends tried to persuade him, but all he wanted was to lie down. Draining the dregs of their tankards, his friends rose unsteadily to their feet.

'You be all right? I could come back with you,' Frank offered, slurring his words.

'I'll be fine. I just need to use the privy and then I'll head back. You go with the others. I'll see you in the morning.'

Jim led the others out as Isaac wove his way around the crowded tables and drunks towards the rear yard. Almost at the door, he felt a hand on his shoulder.

'Hello. Fancy seeing you here.'

Surprised, he turned to see the red-haired lad he had collided with a few weeks ago.

'On your own?'

Isaac glanced over to where the lads had sat. 'I was just on my way to the privy, then I'm heading back to the stables.'

'I was just thinking the same. Funny how we always seem to both be going the same way. Then maybe you can buy that drink for your old friend Jack?'

Isaac tapped his pocket. 'I'm out of money and I've had enough anyway.'

'Just one? Jack will sort it.'

Isaac brushed past, hoping Jack wouldn't follow, desperate to relieve himself. But once he had finished, Jack ushered him back into the inn and with a wink turned and edged past a table where two worn drunks sat, eyes half closed. Deftly, he lifted the jug, quickly concealing it behind his back.

'That's stealing,' Isaac said.

'Oh, come on, they're so far gone they won't even notice.' Jack winked as he sat down at a small table and emptied the dregs from two abandoned tankards onto the already wet floor.

'I'm leaving,' Isaac said, desperate to be away from the inn and this youth who seemed intent on stopping him.

'Just one, seeing as you put me in the mud – least you can do. Here, sit down.' Tankards filled, Jack handed one to Isaac and raised his arm. 'Your good health.'

Isaac sat and took a swig from the tankard, reckoning he'd be rid of Jack quicker if he just drank a bit and left.

'Here, let's liven it up a bit.' Jack pulled a silver flask from his pocket and poured a shot of clear liquid into the tankard. 'Drink up.'

Determined to leave, Isaac drained the tankard and placed it back on the table. All around him, faces blurred, a noise like a thousand flies filling his head as he stood. Eyes fixed on the door, he steadied himself against the table and pushed all other thoughts from his mind. If he could just get some fresh air.

Outside in the street, a fine drizzle was falling. His head drooped as he fought a strong desire to sleep, his limbs numb and heavy. Aware of someone behind him, he willed his legs to carry him as he weaved his way across the street. If he could just get back to the yard, he would be all right. His eyes closed for the umpteenth time as he leant against the rough brick wall and rummaged in his pocket for the gate key. His fingers felt for the keyhole of the black metal lock as he fought to open the gate. Unable to find the slot, panic coupled with helplessness surged through him, the world no longer real as he lost his grip on the key and it clattered to the wet pavement. Unable to see where the key had fallen, he stooped, running his hands over the wet ground, nearly toppling as he bent down. As his legs gave way, he slumped to the floor, aware of the sound of a soft voice.

'Now, why don't you let me help you with that?'

ELEVEN

Isaac tried to sit up, a curious numbness in his limbs. Somewhere beyond the room he could hear loud shouts as he struggled to focus. His head heavy, a sudden shot of light caused him to screw up his eyes, as the outline of two figures blocked the doorway. His stomach churned. The figures came closer and he felt himself hauled upwards, his legs scraping across the floor as they dragged him out into the daylight.

'This him?' a man's voice said.

'That's him.' A woman's voice this time. 'I told everyone he was no good, but would anyone listen? Now see what he has done. Make him tell us where they are.'

Isaac squinted against the blinding light to see who was behind the words. Where were what? The voices sounded familiar, yet angry. The world revolved; there was an abrupt rise in his throat as he doubled over and purged his stomach onto the cobbles, a bitter aftertaste left in his mouth.

'Filthy little beggar.' Isaac felt the grip on his arms tighten. 'Stand up straight and tell us where the horses are.'

Where the horses are? Isaac raised his head, a sticky string of spittle hanging from his mouth. Some of the stable doors were wide open, the boxes beyond empty.

'Don't waste our time,' the man demanded, his boots splattered with the contents of Isaac's stomach.

Isaac tried to remember. The celebrations, the inn, Jack... Stricken, he felt the bile rise again, adding to the slimy mess around him.

Suspended between the two men, Isaac swallowed. 'I-I-I...' Isaac crumpled, his head falling onto his chest.

'Isaac, can you hear me? I can't believe you are part of all this.'

'Stand up when the colonel is speaking to you.'

Isaac winced as he was roughly dragged to his feet.

'Speak up, Isaac,' the colonel said. 'I know you lads all went off to celebrate last night, but Solomon said you left the inn with a well-dressed character.'

'Give him a feel of the whip, constable, that will loosen his tongue,' Mrs Stokes cut in. 'He's clearly been celebrating on his share of the proceeds. Like as not he would have disappeared in a few days.'

'I don't remember, sir. Please, you must believe me.' Isaac looked to where his friends stood, puzzled looks on their faces.

'Isaac,' the colonel sighed. 'When the lads started work this morning, three of the boxes were empty. Someone must have let the thieves in and then locked the gates behind them.'

Trying to find the words again, he stared down at his soiled feet. Stolen. But he hadn't stolen any horses. If he could just lie down for a bit, maybe he could remember what had happened after he left the inn.

'Colonel, Mrs Stokes,' the man holding his arm said, 'this young man is in no fit state to tell us anything. I suggest we take him to the bridewell while we continue the search. Maybe when he has had time to sober up, we can get some answers out of him.'

Isaac felt the bile rise in his throat again as they dragged him across the yard, his bootless feet bumping on the cobbles before they forced him through the gate. Outside, a small crowd had gathered in the street, waiting, curious to know what events were unfolding in the confines of the yard.

The men hauled him past the familiar shops and stalls of the high street, before they turned left along a narrow lane that led to the single-storey building that served as the local lock-up. Opening the black door, they pushed him roughly past an empty table and through another door into a tiny room, with a small square of light, cut by the bars from the solitary window set high in the wall.

He was brought back to a sense of awareness as he landed on the cold floor and the door banged shut behind him. Lying on his side, he started to shiver; a sense of helplessness overcame him, the stink of his soiled clothes filling his nose. Shuffling upright, he leant against the crumbling wall and drew a ragged piece of sacking towards him, draping it around his shoulders. His stomach ached and his head pulsed. It was clear something terrible had happened: the empty boxes, the questions. He had only had two or three tankards of ale and… it must have been the drink from the flask that Jack had poured him. It had tasted bitter, but the effects seemed different to ale. It had been as if he was outside his own body, peering at himself. His head whirled as he tried to remember what had happened after he had left the inn. His toes throbbing from where they had scraped across the ground, his throat raw from retching, his head pounding, he pulled the sack tighter, drew his knees up to his chin and closed his eyes.

TWELVE

The scrape of the bolt being dragged back caused him to look up, fearful of who might be about to enter. Ordered out by the constable, he was led into a closet, a washstand with a chipped white jug and bowl in the corner. He was told to clean up and change into the tunic and breeches that hung on the hook, then they left him and locked the door behind them.

Isaac welcomed the chance to rid himself of his rancid clothes, sluicing his face and body until he seemed half human again. Clean, he transferred the precious horse brass into the pocket of the breeches and gulped down some water from the jug to try and soothe his raw throat.

Unable to tell how long had passed the cell door swung open, the constable grabbing his arm and thrusting him into the room he had first entered, indicating a chair behind the empty table. A second man, his hands clutched behind his back, stood barring the door as the constable sat down opposite and leant forward.

'Tell us where the horses are and who took them,' the man said. 'Colonel Stokes seems to think you are not a bad lad, so care to tell me who you were with last night in the inn?'

Isaac stared at the man. 'I was with my friends from the yard.'

'And after that? A witness tells me you left with a red-haired lad. Headed out just before closing. Care to tell me who they were?'

Witness. What did the man mean, witness?

'Let me help you. The witness, Mrs Stokes's nephew Solomon, saw you leave the inn with another lad. Can you tell me his name?'

'Jack, that's all I know. I only met him once before last night. He made me drink some ale with him.'

A hand slammed onto the table. His body jerked with shock and a snap of realisation they thought he was part of the gang that had stolen the horses. The man leant forward again. 'Let me enlighten you. Sometime between midnight and dawn, three horses, worth a considerable sum of money, were taken. Colonel Stokes is eager to recover the horses quickly before any harm comes to them. Tell us where they are, and maybe the judge will spare you the gallows when your time comes. The longer you hold out, the further away and richer your associates are going to be.'

'But I didn't steal any horses, I don't know where they are.'

'That's not how we see it.' The man stared at Isaac. 'You admit you know this lad, Jack? How much did he pay you for letting him into the yard?'

'I didn't let anyone into the yard. Honestly, I didn't…' Isaac felt on the verge of tears.

Abruptly, the man stood up, his solid frame making Isaac cower down on the worn chair, afraid that the man was about to hit him. Instead, the man turned to the guard who stood at the door. 'Seems they paid him well enough to keep quiet. Throw him back in the cell, let him think a bit.'

Returned to the cell, Isaac tried to recall what had happened after he had left the inn. He was telling the truth and somehow, he had to make them believe him. He felt in his pocket, the cold metal of the horse brass touching his fingers as he wondered what he should do next. If he could get a message to his family, or Mr Downs or Lord Stanton, maybe they could help.

If only he could remember something about Jack. His instinct about the youth had been right: the fancy clothes, the sweet scent, girl-like hands. The youth had mentioned his landlady, but that could be any one of numerous women that took in lodgers around the town. His accent was different, not local, but from where? And how had Jack known he would be at the Wagon and Horses that night? He needed to make them believe that he didn't know where the horses were, that he hadn't stolen them, but how? He knew little about Jack and hadn't told the lads about the encounter in the street. Why was Solomon telling them he had seen him leave the inn with Jack?

Arms wrapped around his knees, he rested his head. So many things weren't right, but without any answers, he knew that he was in deep trouble, and that Jack was nowhere to be found.

THIRTEEN

Three days later Isaac was bundled into an enclosed black wagon, his wrists cuffed, heavy shackles making it difficult to walk. He was to be taken the short distance to the Jockey Club's Subscription Room, where the magistrate hearing was to take place.

The fuzziness of the past few days had gone, but no matter how hard he tried, he still couldn't remember anything after he had reached the gate. The constable had said Solomon had seen him leave with someone, but he didn't remember seeing Solomon at the inn – the boy hardly ever left the yard.

Dragged from the wagon as it drew to a stop, he hoped to see one of the lads or his family. He had asked the constable to send a message to his mother, or for paper so he could write, hoping she would come to help him. But his requests had been forgotten, or ignored, unfamiliar faces filling the path as he was led through heavy double doors, a long, wide hallway floor, shining like ice, stretching ahead of him. Instructed to sit on a wooden bench, Isaac hung his head, his clothes damp and crumpled, and waited.

The constable stood opposite. He waited until the door opened and a clipped voice called Isaac's name. Ushered into the room, Isaac looked up to where an elderly man, his scraggy neck hanging loose over a stiff white collar, eyes red and watery, sat behind an enormous desk studying some papers. A younger man was sitting at a smaller desk on his right. All around, paintings of racehorses and landscapes hung against red-flock walls, with a tall window at their centre, framing brightly coloured flower beds and perfectly cut lawns. Isaac felt in his pocket, gripping the brass tightly as the younger man rose, a piece of paper in hand, and cleared his throat.

'Isaac Bone. You are charged with the theft of horses from the stables of Lord Beaumont. How do you plead?'

'I didn't do it, sir, it was—'

'Silence,' the elderly man croaked, turning to the clerk. 'Enter a plea of not guilty.'

'But, sir.' Isaac knew he had to make the man listen, to see it was all a mistake – then they would let him go.

The magistrate looked up and wiped his mouth with a white handkerchief.

'I have reviewed the evidence, and as such, the crime that you are accused of does not fall within my jurisdiction. Therefore, I commit you to be sent for trial at the next quarter sessions. You will be taken from here and held in gaol until your case is heard. Constable.'

Without another word, the man rose unsteadily to his

feet and handed the papers to the clerk before leaving the room.

Isaac tried to make sense of what had just happened as the constable grabbed his arm and steered him back the way they had come, though the crowd and into the covered wagon, where an unfamiliar man sat waiting. The metal cuffs chafed at his wrists as he shifted to find some comfort on the narrow bench, the sounds of the high street mingling with the rumble of the wheels. A sharp jolt sent him sprawling across the floor, before the wagon lurched forward again, picking up speed as he heard the driver urge the horse forward. Taken aback, Isaac tried to sit up, but a kick from the man sent him back to the floor, his shoulder smacking painfully against the side of the wagon.

'Stay there,' the man ordered.

Perplexed, Isaac looked up. Why was the wagon moving so fast? At the crack of a whip, the wagon lurched forward again, the ground racing beneath him. Shackled, bruised and frightened, Isaac did as he was told, certain the bridewell was now far behind him. Fearing the man would kick out again, he pulled his legs towards him and tried to hide the tears that threatened to overwhelm him.

*

The wagon came to an abrupt halt and the man hauled Isaac to his feet, battered from the journey. Outside, Isaac heard a loud knocking followed by the raised voices of two men, before an unseen hand tugged the door open, a command instructing him to get down. Isaac, feeling stiff after the hours of confinement, was pushed from the wagon, through a doorway into a small yard and towards a pug-faced, stocky man, his unkempt beard littered with remains of a recent meal.

'What's this?' The man wiped his hand across his mouth, smearing crumbs across his cheek. 'I wasn't expecting anyone.'

The constable reached into his pocket and held out a folded sheet. 'Magistrate committed him to the assizes. We don't have space for prisoners at the bridewell.'

The pug face wrinkled as the man seized the paper, his eyes flicking back and forth before he refolded the paper and grunted.

The rumble of the wagon faded as it trundled away, and the man beckoned Isaac forward and into a foul-smelling room, indicating a stool in the middle. As he sat facing the wall, he felt the man move behind him, a metallic clicking as the man grabbed a clump of his hair. Without thinking he jerked away and stood up, the man losing his grip. Nowhere to go, Isaac looked at the shears in the man's hand as he took a step towards him; there was a flash of his fist as Isaac was sent sprawling to the ground.

'Did I say you could move?' The man reached down and grabbed his hair, making him cry out as he lifted him back onto the stool.

The side of his head throbbed as the shears began clicking, black curls tumbling to the floor as the man roughly hacked at his hair from behind. Finished, the man hung the shears on a rusty hook, taking a handful of white powder from a leather pouch and rubbing it into what remained of his once luscious hair before throwing him a set of clothes and a pair of shabby boots. Not wanting to be clobbered again, Isaac stripped, quickly transferring the horse brass while the man's back was turned, before pulling the billowing tunic over his head.

Sore, his scalp stinging from the powder, Isaac stood and waited as the man unclipped a set of keys from his belt and unlocked a heavy door. As he was led down a passageway lit with a solitary torch, the smell of rot and desperation grew stronger, making him feel queasy. His eyes adjusting to the poor light, he made out a row of bars and the shape of ragged people dotted around the walls, as the man unlocked a gate, which swung open.

'In you go.'

He heard the gate slam behind him, the clunk of the lock before the man walked away. No one stirred; there was the odd groan as he looked for a place to sit down, weary from the day's events. Finding a space against the crumbling wall, a few strands of rotting straw the best he could find to cover the damp floor, he sat down. Fearful of who might be around him, he fought to stay awake as several large black rats scurried across the feet of an elderly man who seemed not to notice; another figure was curled up in the corner twitching and muttering.

Why had everyone abandoned him? Surely someone would know he was here, would come to help him? But things were happening so quickly. It had only been a few days since the horses had been stolen and even if a message had been sent, he was no longer in Newmarket. Tomorrow he'd ask if there was anyone he could speak to. Someone who would listen rather than cutting him off when he tried to explain and would let him write a letter to send back to the Brecks. Unsure what time it was, his eyelids started to droop, the room around him still, apart from the pitter-patter of the rats. His head and shoulder aching, he clutched his arms around himself to keep warm until sleep and nightmares overtook him.

FOURTEEN

Watched over by two black-uniformed constables, both wielding stout batons, Isaac waited in silence with the others beneath the courtroom, his head forced forward by the vaulted brick ceiling. One by one, names had been called, as first a pale young girl and then the scruffy man had been summoned through the narrow iron gate and up the stairs to the invisible hubbub above. Both had returned after a few minutes, the girl sullen and tearful, the man grim-faced and angry.

The weeks that had followed his transfer to the gaol had passed in squalor and hunger, the fear of gaol fever ever-present. No one had come to visit him, the daily routine of thin porridge for breakfast and small bowls of watery stews and soups for dinner broken only by the single hour each day when they shuffled in circles around an inner courtyard, often returning wet and cold. The end of each week was marked by the compulsory Sunday service in the gaol chapel, but it was the nights he feared the most. Some tossed and turned, tormented by their lot; others who had lost their wits roamed and ranted, as he spent the long hours on edge, watchful and scared of a blow or worse. Unable to wash, with red bites from the fleas that crawled the whitewashed walls, he felt wretched, dreaming of his childhood and longing for the cool, soothing waters of the pond. During the days he had tried to recall something that might help, playing out what he would say when the time came. The words formed and repeated in his head over and over. It had seemed an eternity, until one day a man dressed in a clerk's suit with a handkerchief over his mouth and nose had come to the cells and called his name, telling him that he would be brought before the assizes the next day.

Pushed along the bench by some new arrivals, Isaac stared at the wall opposite and pressed his hands to his knees to try to stop them trembling, the chains around his scabbed wrists rattling like a tin bucket full of horseshoes.

'How long you been waiting?'

Wary, Isaac turned to look at the man who had just arrived. His grubby shirt and coat looked as if they may once have been of good quality; he had a round, pale face beneath a thinning crown of unkempt black hair streaked with white.

The man smiled, a warmth behind his brown eyes. 'I'm George —'

Isaac heard his name shouted from above and rose apprehensively to his feet. The weight of the shackles causing him to move like an old man, he climbed the steps to the courtroom above, emerging into the chaos of the soaring chamber, a blast of chatter and jeering like a gust of wind tearing across the Brecks. Pushed towards the front of the box, he grasped the brass rail, still warm from the last occupant. In hope, Isaac looked behind him, above a large white-faced clock, to the balcony, trying to find a familiar face. All around, the crowd bayed and hollered, enjoying the theatre, many settled for the day, bottles and napkins of bread in hand.

Overcome by the cavernous courtroom, Isaac felt small and alone as he turned back to face the front and the large brown canopy which towered above the court. Beneath it a man in a grey wig, his black robe trimmed in white fur, stared down from a high, red-backed chair, a sombre look on his face.

From behind a desk a mouse-like clerk scurried, a sheet of paper in hand, to the side of the court where two rows of men with the appearance of having risen above the masses sat. Standing before them, the clerk's high-pitched voice echoed round the court.

'That the accused, Isaac Bone, did knowingly aid and abet the theft of three horses from the yard of Lord Beaumont, and by doing so, did profit from their sale.'

Finished, the clerk walked across and handed the paper to the judge.

Isaac's skin prickled. Aid and abet – what did that mean?

'How do you plead?' the wigged man barked at him from above. 'Guilty or not guilty?'

His mouth suddenly dry, Isaac drew up all his courage. 'Not guilty, I didn't—'

The crowd rose in a clash of whoops and yells. The rabble blocked out all attempts of the judge to make himself heard, his voice barely audible over the noise.

Unsure what was happening, Isaac looked nervously up at the judge before, out of the corner of his eye, he saw two figures enter the room. The crowd quietened as the unmistakable presence of Mrs Stokes and Solomon took up a bench beside the two rows of men.

Isaac felt all hope drain away. The darkness in Mrs Stokes' eyes seemed to be deeper than ever as she glared, first at Solomon, then at him.

'Are there any witnesses?' the judge barked.

The clerk shuffled the papers on his desk. 'Yes, Your Honour.'

'Well, let's get on with it then.'

'Call Solomon Perry.'

The crowd erupted again as Solomon made his way down from the benches and onto a small stand. Delighted at the awkward gait of the chubby figure, shouts of 'put him on a spit' and 'oink-oink' followed him across the room, the crowd now in full flow.

On being handed a Bible, his voice hardly more than a whisper, Solomon repeated the words read out by the mousey man.

The judge looked down on the shaking figure. 'Can you tell the court what you saw on the night of the theft?'

Solomon looked across at his aunt, small beads of sweat standing out on his forehead. 'I was in the Wagon and Horses when I saw...' he paused, swallowing hard before continuing, 'saw the accused cross the bar and speak to a lad with red hair. They disappeared out back for a moment, and when they came back were drinking together. After a while they got up and left.'

'And did you see where they went?'

'I looked out the window and saw them walk across the street together.'

'Them?' the judge asked.

'The ginger-haired lad and another boy who followed them out of the inn. They headed in the direction of the stables.'

'Lord Beaumont's stables?'

'Yes.'

Isaac couldn't understand why he or one of the lads hadn't noticed Solomon. They hadn't invited him, yet he claimed he was at the inn, that he saw him with Jack. He had tried and tried to recall if he had glimpsed him that night but without success. He was sure one of them would have noticed. It all seemed so wrong.

'You may sit down,' the judge directed. 'Is there anyone else we should hear from?'

The clerk glanced down at his papers.

'Mrs Stokes, Your Honour.'

Isaac watched as Mrs Stokes marched, head held high, to the spot that Solomon had just vacated. Dressed in her usual black, Mrs Stokes cleared her throat and repeated the oath before shifting to face the judge.

'Mrs Stokes, I believe you know this boy Isaac Bone. Could you tell the court how he came to be employed at the yard?'

Mrs Stokes gave the judge her best smile before she told how Colonel Stokes had brought him to Newmarket and how they had given him a place to stay and fed him.

'But you believe he was part of the gang who stole the horses?' the judge asked.

'Undoubtedly, Your Honour. The only way into the yard is via the side gate, to which he had the key. My nephew saw him and his accomplices together on the night of the theft and saw them leave the inn and head for the yard. He let them in and then tried to make it look like he knew nothing about it. My suspicion is that in a few days he would have run off and joined his friends and we would never have seen him again.'

'I see,' the judge said. 'You may step down, and thank you for your brevity.'

Isaac watched as the black figure strutted back to her seat, settling beside a sweating Solomon. Why would she say that? He felt the rage surge inside him. And Solomon being at the inn… it seemed so unlikely. Taking a long breath, he turned back to the judge, ready to explain that he hadn't stolen any horses, as the crowd behind him hushed in anticipation.

'Jury, you have heard the evidence,' the judge said. 'Please consider your verdict.'

FIFTEEN

Like a blacksmith's hammer, Isaac felt the blow as the foreman uttered a single word.

'Guilty.'

His legs wavered beneath him, threatening to send him crashing to the floor; a jolt through his chest made him grasp the rail as hard as he could. The courtroom was in uproar as the judge called for order; the raucous crowd were on their feet, calls to string him up ringing in Isaac's ears.

'Sir!' Isaac tried to make himself heard above the continuing din, fighting to keep back the tears.

Expectant, the crowd fell silent, eager to hear the sentence. Clearing his throat, the judge glared down.

'Sir. It wasn't like that. I didn't—'

'Silence,' the judge roared, hammering the desk with his fist. 'The court has heard the evidence and you have been found guilty of the crime of which you were accused. It is now my duty to impose sentence on you.'

Tears streaming down his cheeks, Isaac looked across to where Mrs Stokes sat, her arms folded, the trace of a smile at the corners of her thin mouth.

'But, sir…'

The judge raised a hand and beckoned the constable forward.

'Isaac Bone, you have been found guilty. Horse theft is a serious matter and I understand that the horses are still missing, yet you continue to say you do not know where they are. In the past, you would have hanged, but in accordance with the law I hereby sentence you to seven years' transportation and penal servitude. From here you will be returned to the gaol and held until such a time that you will be taken to the port for your departure.'

Seven years? Transportation? Isaac threw himself at the edge of the box, shouting at the judge, pleading with him as the chains that hung from his wrists slammed against the dark wood. The crowd erupted, enjoying the theatre, egging him on as he tried to scramble from the dock, calling him a ferocious mouse, a pipsqueak.

Why wouldn't they let him explain? Where were his family, his friends? Why hadn't they come?

His feet unable to find a hold on the smooth wood, he felt a sudden blow, pain searing down the back of his skull. Around him, the courtroom spun. No longer able to see the crowd clearly, Isaac put his hand to the back of his head, a warm trickle running down his neck, his fingers wet with blood. In front of him the lips of the judge moved silently as his legs crumpled beneath him. The constable moved closer, slapping his baton into the palm of his hand as a warning. His determination overcoming his fear of another blow, he attempted to raise himself from the floor, everything distant and muffled, slivers of light dancing before his eyes. Falling back, he felt the rage that had surged through him seep away, his place in the world no longer certain. Beaten, he dropped his shackled wrists to the floor, his body no longer part of him as a wave of darkness crept over him and everything faded.

SIXTEEN

Isaac opened his eyes and made to raise his head, sharp pain surging through his brow, the bite of cold metal on his ankles. Confused, a wave of nausea caught in his throat. Unable to focus, he heard the low voice of a man, the words indistinct but close by. Was the man talking to him? His thoughts collided and bounced, the throb of his skull, the dim light, the cold, the sound of mumbled words. The space around him swirled as he tried to sit up, the floor damp and gritty. The courtroom, the crowds, the judge, then it had gone dark. He had to explain, find someone who would listen to him.

'Careful.'

Isaac felt a hand gently grasp his arm and help him sit up, the chill of the wall against his back making him shiver. Upright, the world spun again as he reached behind his head, the touch making him wince.

'Bit of a gash,' the man said. 'Best stay still.'

Isaac blinked and looked at the man who knelt next to him. 'Where are we?'

'Back in the gaol.' The man held out a hand. 'George

Thompson, apothecary, formerly of Sudbury. We met briefly at the court.'

Isaac took the hand and shook it feebly, the movement sending another jolt of pain across his skull. 'Isaac Bone. George, can you help me? I need to tell them I didn't steal any horses, that I'm not guilty. That it was Jack.'

'Shush.' The man looked down at Isaac. 'It's no good you getting all worked up. The trial's over and there is little you can do about it. How many years did they sentence you to?'

'Transported for seven years. But I never did it.' Isaac hung his head.

'Same.'

They sat in silence for a while, his eyes closed against the flicker of the torch outside the cell. Unable to sleep, he shuffled on the filthy floor he turned to the man beside him. 'So how did you end up here?'

'Because I'm a fool, that's why.' George told him how one day a man had come to his shop saying that a friend had had an accident and driven a spike into his leg. He had gone with the man to where his friend lay delirious, clothes wet with sweat. The flesh around the wound was red and burning, the centre yellow and pus-filled. He had given the man some laudanum and set some maggots on the wound and covered it loosely, returning each day until, on the fourth day, his fever had dropped and the maggots, full and swollen, had done their work. When he had presented the bill, the men said they could not pay but offered some plates and other household items instead. He had taken them in lieu of payment, and when a week or so later some cheapjacks came to the shop to buy stock for their next roving, he asked them if they were interested in the items. They had examined them and offered a price, which was more than the maggots and medicine had cost.

'I don't follow,' said Isaac. 'You just helped a sick man.'

'So it seemed.' About to go on, the warden called for silence, snuffing out the torch, plunging them into darkness.

'Best try and get some sleep,' George whispered.

The throb in his head subsiding, Isaac stared into the darkness. Guilty, that is what the judge had said. Guilty. Now he was destined for the other side of the world and didn't know how to make them believe him. He would ask to see the Governor in the morning; ask for a message to be sent to his family; they would speak to Lord Stanton. Resolved to make them listen, he tucked his hands under his arms to stay warm and waited.

SEVENTEEN

Roused by shouting and the rattle of the key in the lock, Isaac and George were led out to the yard, the brightness of the June sun making them screw up their eyes as they were herded into a covered wagon where four others already sat waiting. Pressed together, a heavy chain was threaded through their fetters, the end secured to bolts driven through the floor. It was impossible to move more than a few inches.

Isaac looked at George. 'Where are they taking us? The judge said we would be held in the gaol.'

'Hush down, boy,' a stocky, thick-necked man, who was wedged against the side, growled. 'Don't need your whining; they'll take us where they want and nought we can do about it.'

'Leave the boy alone.' This time a woman spoke. 'Heard we are set for the hulks, then onto the ships and off their hands.'

Isaac pulled at his fetters. Near to panic, he felt George's hand on his arm.

'Best not cause a rumpus – that gash on your head needs to heal, and it won't do any good.'

'I need to speak to the Governor; I can't go, George. I can't. I can't even swim; what if the ship sinks? My sister went to the coast once, said there were waves so big they could sweep a man off his feet. Me and my friends used to splash around in the ponds back in the Brecks, but you could feel the sand between your toes. I'm sure I'll drown.'

'It's not always rough. I been to Amsterdam a few times, to learn about herbs and plants that can cure pain and illness. It was so still it was like gliding over ice.'

A thud on the side of the wagon, a command for silence, and the wagon jolted off. The town was only just stirring as the rattle of their chains merged with the rumble of the wheels. Packed together, they soon began to swelter, with a driving thirst as the hours dragged by. Sometime around the middle of the day they had stopped and been led down from the wagon. Still chained together, those needing to relieve themselves had to do so while the others averted their gaze. Thrown a few husks of bread and a cup of gritty water each, they had climbed back up and continued.

The air had cooled as the wagon came to a halt for the day. Stiff and bruised, Isaac eased himself down with the others. Made to drink like cattle from a stone trough, they were led inside a squat wooden barn, the chain secured to a thick upright pillar. The barn door locked, Isaac slumped to the floor, the thin layer of straw crackling as he lay down as best he could.

'So, who's this Jack character?' George asked.

Isaac sat up, prompting a grunt from the man next to him. Not wanting the others to hear, he told George how he had met Jack when he sent him flying in the street, about his clothes, his delicate hands and sweet scent.

'After that I didn't see him again till he appeared at the inn. I tried to get away, but he made me drink with him. He had this silver flask which he poured into the ale, and it was after that the room began to spin and I felt strange. I tried to get back to the yard but when I reached the gate I must have passed out.'

'My guess is that he drugged you. Maybe laudanum. Lucky he didn't kill you.'

'Maybe it would have been better if he had.' Isaac turned away to hide his tears.

'And you think this Jack was behind the horse theft?' George said.

'It must have been Jack, but everyone thinks I was involved, that I stole the horses. But I didn't, George.'

'Well, that may be the case, but there is no way to prove it. Just like I can't prove I didn't know the goods I handled were stolen.'

'Stolen? You said you helped a sick man, that they paid you with goods.'

'That's right. But a few weeks after I'd treated the wounded man, he and his friend came by the shop. I told them about the cheapjack and how he had given me a good price for the items. They said they had some other bits and pieces, inherited from a relative. If I offered them to the cheapjacks next time they called, they would give me a share for my trouble. Then one day two constables arrived and demanded to search the shop. It was then that I realised that the items were stolen.'

'But how were you to know, George? It's not like you stole them.'

'That might be, just like you didn't steal anything. However, those who did are long gone and we are left behind to take the blame.'

Close to despair, Isaac closed his eyes.

'What will happen to your shop, George? Your family?'

'No family, Isaac, just me.'

'Will you two quit chattering?' The man next to Isaac turned over, yanking the chain as he did.

'Best we get some sleep, Isaac,' George said. 'Expect we have another long day in front of us, and who knows what comes after that?'

EIGHTEEN

After the gaol, Isaac never thought there could be anywhere more squalid. It had been nearly dark when they had arrived at the hulks. With their sails and masts stripped away, the blurry outlines resembled giant stranded sea creatures. Escorted by men in thick grey coats buttoned tightly against the biting wind, they were led from the wagon and up the narrow gangway. The chain that had bound them was removed before they were ordered down a ladder into the belly of the wooden prison, lit only by a solitary lamp. The stench turning his stomach, Isaac looked among the bodies, trying to find a space, as the hatch slammed behind them, with the sound of a bolt being pushed into place.

Their eyes becoming accustomed to the gloom, he and George picked their way among the men who filled the cramped space. About to sit down, a piercing scream filled the deck. Rooted to the spot, Isaac could make out the shape of a colossal man, his head stooped by the confines of the deck, a rake-thin man cowering at his feet.

The rest of the deck turned in silent horror as the giant man stroked his shaggy beard, his hirsute arms bulging, hands so large that Isaac trembled at the thought of what he might do. His face empty of emotion, the giant stared down before reaching out and grabbing the man's tunic, hurling him across the cage, like a sparrow tossed about in a gale. Everyone winced at the crunch of breaking bones as the man slammed against the wall and slid lifelessly to the floor. Still as a statue, a deep, animal-like growl came from the giant, and a gap hurriedly appeared as people cleared a space, keen to get away from the man who thundered between them.

'Blimey, who was that?'

'That's Jeffrey, or the Magpie as he is better known,' the man beside him whispered. 'Likes shiny things and doesn't worry whose they are. Rumour is he ripped half of a man's face off just to get a silver earring he was wearing. Likes to welcome new arrivals, see what they might have about them, so I'd keep your distance if I was you.'

Shocked, Isaac felt deep in his pocket for the precious brass, grasping it tightly in his palm. With the light of the lamp now a meagre flicker, the damp timbers creaking with the decay of long-ago battles, dried blood and crushed bones, he sat down next to George. One eye on the giant, Isaac listened to the water as it slapped against the rotten hull, terrified it would break through and drown them all while they slept. Somewhere in the long, dark hours, the lap of the water lessened, the grunts and coughs of all those around him replacing the rhythm of the waters until slivers of early light crept through the cracks of the twisted hull.

The thud of the hatch smacking against the hull, a shaft of square light broke the darkness, waking them all from a listless sleep. Unsure what to do, Isaac fell into line with the rest of the men, following them up the ladder and onto the deck. As he stood waiting, Isaac looked around. A low mist obscured the horizon, hanging above muddy inlets; a thin trickle of water carved its way through the grey silt. Where he had expected to see busy warehouses, a solitary wooden shack stood, two red-coated soldiers seated around a brazier the only sign of life.

The deck was filling, and Isaac saw the man they called the Magpie squeeze through the hatch, dwarfing the men on either side, who tried to keep their distance.

A shout of 'Rations' and a barefooted man dressed in rags dragged a bucket towards them, a consumptive-looking young boy behind him struggling with a dirty sack. Waved forward, the men picked up a wooden bowl from a trunk and trooped past the barefooted man, who ladled the lumpy liquid from the bucket, before the men retrieved a wedge of bread from the sack. The soup was cold and smelt of cabbage. Isaac dunked the rock-hard bread furiously into his bowl to try to soften it. After only a few mouthfuls the command to 'Finish up' rang through the air, and bowls were hurriedly emptied and returned to the trunk. Scattered around the deck, the guards who had met them the previous evening seemed even more menacing, their wooden clubs dotted with nails, others holding curled whips.

'George,' Isaac said, 'what's happening?'

'No talking,' a guard snarled, 'or you'll be on half rations.'

Fearing the loss of even the meagre morsels, Isaac and George fell silent and waited. Marched past a mound of old rope, each of the men picked up a length and began to pick the strands apart. The rope was coarse and tightly woven and Isaac's fingers were soon raw and bleeding, the pain unbearable.

'See if you can find a splinter of wood or the like,' the man seated next to him said. 'It will help; just don't let the guards see.'

*

Over the following days and nights, Isaac and George found a kindship with the others. Some had been on the hulk for months; others like them had recently arrived. On days when there were no ropes, they were given planks covered in barnacles to pick clean, the guards wandering between them, clubs wielded, a kick here and there. Sitting among them, the Magpie had remained silent, a glance or grunt enough to make men flinch and divert their gaze, the guards seemingly happy to leave him alone. Some days the drizzle and mist never ceased, the breeze that blew in from the sea piercing them all to the bone, the return to the cramped confines and relative freedom of the hull each night a blessed relief.

Once the hatch was closed for the night, George reached into his pocket. 'Still want to write to your folks?'

'How did you get that?' Isaac looked at the folded piece of paper George was holding.

'Let's just say I found it on the way back from the head. I have a piece of charred wood as well; that will have to do to write with and we will just have to hope it doesn't get wet.'

'Thanks George. Could you help me write it please?'

'Happy to. But we need to do it soon. Rumour is that the next fleet is getting ready to sail and we still need to find a way to send it.'

Finally able to write home, Isaac was at a loss for what to say. George, with his never-ending patience, listened, making suggestions until finally the page was filled with grey words.

'Do you think there will be enough time? It's all happened so quickly. If only I could have written before.'

'Least they will know you are alive and hopefully someone can speak up for you. Fold it and try to keep it dry. There's a couple of guards seem decent – I'll see if we can get them to help.'

'Thank you, George. Seems the only good thing to come out of all of this is has been meeting you. Although I wish it could have been in better circumstances.'

'I know. Me too but if we can get the letter sent there may still be a chance.'

*

Two days later, as they climbed the ladder towards the low grey sky, Isaac noticed that the gangway between the hulk and the shore was in place, a dozen armed soldiers at its end. Standing in the shadow of first light, he looked for the now usual spirals of rope, his cracked fingers already protesting. Ordered to line up, he stood gazing out as a heavy chain was once more fed through the fetters they clamped around his grimy ankles.

Finished, all the guards but one stood back. Hand behind his back, he smiled knowingly. 'When I say move, lead off down to where those lovely boys in red are waiting for you, and enjoy your walk. It will be the last one you take on English soil.'

NINETEEN

August 1839

The low, unbroken drab sky wrung its misery onto the waiting men. Closely watched over by red-coated marines, the long snake of shivering men had shuffled slowly forward, growing as they added more men to the line.

The docks were busy with the rumble of carts, traders heaving bulging sacks and boxes, men hauling bundles from the towering warehouses to the waiting ships. On stalls set up along the quay, fishmongers fought the screeching gulls who swooped to peck away at the discarded guts, their white deposits splattering the cobbled pavement. Alongside a black carriage, two men quarrelled furiously, their words vulgar and blasphemous.

'How are you doing, George?' Isaac looked straight ahead so as not to attract attention.

'Cold. Could do with the jakes, I've been standing here for so long. What about our transport? The *Marquis of Bath* sure sounds la-di-da. Maybe they will give us a private cabin.'

Despite George's attempt to lighten his mood, Isaac looked up at the ship that scraped against the dock, tugging at the tight cables, restless to be free. From where Isaac stood, he could see a latticed window stretching wide across the rear end of the ship, three shadows of yellow light inside. Along the side, uniform rows of square hatches – some open, others closed – ran to the front; the calls of the men inside could be heard as they readied the ship. High above, three masts – the tip of the tallest lost in the shroud of drizzle – swarmed with men who scurried around the spider's web of ropes.

As he watched a dozen bleating sheep being swung over the side in a large net, he tried to imagine how everyone in the line that stretched in front of and behind him would fit on the small vessel. He had become used to the cramped confines of the hulk, but that was moored alongside the bank of the river, far from the sea. This ship looked tiny in comparison. Terrified at the thought of weeks at sea, Isaac looked towards the front of the line where the distinctive bulk of the Magpie towered over a clerk, who sat huddled against the damp at a makeshift table at the bottom of the gangway. The routine that preceded entry to the ship began for the umpteenth time that day. As Jeffrey drew his tunic over his head, Isaac gasped. A dense coat of black hair covered his entire chest and back, his appearance more that of an animal than a man. When he was stripped to the waist, a man in a sturdy blue coat, a tricorn hat atop his head, circled slowly round him. Tall, but still overshadowed by the giant, he waved the Magpie forward, the timber planks groaning and twisting beneath his weight as he made his way up onto the ship.

Wet and cold, the chain of men shuffled forward. When only a handful of men were left in front of him, Isaac heard a thick, rasping cough break the air as a frail, elderly man lurched towards the desk. Isaac had seen him fall from one of the wagons earlier, and by the way the man's chest heaved, it was clear he was unwell. Barely able to stand, the man tried to remove his shirt, revealing a glimpse of exposed ribs as he struggled to move his arms. Isaac listened as the man in the blue coat turned to the clerk at the desk.

'This man is sick. We can't risk contagion on board. Have him removed and taken back to wherever he came from.'

'Yes, Doctor Wheeler,' the seated clerk said, signalling for the guards.

The emaciated form turned, another thick cough rattling from his wasted body; as he bent double, one of the guards stepped quickly away from the old man, his face speckled with red droplets.

'Filth!' The guard drove the butt of his rifle into the back of the half-standing form, sending him crashing to the ground. The man fought for breath, his sunken eyes staring upwards as his shallow face turned blue.

'George, why doesn't someone help him?'

'Shush, there isn't anything that can be done for him. Better he ends his days here, rather than in some deep ocean or unfamiliar land.'

Now at the head of the line, Isaac glanced back towards the lifeless man with pity, watching as the marines kicked the lifeless body towards a filthy canvas.

'Shirt off,' came the instruction.

Isaac clutched the bottom of his tunic and dragged it over his head.

'Arms up above your head and turn around slowly. Any red spots, breathing difficulties, diarrhoea, fever or cramps?'

'No, sir.'

'Good, mark him as cleared.'

As he pulled his shirt back on, Isaac watched the blue eyes of the man who had examined him flicker. The man's skin was pale and smooth, his posture that of a gentleman, but Isaac felt he had a hint of sadness about him. About to head onto the ship, Isaac hesitated, sad at what his life had become.

'Sir.' He hesitated, nervous at what he was about to ask. 'Could you send this for me?'

The man frowned. 'Speaking to an officer is a punishable offence on ship. Don't you know that?'

Isaac dropped his hand to his side, the letter held tight.

'But seeing as we are not on ship yet, leave it with my clerk.'

A hint of a smile flickered across the man's face as Isaac laid the letter on the table. 'Thank you, sir.'

Feeling a wave of relief, Isaac trudged up onto the ship and joined the rest of the men who stood huddled between coils of ropes, crates and barrels piled high. Overhead, barefoot men swung from ropes, their movement like the squirrels that filled the trees of the plantation back in the Brecks. At the far end of the ship, a small group of women huddled together, tiny infants screaming as they gripped ragged skirts.

George appeared, tucking his shirt in. 'Isaac, what were you thinking? Speaking to the officer. Asking him to send the letter.'

'I just panicked, George. I thought if I didn't ask then it would be too late.'

'You were lucky not to get into trouble. What did he say?' George said.

'I know, but he said to leave it and that's as good as I could have hoped for. Hopefully it will get back home, too late to save me now, but like you said, at least they will know I'm alive.'

Men still climbing onto the deck, the pace of the sailors quickened, words Isaac didn't understand bellowed by a short-set man, whose limbs were thick with muscle. Sent down into the belly of the ship, they were told they would be held below deck until they were out at sea. After that the captain would address all convicts on deck.

Isaac swallowed. A convict; that was what he had become. No longer Isaac Bone, a furrow boy, a stable lad or apprentice jockey, just a convict. Apart from George, he knew no one, and feared what lay ahead. Below deck, the smell of tar and stale air mixed with fear at the voyage to come. They squeezed together as the slam of the hatch extinguished the light overhead. The last time he would look at an English sky.

TWENTY

The sway and creak of the wooden prison increased; loud commands rattled through the deck to meet the rumble of the men below. Isaac tried to count how many people had been crushed onto the ship. He had watched the line of convicts gradually walk up the gangway; then there were the women and children, the men in red tunics, the sailors and officers, the animals – all crammed onto the tiny ship.

At an abrupt gurgle from his stomach, Isaac sat down and wrapped his arms around his knees, the churn of the sea just a few inches away. In a futile attempt not to join those around him, he swallowed hard, but the swaying of the packed hold was too much as he added to the already slimy mess.

'I can't stand this for months on end.' Isaac wiped his mouth on his sleeve and looked at George.

'Try to concentrate on that beam over there...' George stopped mid-sentence, retching hard. All night they had floundered in the terrible darkness, powerless to escape the rancid mess that slopped around them. His stomach empty, Isaac gave up any attempt to evade the slime.

The ship still rocking, a blast of cold air rushed into the hold as a man with his arms decorated in blue letters and shapes peered down. Clearly taken aback by the acrid smell and the sight of the convicts, he had disappeared, returning with a cloth held to his mouth and nose. Beckoned by the man, Isaac followed the others up and out, the whip of an icy breeze a welcome respite from the slippery mire below. No land in sight, a grey sea enveloped the small ship, the shape of two more ships silhouetted against the horizon.

Like moles, men spilled up from the depths, nudging against each other so everybody could fit on the congested deck. Clearly, many had had the same grim night – pale faces and red eyes everywhere. They were told to be silent. A man in a dark navy coat, gold braid on the shoulders, appeared above them, hands behind his back, as two younger men in similar uniforms flanked him. A step away was the doctor who had marked Isaac off when he had boarded.

The uniformed man spoke with authority, his voice crisp and commanding. Even the breeze briefly calmed as he addressed the packed deck.

'My name is Captain Crane and I am the commander of this ship, and these are Lieutenants Stone and Shepard. We are bound for Tasmania and the penal colony at Port Arthur. Those under the age of eighteen will transfer to the boy's prison at Point Puer when we arrive. I would remind you all that you are convicted criminals, and you will work hard and obey orders during this voyage. In return, you will get your rations and fair treatment. Anyone who breaks the rules will feel the lash; boys will kiss the gunner's daughter. This is Doctor Wheeler.' The captain waved a hand at the man who had examined them the previous day when they had boarded the ship. 'He will attend to you if you are unwell. I expect you to attend service every Sunday, and I will not stand for squalor and filth.'

With that, he turned, acknowledging a salute from the two lieutenants who fell in behind him, leaving Doctor Wheeler looking down to where the exhausted convicts stood.

'Early days at sea can be difficult but let me reassure you it will get easier for most of you. The mate tells me that the decks below need to be swilled out. We will show some of you how to do this. The rest of you will wash yourselves and your clothes. Carry on, bosun.'

Isaac looked at the grey sea that surrounded him and tried to not to vomit again. Above, the sails strained against the wind, the ship leaving a trail of white as it began its voyage.

Glad not to be sent down into the mess of the hull, Isaac and the other convicts were shown how to lower wooden buckets over the side and then haul them, hand over hand, back to the deck, before the convicts were directed to remove their soiled clothes and place them in a bucket.

Struck with alarm, Isaac felt in his pocket, not wanting others to see the brass. Men already half naked, Isaac shyly stripped off his sick-stained shirt and stepped out of his trousers, concealing the precious metal under his bare foot. Standing in only his underclothes, Isaac shivered as he waited his turn to scrub his clothes in the ice-cold water. His hands numb, he pulled the still sodden clothes on and bent to pick up the brass. Fingers blue with cold, he fumbled the cherished item; a loud crack as the brass hit the timbers. Despite the harsh cold, a pulse of blood made him rush with heat as he stepped hastily to cover the precious keepsake. Glancing around to see if anyone had noticed, he willed his fingers to grasp the glistening metal, desperate to stash it away out of sight.

As he slipped the brass into his pocket, the sky around him darkened as Jeffrey's shadow loomed over him. Filled with terror, Isaac saw the man's battered face up close for the first time. Beneath the wide bush of eyebrows, narrow iniquitous eyes snapped back and forth. His nose was lumpy and misshapen with long hairs protruding from each nostril. Isaac took a step back, afraid the man would grab him as the brute's eyes bore through him, making him think of the wretched man from the first night on the hulk.

'Nice sparkling trinket you have there,' Jeffrey growled. 'Maybe you should turn it over to me for safekeeping, or perhaps I'll just crush your scrawny little carcass and help myself.'

Isaac readied himself for a strike, convinced the man's threats were not a bluff, as he reached into his pocket.

'Move.' Isaac felt a wave of relief as a marine waved his rifle at Jeffrey.

A look of fury crossed Jeffrey's face as he shoved his way between two shivering convicts, kicking the bucket over as he moved away. Retrieving the brass and slipping it into his pocket, Isaac cursed himself for being so careless. Now Jeffrey knew he had the brass, and everyone knew that what Jeffrey wanted, Jeffrey got.

TWENTY-ONE

Days passed. Some still clung to the rails, unable to stand the constant motion, which bothered Isaac less and less. He was now able to eat a few mouthfuls of rations without the need to rush for the side, and the rocking of the ship began to remind him of the steady canter of the horses he used to ride.

The air grew warmer as the sky turned blue, the chill wind replaced by a tranquil breeze. A twice-weekly dose of vinegar, lime juice and sugar to ward off scurvy had now become every other day as the supply of fresh vegetables and fruit dwindled. Anything still edible was reserved for the captain's table.

The daily routine had developed much like those of the gaol and the hulk. Burnt red, the convicts had worked on the wooden deck, endlessly scrubbing, cleaning or whatever else they were ordered to do. High above, barefoot sailors hollered and sang in rhythm as they perched precariously on the ropes and masts.

As they knelt in line, worn brushes in hand, George had shaken out some of the coarse sand used for scrubbing the decks and drawn a rough map. 'Look, Isaac. See, we don't run in a straight line.' George traced a zigzag across the powdery map before running a line round the bottom to a large island. 'By taking this route we can run the winds, which makes it quicker and we can take on fresh water and supplies more easily.'

'If you say so, but can't see why we don't go straight down and round.' Isaac sighed, trying to remember the map from the flint schoolhouse back in the Brecks.

George looked serious. 'Because the winds would push us onto the rocks around that coast. Look lively, here comes the bosun.'

George plunged his hand into the nearby bucket and washed away the crude map. A loud bellow from the bosun cut the air as a rush of marines barged through, a racket coming from the rear of the ship. Everyone turned to see a blur of red-coated marines trying to wrestle a wild-looking Jeffrey to the ground. The brute seemed possessed as he hit out at a skinny marine, sending him skidding across the deck in a daze.

A single rifle shot rang out, an array of rifles now pointed at Jeffrey. Isaac waited for Jeffrey to fall but he stood defiant, a human oak tree surrounded by rifles.

'On your knees,' the marine sergeant commanded. 'Or I'll order the men to shoot you where you stand.'

'Sergeant.' The voice of the captain came from the deck above. 'Get that man in irons and down below. Now.'

Jeffrey didn't flinch as they edged towards him, letting them bind his arms behind him and be led away.

Isaac turned back to scrubbing the deck. 'What was all that about? Did you see the rage in him? Six of them couldn't get him down. Do you think they would have shot him, George?'

'No telling. Every man that they get there alive is a profit, but I suspect he is going to pay for that outburst.'

*

The following day at muster Isaac noticed the grate that normally covered the hatch was leaning against the mast. 'What's going on, George? Why is the grate like that?'

'I think Jeffrey is going to pay for yesterday,' George whispered.

Isaac watched as a tall young man was led across the hushed deck, followed by the imposing form of Jeffrey. Behind them a line of marines' bayonets was fixed on them, preventing any retreat.

Hands clasped behind his back, the captain waited as the doctor and one of the officers made their way down towards the grating.

'Convicts,' the captain addressed the crammed decks; men, women and children hushed at the dread of what they were about to see. 'I have gathered you here to witness the punishment of these two men. I will maintain order on this ship and anyone who thinks otherwise should take note of what they are about to see. Lieutenant, if you please.'

'Isaac,' George whispered, 'look straight ahead and don't close your eyes. Try to think of a song in your head.'

Lieutenant Stone stepped forward, a nervous flick of his tongue around his lips before he spoke. 'John Harris. You have been found guilty of stealing food; sentence: two dozen lashes.'

The young man struggled against the two sailors who pushed him towards the grate, spread his arms and fed his hands through rope loops, tightened with a sharp tug. One of the sailors stepped behind the now sobbing man and ripped open his shirt to expose pale white skin, stretched over a rack of bones. As a wooden gag was forced into his mouth, the young man twisted against the grate, trying to look behind him, his face wet with fear.

Satisfied everything was ready, the lieutenant nodded to a single drummer. At the rumble of a drum the bosun stepped forward, a vicious-looking whip with knotted strands gripped in his hand. Isaac had become used to seeing the man around the deck, the ease with which he carried barrels and hauled on the ropes a testament to his strength. The drum stopped, and a weighty silence hung over the deck as the lieutenant shouted, 'One!' The bosun's arm was a blur as it swished through the muted silence, the slap clearly heard as it hit the back of the man hanging from the grate; a muffled scream escaped the man's gag as his pale body writhed on the grate. Isaac winced as the lashes fell with the steady beat of the drum, the count rising. The lines on the man grew from thin pink lines to deep red gashes, the blood from the open wounds soaking into the waistband of the man's trousers. The count reached twenty-four. The man sagged to the deck when the ropes were loosened, whimpering, the sides of his mouth trickling with blood from where he had bitten down on the gag.

The young man was dragged away, and Jeffrey was led forward, the marines wary as he was secured to the grate.

The officer cleared his throat. 'Benjamin Jeffrey. For striking a member of the crew: five dozen lashes.'

Offered the same gag used by the young man, Jeffrey clamped his mouth shut. This time there was no grunt, no struggle on the grate as the whip fell time after time. The man with the lash swung with force and power until the count reached thirty. The hair-covered back was now a raw mess of ripped flesh and crimson blood. The man paused and dipped the whip in a bucket; the water that ran across the deck when he pulled the strands through his hand was a deep crimson. All on deck watched as Doctor Wheeler stepped forward and examined the spreadeagled Jeffrey. A solemn expression on his face, the doctor indicated for the flogging to continue. Steadily, the beat continued until the final stroke was delivered, the drum falling silent. Untied, Jeffrey stood upright, his chest heaving, his back a matted carpet of hair, skin and flesh. Beaded with sweat, the bristled face showed no emotion, but from behind the dark eyes a deep defiance still burnt.

The marines clamped the irons back around Jeffrey's wrists and led him away. Glad the flogging was over, Isaac wondered at Jeffrey, how he had acted as if he never felt a thing while the young man appeared half dead. Jeffrey deserved his flogging – they weren't going to let him get away with attacking the marines – but it seemed unfair to whip the other man when all he had done was try to get some extra food.

The deck was clearing as the convicts went about their work when one of the crew handed Isaac a bucket and brush, indicating the area beneath the grating. Knowing what was expected, he dropped to his knees and began to scrub the bloodstained deck.

TWENTY-TWO

In the days that followed the flogging the ship ran with chatter, men huddled together in small groups, mutiny on their lips. Rumours went around the smouldering decks that the young man was close to death, his spirit broken as much as his body. Some, harsh in their judgement, said he deserved his punishment – they were all hungry. Others shook their heads and said men like Jeffrey just became harder at the end of the lash.

His mood low, Isaac stooped and picked up the bucket and made his way over to the side of the ship. As he dropped it over the side, his attention was caught by the doctor and one of the sailors who stood by the cages filled with chickens that occupied part of the deck out of bounds to convicts.

'Is there no one capable of looking after a few chickens and sheep?' the doctor reprimanded the embarrassed-looking sailor. 'Heaven knows we are short enough of food without the sheep dying or the chickens flying overboard!'

The sailor looked uncomfortable. 'With respect, sir,

we are seamen, not farmers. More used to hauling rope and anchor than caring for animals.'

The doctor sighed. 'There must be someone on this ship who could clean them out, water and feed them. Are you telling me among all these crew and convicts not one single man, woman or child has any experience of looking after animals?'

Forgetting the rules, Isaac hauled the bucket back up and approached the two men. 'Excuse me, sir, I've looked after chickens. I could care for them.'

The doctor looked down, his once pale face now a light brown. 'You again. I thought I made it clear before that approaching an officer is an offence? Maybe I should take you to the captain – see what he makes of your insolence?'

'Sir, I only meant—'

'Be quiet,' the doctor instructed. 'Remind me of your name.'

'Isaac Bone, sir.'

The doctor leant over and whispered something to the sailor who turned and made off in the direction of the cabins at the far end of the ship.

As he shifted from foot to foot, uneasy he had been so foolhardy in approaching the doctor, he waited until the sailor returned and handed the doctor a scrap of paper.

'Isaac Bone. Born Norfolk. Convicted of horse theft, sentenced to seven years' transportation. Country boy. Do you think you could look after sheep as well?'

'Yes, sir. I grew up in the country and we had chickens at home, and I know how to look after horses. Sheep aren't that different.'

The doctor suppressed a smile. 'I'd like to see you ride sheep. Is there anyone who could help you?'

'Yes, sir, George Thompson. He is a good man and knows about medicine as well.'

'Fair enough. Well, get these chickens cleaned out. The sheep are in pens on the lower deck. It will be your responsibility to make sure all the animals are kept safe and cared for. I'll speak to the bosun and get your friend reassigned. Oh, and you will sleep on deck to make sure the chickens and eggs don't go missing. Is that clear?'

'Yes, sir.'

Barely able to believe the endless hours of scrubbing the decks might be over, and that the constant noise and threat of disease could be behind him, Isaac ran to find George.

'George, you won't believe what has just happened.'

'Isaac.' George rolled his eyes in disbelief. 'Will you never learn? You're lucky that you don't find yourself bent over a canon for approaching the doctor like that. You were lucky the first time.'

Isaac's face fell. 'I thought you would be pleased. Means we don't have to sleep below deck anymore. We can rig up a shelter by the coops. You said fresh air was better than being crammed down in the bowels of the ship with all the filth and noise.'

'Well, you will need to show me what to do – you know I can't tell one end of a sheep from the other.' George grinned. 'I'm sorry, Isaac, of course it will be great, but you must stick to the rules otherwise you will find yourself in hot water.'

'I will,' Isaac promised. 'So shall we see what needs doing?'

Over the next few days, they cleaned and repaired the coops, just managing to grab one of the birds as it flapped its way towards the side. The sheep pens shared one of the lower decks with the women and children. The bedraggled woolly creatures smelt like damp blankets, so each day they manhandled them up into the fresh air for a few hours.

At night, they slept under a tatty piece of unused sail, rigged between the coops. The salty air was chilly after the warm days. The welcome peace of the moonlit hours was broken only by the ding of the bell as it signalled the change in watch, and the occasional fluttering of wings. Grateful to be away from the dangerous confines of the decks below, their spirits lifted. With the stars twinkling in the clear night sky above, the sails puffed out and full, for a moment the world almost seemed a better place.

TWENTY-THREE

Late in the afternoon, the clucking chickens secure in their coops, Isaac saw the sails billow against their ropes, the ship rocking on an unseen wave. Far away on the horizon the specks of the two following convict ships danced up and down, a strip of intense light separating the dark blue sea from a wall of towering black cloud. Disturbed by the approaching storm, the chickens began to flutter in the small coops, sensing the change as the sea beneath the tiny ship began to churn and froth. The wind increasing, a flurry of activity saw the captain, flanked by the two lieutenants, appear on the upper deck by the ship's wheel.

The sky above the ship darkened, the trailing ships now swallowed by the thunderous sky as heavy spots of rain peppered the deck. The captain's voice lost in the wind, Lieutenant Shepard climbed down onto the deck, orders bellowed against the wind sending sailors swarming like lines of ants up the masts. The usual collective chorus that rose in the air when there was work to be done was snatched away by the now howling wind, the ship pitching in the ever-growing waves.

'Get those chickens down into the hold,' one of the sailors ordered. 'Then stay down there.'

'Need a hand?'

Isaac was pleased to see George appear. 'Are the sheep secured?'

'Best they can be, but it's getting noisy down there and folk are fearful of what's coming.'

The sky and sea now one, the hellish wall of cloud had turned day to night, no way of telling where the horizon might be.

'Do you think we will drown?'

'Time for that when we are down below. Grab that last coop and let's get moving,' George said.

George and Isaac fought their way to the hatch, the pelting rain lashing against them, a flash of lightning revealing surging waves, the coop in danger of being torn from their grip as they battled across the deck. Sailors frantically roped down anything that wouldn't fit through the small opening. A deafening crash of thunder made the deck shake.

'Be quick, you two, or you will find yourself up here when she hits,' a dripping sailor warned.

Knocked sideways by a wave, George and Isaac struggled to stay upright, the coop almost lost. The hatch was battened down behind them, leaving them in near darkness, the clatter of the rain on the deck now sounding like large pebbles being dropped from the sky.

Wedging the coop between some crates, his clothes sodden, Isaac shouted over the deafening gale.

'George, can you find your way over to me? There is

just enough space for the two of us by these crates, and there are some old sacks we can use to bed down.'

Unable to make themselves heard over the din raging above, they fell into a fearful silence. The small craft creaked and groaned, lifted into the air by some giant unseen hand before being slammed down again and again. The claps of the thunder mixed with the screams of terror from those in the decks below begging to be let out. A mighty crash pushed the ship over on her side, everything sent topsy-turvy as the ship twisted and groaned, water pouring through the warped hull. Chaos tore through the dark air as Isaac scrambled to find a grip, the sound of a coop splintering as it crashed against the wall. All around, timbers cracked, and a trickle of freezing water began to fill the devastated deck. Convinced the ship would break in two, a drawn-out screech echoed all around before she fought back, debris sent spinning through the air once more as she righted herself.

'We are going to die, George.' Isaac felt the water lapping around his calves. 'That last wave nearly sunk us. If there is—' Another crash of thunder shook the ship, the scattered chickens flapping frantically around the rapidly filling deck.

The storm had raged on as the wind and sea fought a mighty battle amid the darkness, trying to rip the small ship apart and consume its human cargo. The anguished shouts of men and women rising through the floor that divided the decks, water poured through the hatches and any other cracks it could find as the battered vessel lurched and flipped like an autumn leaf blown across the heath.

Somehow the ship stood firm, the wind and rain weakening and the decks falling silent. Drained by fear and the thunderous noise of the last few hours, Isaac gathered up the chickens and, with no hope of finding a dry place, they huddled together until, exhausted, sleep overtook them.

TWENTY-FOUR

Filled with terror, Isaac jerked awake, the smell and force of a hand pressed over his mouth making it difficult to breath. Unable to see in the feeble light that struggled through the broken hull who had him pinned to the sodden deck, Isaac kicked and punched against the shadowy figure, the frenzy of blows useless against his attacker. Strength fading, Isaac froze in sudden realisation as the man spoke.

'Why don't you give me that little trinket of yours?'

'Leave the lad alone.' Isaac glimpsed George out of the corner of his eye as he moved towards them, pleading with Jeffrey, a slight tremble as he spoke. Still held down, Isaac watched with horror the grey outline of the man's hand swinging through the air, a sharp cry as it smashed into George with such force it knocked him from view. Finding a surge of strength, Isaac kicked out as he fought to get free, the thought of George lying hurt more than he could bear. Without warning he felt the weight lift as the man let go. Momentarily confused, Isaac put his hand to his jaw and sat up, desperate to find George as the jolt of the giant's footsteps echoed across the timbers. Hearing a muffled groan he looked on with horror at the enormous hairy foot now pushing down on George's already bleeding head.

'Shall we make this easy?' Jeffrey mocked. 'Give me that shiny piece and I won't crush his head like a rotten apple. Or would you rather see his brains all over the floor? Your choice.'

Isaac felt for the precious piece in his pocket, his fingers running over the familiar shape.

'Don't give it to him.' Isaac watched as a trickle of blood ran down George's face as Jeffrey pushed down harder.

'I must, George. He'll hurt you otherwise.'

Tears running down his cheeks, Isaac placed the precious brass into the outstretched palm and watched dirty fingers curl over it.

'There, wasn't too hard, was it?' Jeffrey smiled before he slipped the brass into his pocket and turned towards the hatch, the lined and scabby mass of back disappearing in the early morning light.

Isaac slid over to where George lay and helped him sit up. 'You all right?'

'Not too bad, lad, bit of a clump and my ears are ringing but sure I'll be fine. Must have been the storm set him loose. I'm sorry you lost your keepsake, Isaac. I know how much it meant to you. I just couldn't stop him – he's too big and strong for a country man like me.'

Isaac swallowed as he looked at George's battered face.

'I'm sorry too. It was brave of you to try but it was only a brass, not even that valuable.'

Isaac looked at his friend, a deepening red swelling already visible on the side of his face. As streaks of light found their way through the split hull, they waited, unsure what would greet them when they were finally allowed on deck or even if there was anyone left to unlock the hatch. Eventually, the sound of the wooden planks being slipped from their brackets brought them to their feet as the hatch flew open, a perfect blue square framed high above.

Assembled amid the tangle of rope and fallen canvas, the shivering convicts took in the destruction around them. The main mast hung like a broken match above the deck, the rails around the sides riddled with gaps, the sailors bedraggled and exhausted, the marines as bedraggled as the rest.

The strain of the storm etched on his face, the captain, followed by the officers and Doctor Wheeler, took up their usual places. As hush descended, Lieutenant Stone stepped forward. 'The captain has ordered that the ship be repaired as best we can. Progress will be slow but we will continue towards our destination. Rations will be halved, as much of the provisions have been lost to the seawater and are inedible. If any men think they could be of assistance working with wood or have a head for heights, then make yourselves known, and you will receive extra rations and your record will be marked for good conduct.'

A rumble of dissent rose from the convicts. Rations had been sparse before the storm, their diet little more than rock-hard biscuit infested with weevils.

Grim-faced, the captain stepped forward, cleared his throat and addressed the convicts. 'From this moment on, theft of food, no matter how small, or any talk of mutiny, will see the culprit hang. Carry on, Lieutenant.'

TWENTY-FIVE

Night and day after the storm had passed, the sound of banging and sawing filled the air as the sailors worked to rig a makeshift sail from the broken spars and tangled ropes. Helpless, the ship drifted, unable to resist the gentle current that now lapped at her battered hull. Lookouts scanned the horizon, clear cloudless skies in all directions, looking hopefully for the other ships. The sailors coaxing and cursing the stricken vessel to do their bidding, the single sail flapped forlornly in the breeze, the patched-up vessel making little progress across the rippling expanse. Below in the flooded decks convicts scooped seawater into buckets to lighten the ship while others worked to heal the wounded hull, pressing caulk into the weeping cracks till their fingers bled.

The sheep, rigid and bloated, joined the rest of the spoiled rations, tossed over the side to float away or sink beneath the rippling waters. Now left with nothing but a few scraggy chickens to mind, George and Isaac worked alongside the other convicts, able to return each night to the airy deck to guard the few birds that remained.

As the weeks passed, the reduced rations took their toll; the convicts and many of the crew could barely muster the strength to stand, let alone work. Gums raw, a never-ending ache in his joints, Isaac watched another body despatched to a watery grave.

Brooding, Isaac knotted a piece of twine around the corner of the chicken coop, unable to shift the unending pangs of hunger and thirst, his memory of the storm fresh in his mind. George's bruises and scabs had faded, but frequent sightings of Jeffrey brought back to Isaac the loss of his precious keepsake with a jolt.

'Penny for them?'

'Penny for what, George?'

'Your thoughts. Penny for your thoughts.'

'Oh. I was just wondering what Jeffrey did with my brass.'

'He'll have it stashed away somewhere if the storm didn't take it, and there isn't any way he is going to give it back.'

'But it was all I had.'

Isaac turned away, not wanting George to see the wetness in his eyes. Apart from the tatty clothes he wore, he had nothing; the brass was the only thing that he had managed to keep; now that had been taken from him. 'Do you think my letter will have arrived yet, George?'

'Fingers crossed, lad, but don't get your hopes too high; even if it has, it will take time given how far away we are.'

Distracted by a shout from the small platform perched precariously atop the makeshift mast, Isaac followed the sailor's outstretched arm, his finger pointing towards the horizon.

'Can't see what he is pointing at, can you, George?' Isaac said. 'Is it the other ships? We haven't seen them since the storm.'

'I think it may be some birds. We might be near land.'

'I can hardly remember what it's like for the ground not to be constantly swaying, and it would be lovely to have some fresh water and food instead of the dry biscuits.'

For the next few days everyone had scanned the sky, the lieutenants gazing through telescopes. Isaac was doubtful that the birds had been little more than a trick of the light.

One fresh dawn, a sharp cry of 'Land ho!' cut the air. Fatigue and hunger momentarily forgotten, Isaac joined the marines and sailors as they hurried to the side of the ship. Still indistinct, a mass of dark cliff fused with the lightening sky, the blue of the sea contrasted at the base. Isaac had prayed for the journey to end, to stand on dry land once more. But now he was nervous; the thought that he would be separated from George when they arrived was unbearable.

All day they skirted the coast, the cliffs descending to dense trees that almost reached to the sea. Night had come and gone but still the ship lurched on, no sign of life apart from a wisp of white, which may have been a fire or just mist.

Since the storm there had been little to do, the few balding chickens long since boiled for the captain's table. The convicts were allowed on deck, most sore-gummed and weak from the reduced rations, the marines faring no better as they kept watch.

When, finally, the shout came, few moved, most convinced it would be another false alarm. As George and Isaac hauled themselves up, they saw that the landscape had changed: a large cove rose high towards steep hills and a small town nestled at their feet. Isaac had always imagined that the land would be barren, with grey buildings surrounded by towering walls, just like the gaol. Instead, a green landscape reached up and away from a rocky shore. Scattered among small groups of trees, two red-brick buildings, each four storeys high, smoke rising from a tall chimney, filled the centre of the colony. To one side sat the recognisable outline of a church, smaller squat buildings made of similar red brick all around. Behind, the land sloped up and away to broad lush mountains which stretched along the skyline. As they edged closer, Isaac could make out white painted houses, one larger than the rest, with a veranda across the front. To the other side a small creek ran down from the trees to the sea where there was a group of faded tents, and figures in dresses bent double at the water's edge. Hemming the colony, enormous rocks, battered by white-crested waves, ended in high cliffs.

Convinced this couldn't be the penal colony, Isaac jumped at the rattle of the anchor chain as it snaked across the deck, a loud splash as it entered the water and plummeted down to the seabed. Ordered away from the side, their chatter replaced the usual moans and groans, everyone hopeful that the feel of earth and grass would soon replace the battered timbers of the ship beneath their feet. Thick clouds passed overhead as a small boat, rowed by men in rags, struggled across the waves towards them, knocking against the side of the ship. The captain and officers were out on deck in full regalia. A rope ladder was thrown over the side and a man in a tired, dusty uniform climbed onboard and saluted. The face of the captain remained stony, the salute barely acknowledged, before the party headed off, reappearing late in the afternoon. The men from the colony clambered back down to the waiting boat and headed away.

With the last slit of daylight on the horizon, Isaac looked down at the brown feather in his hand. 'I don't know how I'm going to survive without you, George.'

'You're a smart lad.' George put a fatherly arm around Isaac's shoulders. 'Just keep your wits about you and steer clear of trouble. We made it this far, and, well, can't say it has been fun, but it might have been worse.' George fought back the tears. 'Now we have a new challenge in front of us.'

TWENTY-SIX

December 1839

Isaac woke to the splash of oars, the first glint of light cracking the horizon. Not wanting to wake George, he tiptoed to the rail; the same small boat that had brought the men from the colony the day before was returning. Joined by George, they watched in silence as the silhouettes of the men rocked back and forth, each stroke bringing them closer.

A whistle pierced the morning calm as marines in full red uniform, rifles ready, lined the deck. Assembled with the other convicts, Isaac thought the deck seemed less crowded than the day they had set sail. Men, some leaning on others, stared apprehensively at the marines, while children so thin they looked like matchstick puppets from a visiting fair flopped by their mothers. Among them only Jeffrey seemed unchanged – his bulk no doubt maintained at the cost of those poor helpless convicts whose meagre rations he frightened them into giving to him.

Lieutenant Shepard waited while a curled rope, one end tied to the makeshift mast, dropped over the side to the waiting boat. Sailors heaved on the anchor, the helmsman fighting to steer the vessel against the current as the grunting rowers heaved on their oars. Inching towards the wooden jetty that reached out from the shoreline, the ship finally bumped to a halt, pairs of waiting hands tethering the exhausted vessel to a rest.

'Well, that's it, George,' Isaac said. 'I'm glad we won't have to spend any more time at sea, but I wish we could stay together.'

'Probably for the best, Isaac. You'll be safer with boys your own age.'

A grating of wood saw a side of the ship's splintered rail drawn back, the narrow gangway they had climbed up all those months ago lowered into position. From between the two brick buildings the tramp of boots grew as a line of marines from the colony, rifles readied, marched towards the jetty and formed a wall of red along the shore. Eager to be rid of his troublesome cargo, the ship's bosun instructed first the women and infants, then the boys, and finally the men to move to different parts of the deck.

Unable to speak, Isaac threw his arms round George.

'Stay strong, Isaac,' George said.

'I will. You look after yourself too.'

Separated, Isaac joined the rest of the boys standing by the mast. Several were taller than Isaac, but their childlike, hair-free faces made him think most were younger.

Isaac watched as first the women, some with babies in their arms, stumbled off the ship and made their way towards the group of tents he had seen from the ship. Next, the long line of men trooped down the gangway,

Isaac catching a last glimpse of George as he walked with the others towards one of the large red buildings.

The area at the foot of the jetty now empty, two marines herded Isaac and the other boys from the ship. As he felt the dirt of solid land beneath his feet for the first time in months, three men approached. Dressed in shabby clothes held together with patches of all colours rather than the red uniforms of the marines, the leader swished a vicious cane through the air as he walked towards them, the two men on either side tapping long sticks on their legs reminding him of the jockeys back in Newmarket.

Halting a few paces in front of the small group, the men remained silent. Isaac looked at the ground, his arms clasped behind his back to disguise his unease. Around him he could feel the tension. The small boy on his left, his shirt hanging from his shoulders, with stained short breeches, was sobbing loudly. Without warning one of the men stepped forward, a loud thwack as the crying boy let out a sharp yelp, a thick welt already rising on his pale legs.

'Shut up!' the man bawled.

Isaac willed the boy to be quiet, to stifle the sobs that came now in quick gasps as he bent and rubbed at his leg. The man snatched the boy by his collar and pulled him upright.

'I said *shut up*.' The cane cracked again, the boy's body arching as the blow landed on his back. 'Didn't you hear me?'

The man tossed the boy towards one of the other men, who gave the boy a crack round the head with his open hand, sending him to the ground with a yell, his arms wrapped tight around his head against another blow.

'Pick him up.' The man stabbed his cane towards two boys who stood rigid with fear beside Isaac. 'Then follow me, and no snivelling or talking, otherwise you'll get the same, only a damn sight harder.'

Isaac saw the boy wince as they lifted him to his feet, his shoulders slumped in utter defeat. Unsettled and angry, Isaac filed along the shoreline with the other boys. That boy didn't deserve to be beaten. Whoever these men were, they didn't act like marines. His heart thumping, he quickened his pace, intent on asking the man what authority he had to hit the poor frightened boy.

'Don't.' He felt a hand on his wrist. 'Better he got it than us.' Isaac felt the pressure on his wrist lessen as a tall boy next to him released his grip.

The buildings they had seen from the ships now out of view, only a white spiral of smoke visible against the sky, they rounded a rocky outcrop onto a wide beach, the sand a deeper yellow than even that of the Brecks. About fifty yards out a small boat waited, four men seated at its centre, a fifth man perched at the front.

'Out you go.' The man pointed his cane.

'But I can't—' a boy started to say and was rewarded with a stroke across his shoulders from the man standing behind him.

'Do you think I care?' the man said. 'My job is to walk you down here and send you off to your bit of paradise. Now get a move on. I haven't got all day.'

Isaac stared out across the water, fearful of how deep it was. All around he sensed the same fear, doubtful many of them could swim as far as the waiting boat.

'Move.' The three men raised their sticks, the threat clear.

Hearing the boy whom they had beaten earlier sobbing again, Isaac took his hand and stepped forward, the water lapping at his ankles, but the boy stood firm, unwilling to enter the water.

'I'll go first.' Isaac squeezed the boy's hand and took a step forward.

As the water rose past his knees, he half-led, half-hauled the quivering boy forward. Overtaken by two taller boys, he paused, watching one take a few tentative steps, the other following, then repeating the process over and over until the water reached their chests. The boat within reach, Isaac gasped in horror as one boy disappeared beneath the slate-coloured water, a muffled cry as he vanished. No one moved as the other boy grabbed at the sea, desperate to find his friend, convinced he had been washed away, but then a pair of flailing arms broke the surface followed by a face choking in panic as water flew from his mouth before he disappeared again.

Isaac watched the men manoeuvre the small boat, grunting as they rowed towards the spot where the boy had been. This time, as the boy surfaced again, he was grabbed by a pair of muscular arms, which hauled the spluttering boy over the side and into the bottom of the boat.

Not waiting to be asked, the boy who had searched for his friend grabbed at the side and pulled himself in.

'Quick,' the man at the front of the boat said. 'The tide's on the turn and we can't hold here too long.'

Hoping that the current wouldn't sweep them away, Isaac struggled forward, his grip still tight on the petrified boy. Water now up to his chin, Isaac pulled with all his might, swinging the boy round before he had time to protest, urging him to grab the side of the boat as he nearly collided with it.

One by one, they lunged at the small craft until finally the heap of sodden arms and legs lay exhausted on the floor. Panting with effort, the sailors rowed towards a low mass of land dotted with shrivelled bushes and trees, the black water pushing against them. The main colony now a line on the horizon, they heard the bottom of the boat scrape along the sand. Ordered into the water once more and told to wait on the beach, they dropped over the side of the boat and watched the men turn and row away.

TWENTY-SEVEN

The bedraggled group lay on the sand, grateful for the warmth beneath them.

'What we got here then, lads?'

Isaac looked up to see a lanky youth, jowls covered in a light whiskers, flanked by two more callow youths. 'A new batch of little villains to make our lives nice and easy.' The youth's accent was harsh, his green eyes small and birdlike.

The boy stooped down and grabbed Isaac's hair. 'Look at this one. Think he'll make an obedient servant?'

The two sidekicks laughed.

Isaac twisted against the boy's grip. 'Best you learn quick how things work round here. The guards are old, most of them drunks. It's me that's in charge. So, if I say I want something, then you just hurry along and get it, got that? And that goes for the rest of you.'

'Fraser,' a voice boomed. 'Leave him be or I'll knock your block off.' Isaac felt the youth release him.

'You'll keep,' the youth he took to be Fraser said under his breath before he sauntered away, followed by the others.

The warning came from a scruffy, bearded man who now stood with his hands on his hips. A few paces behind him, two boys waited alongside an elderly man, who swayed from side to side. The first man grinned to reveal a mouthful of black stumps. 'Now pay attention to the warden. He's here to make you feel nice and welcome.'

Isaac watched the older man stagger forward, his ragged trousers snagging on a small bush, causing the two boys to giggle; the one nearest to the bearded man was rewarded with a sharp cuff round the ear. The warden started to speak; his words slurred, and there were long lapses as his eyes drooped before they fluttered open again. Finished, the man belched and pitched forward before he pulled himself upright and lurched away back down the path.

Unable to understand what the warden had said, Isaac looked at the two boys. Up close, Isaac thought one of the boys was close to his own age, the other younger, but he noticed a resemblance between them: their snub noses, straight blond hair and full cheeks a perfect match. 'That was Warden Taylor, my name is Arthur Williams. These two ruffians will show you the ropes and hopefully keep you out of trouble.' The bearded man smiled before becoming more serious. 'But we have rules here, and if you break them, there is a nice solid stump waiting for you to embrace while we give you a little reminder.' With a nod to the two boys, the man turned and walked away.

Rubbing his ear with one hand and still grinning, the boy flung his arm in a wide arc. 'Welcome to Point Puer,' he said with a broad country drawl Isaac immediately recognised. 'I'm Tom and this is my brother Edmund. Half of you follow me and the rest go with him, and we'll show you your digs.'

Falling in behind Tom, Isaac made his way across the parched ground. Unlike the main colony, there seemed to be no brick buildings, just a scattered assortment of crudely built shacks and canvas shelters. The only thing that passed for a proper building was a lonely cottage, its once painted wooden slats blistered and peeling, a white picket fence broken and forlorn.

Pausing at one of the low timber shelters, Tom drew back the ragged sacks with a flourish. 'It isn't a palace, leaks when it rains, and there's no doorman, but it's what we call home. When it's time to bed down, you'll find some blankets in the corner.' Tom wiped his brow. 'Best we get out of this heat and find some shade. Even though there's a bit of a breeze, it gets mighty hot round here,' he said. 'Best not to move around too much in the middle of the day if you can help it.'

The boys settled under the only thing that passed as a tree that stood proud of the scrub and bushes. 'So, my new friends. You won't have got much of what the warden said. Today was a good day. Usually, he is too drunk to stand. Williams is really in charge, but here's how it works. If you hear a bell ring, it is time to do something. Get up, roll call, lessons, eat – that sort of thing. You'll soon get the hang of it.'

'Tom,' Isaac said. 'Do you come from Norfolk?'

Tom raised his eyebrows. 'Well, bless me, a fellow Norfolk boy…'

A loud ringing made them look round.

'That means it is lunchtime,' Tom said. 'Let's see, it's Tuesday, so meat soup, bread and dumplings.'

Isaac felt the emptiness inside and jumped up. Meat, fresh bread. Isaac's mouth watered at the thought after so many months on poor rations. Tom led the way to two larger structures with open sides, a twisted wooden table down the middle, rough-cut benches down each side.

Joining the queue, Tom indicated a battered bucket. 'Grab a mug and a spoon from there. They don't give us long, ten minutes at most to get the scran and eat it. Want some bread?'

Isaac looked at the pile of hardened slices.

'Don't look so disappointed,' Tom said. 'This is as good as it gets. When I said meat on Tuesdays, it's just a game we play. We get the same every day. We torture ourselves. It's a big beef roast or a tasty chicken just off the spit, but it is the same every day. Hold your mug out.'

Isaac stretched his arm towards a skinny boy, his eyes sunken and dark, who swiftly dipped a battered ladle into a large black pot and, without looking up, poured a stream of lumpy liquid into Isaac's mug.

Seated under the shelter, the only noise was the slurping and chomping of dozens of mouths. Intent on draining every drop, Isaac dipped his bread into the mug.

Interrupted by the bell again, Tom tipped his mug up. 'Eat up. The old boy who teaches is ancient, but there will still be trouble if you're late. I'll see you later; and pay attention. You may learn something, although you will be the first if you do.' Tom patted Isaac on the shoulder. 'We can talk more after the last bell.'

As they sat crammed together on hard, narrow benches, the stooped, grey-haired teacher spent the afternoon testing them on their letters and numbers. Isaac was stunned as some of the other boys struggled to spell even their own names. After lessons, Tom returned and took them back to the shelter where they would sleep, the sacking along the sides now rolled up to allow the breeze to lessen the heavy heat of the night air.

After a final bell for prayers, Tom and Edmund and Isaac settled down on the dusty mats that covered the floor of the shelter, two boys at the far end already breathing deeply.

'So, where you from, Tom?' Isaac asked.

'Grew up in Great Yarmouth. Moved to Norwich with Pa when Ma died. He wasn't much interested in us, so me and Edmund used to swipe the odd item to get by.' Tom winked. 'That's how we ended up here; been nearly a year now.'

'I knew you came from my parts. I'm from a village called Tottington. About a half day's ride from Norwich. You heard of it?'

'Can't say I have. Best get some sleep now, first bell is at dawn. Suspect we have loads of time to talk.' Tom yawned and lay down, his back to Isaac.

Isaac closed his eyes and wondered how George was. Noticing the strangeness of the steady earth after weeks on the ship, he heard Edmund's voice. 'Oh, and one last thing. Watch out for Fraser and his gang. No brains, but hard as nails. Where he is, trouble normally follows.'

TWENTY-EIGHT

As the first bell of the day rang out, Isaac scrambled to his feet. It had been two months since he had arrived and at first he had been at a loss as to what to do each time the bell rang, but gradually the daily routine of lessons, instruction in working wood or mending clothes, punctuated with muster, prayers and barely palatable meals, became familiar. The prison, although so far from home, reminded Isaac of the Brecks, the thorny bushes and scattered trees clinging to the sandy soil. The land side was guarded by a high fence of wooden trunks, a thick impenetrable bush beyond. Stony beaches and ragged cliffs hemmed the other sides of the peninsula, the waves that crashed against the shore a warning of the swirling currents that would sweep away anyone foolish enough to try to escape.

A single ship had arrived adding to the already crowded shelters on the peninsula, the new boys giving Fraser and his thugs a fresh batch of youngsters to terrorise.

He had found an easy affinity with Tom and Edmund, and slowly accepted that he could do nothing more than make the best of his situation and hope for news from home.

Tom was popular with all the boys. Given to quick wit, a beaming smile on his face, he was often to be found at the centre of any mischief. Edmund, although younger than Tom, was the more serious of the two brothers and often looked upon Tom's antics with a mix of disapproval and concern. Altogether there were nearly one hundred boys, watched over by the drunken, elderly warden, the toothless man who had greeted them, and several freed convicts who had become jailers when their sentences had ended, intent on doing as little as possible other than taking the best food and getting drunk.

Wolfing down the hunk of bread smeared with fat, Isaac heard Williams calling his name.

'Isaac Bone, letter for Isaac Bone.'

Convinced his letter had been discarded among the fish heads and muck of the docks, Isaac had almost given up hope of hearing from his family. Could it be that it had reached them? That they had managed to convince the authorities that he wasn't a thief and he was going to be sent back to them?

Taking the letter, he pondered whether to read it now or wait till he could find a quiet spot. What if it was bad news? Maybe his mother was sick, or one of the girls? Unable to wait, he returned to the now empty shelter, the other boys having made their way to lessons. His hand trembled as he turned the letter over, before running his finger under the yellow seal and beginning to read.

Written in Alice's neat hand, Isaac felt his hope begin to fade. Finished, tears falling onto his lap, Isaac folded the letter and lay it by his side.

'Isaac, there you are.' Tom came into the shelter. 'You all right?'

Isaac pointed at the letter.

'From home? Take it that it wasn't good news?'

Isaac shook his head. 'Seems they tried to find out what happened. Mother went to Mr Downs, asked him to speak to Lord Stanton. Alice even went to Newmarket, but Mrs Stokes slammed the door in her face. She asked around but no one at the yard was prepared to get involved, said Mrs Stokes had warned them not to talk to anyone or they would lose their jobs. Alice says they will keep trying but it's hard to get to speak to anyone and they don't get a reply to letters.'

'I'm sorry, Isaac. You deserve better, but neither of us were born with a silver spoon in our mouth and that's what counts. They will have made up their minds we were guilty even before we were in front of a judge, that's the way it is.'

'Guess you are right, Tom, just I always hoped…'

'I know.' Tom put an arm around the heaving shoulders, drawing Isaac to him. 'But best wipe your face and we get to lessons before we are both bent over getting our butts warmed.'

The letter folded in his pocket, Isaac followed Tom, taking his seat on the narrow bench beside the other boys. At least he knew his family was well, his younger sisters now at the village school, Alice still at the hall. Deep inside, he had known that there was little chance of anyone believing he hadn't been involved. He couldn't tell them anything about the mysterious Jack, what had happened that night after he left the inn, or where the horses had gone. It seemed unlikely his family would be able to find out any more than he already knew. He would write again when he could, tell them he was well, try to reassure them things weren't as bad as they might fear.

The ding of the bell signalled lessons were over and it was time for chores. Told to present himself to the cook, Isaac skirted the shelters, spying Fraser lurking in wait for whoever was unlucky enough to wander his way, convinced he would never know the truth of what had happened back in Newmarket. That he would never see his family, or his beloved Brecks again.

TWENTY-NINE

The light was still pale when the boys made their way down to the shore to bathe, watchful for Fraser and his two thugs. Despite the relentless days of heat, the sea was always bracing, the rolling swell hiding danger for any who ventured out too far. Edmund had told Isaac of two boys who had tried to escape by swimming to the mainland, only to be swept away into the open ocean beyond.

'Enjoy the warm bath?' Tom joked as he stood shivering at the water's edge.

'Ignore him, Isaac,' Edmund said. 'You'll only encourage him.'

'See those animals over there?' Tom pointed to some rocks where some brown creatures stood upright on their back legs, small paws with large black claws held in front of them. 'Heard them called a "roo" – strange, aren't they? We have tried to catch them, but none of us really knows how, and every time we get close, they hop off into the bushes like this...' Tom brought his hands together in front of him, fingers pointed downwards. Crouching, he leapt forward, imitating the animals. 'Bet if we could catch one, they would taste good.'

'Me and my friends used to catch rabbits back in the Brecks,' Isaac said, thinking back to the ruddy-cheeked gamekeeper who had shown them how to set traps. 'They're a bit bigger, but that shouldn't matter too much.'

'Really?' Tom's eyes opened wide. 'You think you could catch one? We could have such a feast. Most of us here are city boys; wouldn't know where to start.'

'I could try,' Isaac said. 'Know what they eat?'

Tom beckoned Edmund over. 'Isaac reckons he might be able to catch one of those. Just imagine real meat. You know what they eat?'

'Seem to munch on anything green, not that there is much green around here,' Edmund said. 'You know we will get a thrashing if we get caught.'

'Edmund, you worry about things too much,' Tom teased his brother. 'What would we need?'

Isaac stretched out his arms. 'A piece of rope or cord about this long and a place out of sight where we could rig a trap.'

The ding of the bell signalled evening prayers.

'We can talk later,' Tom said excitedly as he pulled on his tunic. 'But we keep it hush-hush. The fewer that know the better.'

After prayers, Isaac was making his way towards the shelters, lost in thought as to where the best place to set the trap might be, when he felt a hand shove him roughly from behind.

'Where might you be off to?'

Isaac turned to see the smirking face of Fraser, his two companions just behind him.

'Nowhere,' Isaac replied.

'Nowhere. Well, that's not good, is it? You should always be going somewhere. Now why don't you go up to the kitchen and get me and the lads here a nice little extra something to fill our bellies?'

Isaac made to move away, but his path was quickly blocked.

'Not so quick, squirt. I want you to sneak into the canteen and bring us some fresh damper.'

'But if I get caught stealing food, I'll be for it.'

Fraser cocked his head. 'That's the idea. You get caught, not us.'

Isaac looked at the freckled face, the small green eyes, unsure how to respond. How was he going to get any extra food?

Fraser stepped close, his breath hot on Isaac's face. 'Just in case you think of grassing me up, the old boys don't care what I do as long as they are left in peace.'

Isaac didn't move as the youth pushed past, a deliberate knock with an elbow finding Isaac's ribs, making him gasp.

Back at the shelter, Isaac slumped onto his blanket holding his side.

'You all right?' Tom asked.

Isaac told him about Fraser.

'That thug is a real pain,' Tom said. 'Thinks him and his cronies can do just as they like and they are the ones in charge here, not the warden. Anyway, this will cheer you up. I found this round the back of the shelter.' Tom pulled the frayed end of a thin piece of rope from his pocket. 'Think it will do?'

'Might do. Could take a time though before we catch anything, and by then Fraser will probably have beaten me to a pulp.'

Tom put his arm round Isaac's shoulders. 'Well, it's the best we have got for now. Let's get together with Edmund later and we can plan what to do next.'

The heat of the day retreated as Tom and Isaac sat and waited for Edmund.

Entering the shelter, Isaac could see something had angered him. 'What's up, Ed?'

'Fraser and his henchmen were at it again. The younger boys are terrified of them. What I'd like to do—'

'Isaac has the same problem,' Tom interrupted his brother. 'Threatened him that if he didn't get them food they would do him in.'

'Thanks, Tom.' Isaac hugged his knees in tight.

'Sorry, mate, didn't mean to make it worse.' Tom pulled the rope from his pocket, gave it a twang. 'So, we are going to do this or not? Seems it might be our only hope to feed our bellies.'

Isaac took the rope from Tom and pulled it tight. 'Should do, but we will need to be patient. Animals sense a trap – and anyone thought how we are going to skin and gut it if we catch one? We don't have a knife, and we can't eat raw meat.'

'I could skin it,' a soft voice behind them said. 'All we need is a shell off the beach.'

Turning, they saw the outline of a podgy boy who slept at the end of their shelter. Isaac couldn't remember the boy ever saying a word to anyone.

Tom shot to his feet. 'What do you know about skinning animals?'

'I used to scale and gut fish on the market. We'd use a shell, sharp as a knife if you know how to fashion them.'

The three of them stared at the boy.

'I'm so hungry it makes me miserable. I used to be twice this size. Please let me help. I won't tell anyone.'

Tom sniggered. 'Twice the size?'

Isaac looked at the two brothers. 'What do you think? He knows now anyway.' He turned back to the boy. 'What's your name?'

'William, William Tuck.'

'But we still don't know how we will cook it,' Edmund said. 'There's not much wood here. It all comes from the mainland, and even if we had some, we couldn't just light a fire.'

Tom suddenly beamed.

'William. Have I seen you at the forge?'

William looked puzzled. 'Yes, it's very tiring, especially in the heat.'

'Don't you see?' Tom erupted. 'We can use the forge after everyone is asleep. No one will think it strange if a bit of smoke drifts up. It often smoulders all night, and it's mostly enclosed so no one would see us. What do you think?'

Isaac and Ed looked at each other. 'Guess we have a plan,' Isaac said, shuddering at the thought of their fate if they got caught.

THIRTY

Ever wary of Fraser, the boys had observed the creatures, trying to determine the best place to set the trap. In the end they decided that a rocky outcrop away from the main camp gave them the best chance to snare their prize away from prying eyes. Sunday was the only day of the week when there were no lessons, and the boys were free to do as they pleased while the warden and other adults drank the afternoon away in the shade. Having arranged to meet after the church service, one by one they wandered to the agreed spot.

'Think this will be enough?' Tom held out a handful of wilted leaves. 'I kept some of my cabbage from lunch.'

'Should be, we only need enough to lure them into the trap,' Isaac said. 'Everyone ready?'

'You know we will get a terrible thrashing if we get caught?' Edmund said.

'Will be worth it, just to have a full belly for once.' Tom licked his lips. 'I can taste it already. Now the old fellas will be dozing, so let's get moving before Fraser or one of his mates sees us.'

Trying to look as if they were combing the beach, they made their way down to the far end, several roos grazing the sparse wiry grass where the sand merged with scrub at the rear of the beach.

'William, you stop here as we agreed,' Isaac said. 'Remember, two sharp whistles if anyone comes looking.'

Leaving William behind Isaac, Tom and Edmund skirted the outcrop. 'Do you think we can trust him? What if he has told Fraser?'

'William wouldn't risk his share of the food,' Tom said. Anyway, I have a feel for folks and I say he is all right. Now let's get on.'

Isaac scoured the beach, rejecting the rocks Tom enthusiastically pointed at until finally they spotted a flat grey slab.

'This should work,' he said.

'Can't you find anything bigger?' Tom replied. 'It's massive.'

Crimson-faced and glistening with sweat, the three boys manhandled the rock towards a stunted shrub, the surrounding area bare and scorched. Laying the slab on the ground, the boys looked anxiously around while Isaac scrunched the cabbage leaves into a bunch and knotted the rope around them.

Satisfied, Isaac got Tom and Edmund to lift the slab, wedging it open with a green stick that bent ominously under its weight. Carefully, Isaac placed the cabbage in the crease where the earth and rock met and fixed the other end of the rope to the base of the stick.

'Hopefully they will take the bait, but like I said, we might need several tries.'

Finished, they made their way back to where William sat waiting.

'See anyone?' Edmund asked.

William shook his head.

'Right then, best we get off.'

'I'm staying here,' William said. 'If anyone comes by, I can make sure they don't go near the trap.'

'You can't stay,' Isaac said. 'The roos might not go near the trap for days.'

'I'm staying.' William crossed his arms.

Unable to persuade William, Isaac, Tom and Edmund made their way back to the shelter. Certain their bellies called out more than usual for food, they dozed the afternoon away dreaming of fresh meat.

Isaac swatted at the tiny flies that plagued everyone when daylight faded, fearful Fraser and his mates would come looking for him or find William and make him tell them what they were doing. Or… A hundred calamities crowded his head as he waited for the muster bell. Startled, he heard the breathless voice of William.

'We caught one.'

'You sure?' Isaac said. 'Seems awful quick.'

'I'm sure.' William hesitated. 'Well, I think I'm sure. I was just sitting there when I heard a crash and then a squeal. When I went to have a look, the slab was flat on the ground. I'm positive there are legs sticking out. You coming?' William was beside himself with the promise of food. 'We should go now before someone else discovers it.'

'Calm down, William, someone will notice.'

Isaac beckoned Tom and Edmund over. 'William says he thinks we have one. Should we go now or leave it till later? The bell will sound soon.'

Tom's face lit up. 'I say we go now and risk it. We can hide it and then go back after last muster.'

Wary of being seen, they made their way back to the trap. The slab now lay flat, two brown legs sticking out. Tom nudged the black paws with his foot. Nothing moved or murmured.

'Here, lend me a hand.' Tom bent to raise the slab.

'Wait. What if it runs away?' William butted in.

Isaac and Tom glanced at William. 'What if it runs away? Well, you'll have to catch it. It will be easy to find. It will be the one with the flat head. Now help me, this is heavy.'

The animal remained lifeless as they hoisted the rock. Isaac picked it up by its legs; a spot of blood ran off the long snout, and its stumpy front limbs were bent backwards.

'What do you think it will taste like?' William asked. 'It's thinner than I thought. Think there will be much meat on it?'

'If we get caught, there will be no meat on us when they have whipped our backsides. Now let's get this strung up.'

It took two of them to haul the furry corpse behind a bush.

'You got that shell, William?'

William reached in his pocket and took out a brilliant silvery shell, the edge sharpened.

'Slit the throat just here.' William indicated where Isaac should cut. 'Then it will drain out ready to skin later.'

With a swift stroke, Isaac drew the shell across the creature's neck, a steady trickle of blood staining the sand. In the distance, the clang of the bell announced muster.

'Best we get back before we are missed,' Tom urged. 'Everyone will be in camp now, so less chance of it being found. There is a full moon tonight so we can skin it here and then take it back to the forge. Agreed?'

Everyone nodded as they set off back to camp.

William was puffing as they rushed to make muster. 'Let's hope no one finds it before we get back. It would be more than I can bear to find it gone.'

*

The moon had pushed up high in the sky, its silver light covered by the occasional cloud. Relieved at the last command from the bell, they had lingered to ensure the other boys were asleep before Isaac and William had crept out and down to the bush, while Edmund and Tom headed to the forge. Isaac's hands were raw as he wrestled to cut the head and feet from the animal, the task more difficult than he had expected. Defeated, he turned over the shell to William, who set to work with an efficiency Isaac had never seen in the usually lumbering boy. Swollen with pride, a sweat-coated William held up a wet joint of pink meat. Careful to bury the skin and throw the guts out of sight, the two boys headed to the forge.

Ducking through the flap, the coals of the forge flared red as Isaac made way for William.

'Wow, there should be enough there to dine like a king.' Tom rubbed his stomach. 'Split four ways we will eat well tonight.'

'I think someone should keep watch,' Isaac said.

'Edmund? William knows how to handle the forge and we can call you when it is ready,' Tom said.

A reluctant Edmund made his way outside as they set to work.

'What do you reckon it will taste like?' William asked as Tom pushed an iron stake through the pink flesh, a puff on the bellows making the coals flare deep red.

'Like rabbit, I suppose.' Isaac tried to remember the last time he had tasted rabbit or anything that resembled fresh meat.

The browning meat was giving off a tantalising smell when a sudden rush of cool air flooded the forge as the flap swept back. Convinced they had been caught, Isaac held his breath as Edmund crashed through, almost knocking them over. Relieved, Isaac let out a gasp and was about to speak as the flap drew back again, revealing the unmistakable silhouette of Fraser and his sidekicks.

THIRTY-ONE

Isaac froze, the silence broken only by the hiss of juice as it dribbled onto the burning coals.

'What have we here? My little pals having a party without us. Now that's not terribly friendly, is it?' Fraser stepped forward and inhaled. 'Smell that, boys.' Fraser turned to Isaac. 'Cooking me a nice roast supper? Good, you understood our chat the other day. Now, what say you hand that over and we'll be off?' Without waiting for an answer, Fraser moved closer to the burning coals and made to take the brown, rich-smelling meat.

Faced with the loss of their prize, Isaac stepped between Fraser and the meat. 'We trapped it, so back off, it's ours,' Isaac said with more courage than he felt.

'Hear that?' Fraser rolled his eyes as he addressed his two cocky accomplices. 'He doesn't want to give us his tasty dinner,' he said, giving Isaac a shove.

Isaac felt a deep fury rise and a surge of anger through his chest and down his limbs. Everything he had ever cherished had been taken away from him, his family, his friends, his future. Condemned to this place on the far side of the world, he was always hungry and he was sick of Fraser and his thugs. Hands clenched into fists, Isaac stepped forward, looking directly into the greedy eyes of the older boy. 'Leave it.' Isaac slapped at Fraser's outstretched hand, knocking it aside.

In the glow of the embers, Isaac saw a flicker of surprise cross Fraser's face before, without warning, the thug flung back his head and brought it sharply forward, the force, as it crashed into Isaac's face, making Isaac stagger backwards, a warm trickle running down his face.

'What did you say?' Fraser growled.

Isaac shook his head, wiping his face, leaving a red smear on the sleeve. 'I said leave it.'

Determined Fraser would not take the roasting meat, Isaac leapt at the unsuspecting Fraser, slamming him to the ground. Isaac sank his knee into the boy's ribs and heard a sharp snap of bone as he unleashed a storm, pummelling the whimpering Fraser who raised his arms to fend off the blows that rained down on him.

Sensing one of Fraser's scrawny sidekicks move, William lunged forward and grasped him round the neck, bending the boy forward. Taking their cues, Tom and Edmund hastily seized the remaining boy, who let out a yelp as Tom twisted his arm behind his back.

'Blimey, Isaac, where did that come from?' Tom asked. 'It was like you were possessed. Edmund, see if anybody heard.'

'What do we do now?' William's voice trembled as, sweat running down his face, his arm locked tight around the neck of Fraser's lackey, who gasped for air.

'Ease up, William,' Tom said. 'You'll throttle him.'

'All clear.' Edmund reappeared.

Isaac rubbed his burning knuckles as he studied Fraser, who lay on the charcoal-covered floor, his knees pulled up, arms wrapped around his chest. 'Let them go.'

'What if they run off and grass on us?' Tom said.

'They won't.'

'How can you be sure?

'They have as much to lose as us if they go blabbing. They will have to explain why they were roaming around at this time of night and what they were doing in the forge.'

'Suppose so.' Tom and William released their grip on the two boys, who stood limply, unsure what to do now their leader was lying groaning on the floor.

'Now listen to me.' Isaac looked straight at the two boys, a new-found authority in his voice. 'If one of us gets hauled up for this, then we all do. They won't care whether it was me, Tom, Edmund, William, or you three – they will thrash us all the same. It is in everyone's interests to say nothing. So, I suggest you two pick up this useless piece of rubbish and get him out of here and keep your mouths shut. Because if we get whipped, so will you, and that will be nothing to the thrashing I will give you after they have finished.'

The boy rubbed at his throat, the other shaking his arm. 'We won't tell.'

Isaac looked at his friends. One by one, they nodded in agreement. 'Good. Now I suggest you get this' – Isaac nudged Fraser with his foot – 'and yourselves out of here before we change our minds.'

Hauling a still whimpering Fraser to his feet, they pulled open the flap and left the forge without looking back.

'The meat.' William grabbed a cloth and drew the meat from the heat, the skin now blackening, but a sweet aroma filling the air.

'Best get out of here,' Edmund said. 'In case they don't do as they said and come back with the guards. William, douse the coals and then we can find ourselves a nice, secluded spot to get rid of the evidence.'

THIRTY-TWO

The following morning, Isaac stood at muster, his normally grumbling stomach hushed for once. A few paces away, his friends stood, with a rosy colour to their cheeks he was sure had not been there the day before. As the tedium of the twice-daily roll call crawled on, Isaac tried to locate Fraser, afraid that he or his two henchmen might have gone back on their word. Hearing Fraser's name called, he barely heard the reply, the normally confident response missing as Fraser stood with his head bowed, a hand across his chest. Dismissed, Isaac waved at the others in relief that, so far, the boys had kept their word, and hurried towards the workshop. In his mind he went over the events of the previous night. He had never raised a hand in anger before, never felt he had it in him to beat thugs like Fraser. Word would soon get round, but few were likely to take Fraser's side and he knew now that he could stand up for himself. Nearing the workshop, he saw Fraser's two lackeys walking towards him.

Face to face, Isaac watched the boys carefully, ready for a blow. 'Out of my way.'

One of the boys swallowed hard. 'Me and Geordie, we reckon... well, we reckon Fraser's done after last night. You gave him a drubbing he won't forget in a hurry, and we're done with doing his dirty work.'

Already late for the workshop, Isaac realised things had changed, but trusting these two was risky. Maybe all they wanted to do was save their own skin, and Fraser would still be a danger once his bones had healed and the bruises faded. Shifting allegiance to whoever was top dog was easy, but for now he had the upper hand. A new-found confidence.

Isaac took a breath before lifting a finger. 'If I find out that either of you have been taking food from the younger boys, bullying anyone, or so much as even speaking to Fraser, it will be me you answer to. I'll be watching you, and if you think you can do it on the sly, forget it. Understand?' Taking their nods as agreement, Isaac shoved his way between the two youths, allowing himself a moment of satisfaction, and headed to the workshop.

*

As the weeks passed after the incident at the forge, Isaac felt more at ease, and the fear that Fraser would tell the guards faded. His country-boy upbringing made him more suited to the open air than those who had grown up in the cities. The fact he could write his name and read put him ahead of many of the boys in the daily lessons.

His chores finished, Isaac sat waiting for the others. Christmas had passed a few months ago, the sweat dripping from everybody as they sang 'Silent Night' in the sweltering heat. Soon the weather would cool, just as back in the Brecks the heath would spring to life. Saddened by the thought of his sisters and mother so far away, Isaac felt in his empty pocket. So much had happened. If he had never met Jack that day, then he might have become a jockey, provided for his family, been someone. Instead, he had been convicted of a crime he didn't commit and shipped to this lump of rock. An unending routine of muster, schooling, instruction and monotony.

Plucking at the grass, he was certain his eighteenth birthday had passed, that his time here was running out and he would soon be transferred to the main colony. He knew the ritual roll call of those due to transfer was close – the last batch had been some months ago. What would life be like on the main colony? Would George have survived? Had the untameable Jeffrey continued to menace his fellow captives as well as his gaolers, helping himself to everything that took his fancy?

'Isaac, Isaac.' Tom appeared in a state of excitement. 'Look, Isaac, can you see them?'

Isaac stood up and peered out to sea as the unmistakable outline of three ships advanced towards them. With little to break the daily monotony, everyone congregated to watch, such was the rarity of the arrival of any ship. Imaginations were fuelled by the sight; excitement about the possibility of fresh food and new clothes was tempered by wondering how many more mouths there would be to feed. Would there be sickness among the new arrivals? Transfixed, he wondered how many wretched men, women and children were on board, innocent like him, or condemned for crimes so small, sent far away from those in authority who feared them, separated from loved ones. Troubled, Isaac felt the world around him shift, something deep, something ominous. As he watched the ships navigate around the headland, the crowd began to disperse. Standing alone, the ships now out of sight, he hardly dared hope that maybe they brought news from home, that he might be pardoned. Isaac shuddered, a strange feeling just like he had all those years ago on his first day at the hall running through him. Turning away, he closed his eyes tightly with a feeling of dread; a premonition that the new arrivals would bring yet more turmoil into his life.

THIRTY-THREE

May 1841

As they gathered for muster, Isaac felt uneasy. After the arrival of the ships a couple of weeks ago, new boys had arrived, most wretched and subdued, some having to sleep under the stars, the shelters already full. Unsteadily, the warden made his way over the uneven ground towards them, along with another elderly man, his head completely bald – and whose stutter the boys began to mimic behind his back. By his side the bald man clutched a sheet of thick yellow paper with curled edges. Isaac crossed his fingers behind his back and closed his eyes tightly as the man began his tortuous summons. The first name spluttered from his lips; a gaunt boy took a moment to register that it was his name that had been called.

'William T-T-T-Tuck,' the man stammered.

Isaac looked across at his friend in surprise. He had never wondered how old William was. It didn't seem possible he was eighteen, his ruddy face still smooth and childlike. Momentarily distracted, he watched a bewildered William make his way to the front and join the first boy.

'Ch-Ch-Charles Fr-Fraser.'

Fraser? Deserted by his two stooges, he had become a lonely figure, everyone now knowing he could be beaten. But with his injuries healed, Isaac knew the youth would bear a grudge and, despite what had happened between them in the forge that night, he was still a danger.

Two more boys joined the waiting group as the stuttering clerk looked down at the paper in his hand. Hope rising that he might slip through the net this time and share a few more months with Tom and Edmund before the brutality of the main colony, Isaac took a breath.

'Isaac B-Bone.'

His heart sank. He had known his chances were slim, but now the days of sleepy old convicts, drunken guards and relative freedom were over. Now he would be forced to do a man's work, the work of a convict, long days of heavy toil with little food in terrible heat and dust.

Ordered to assemble on the shore, Isaac and William went to collect what few possessions they had from the shelter.

'I didn't think you were eighteen?' Isaac said to William as he gathered what few spare clothes he had.

William shrugged. 'To be honest, I'm not sure how old I am. My mother wasn't good at papers and my father wasn't around much. Suppose they must have just put something down when I was arrested.'

'I don't think you ever told me how you ended up here.'

'Same as most,' William began just as Tom and Edmund rushed over.

'You two look after each other. You hear me?' Tom said. 'Won't be long till we are all together again.' His eyes reddened, the jester in him lost as he embraced Isaac.

Isaac held his friend tightly against him, warm tears soaking his tunic.

'Bye, Edmund. Try and keep him out of trouble.'

'I'll try.'

After hugs for William, Tom and Edmund headed back to the workshops.

'Well, guess we still have each other,' Isaac said, draping a brotherly arm around William's shoulders, as William forced a smile.

As the small boat bobbed a few yards from the shore, Isaac remembered the day he had first arrived, the boy that was nearly swept away. The water was no higher than his waist this time.

The small craft crept out towards the open sea, only the gentlest of pulls needed by the men who rowed the boat to steer it towards the main colony and alongside the jetty. Hand over hand, they climbed a rough rope until they stood on the pier, where several rough-faced men greeted them, the recognisable figure of Doctor Wheeler a few paces behind.

'Quiet!' one of the men bellowed, a vicious-looking whip curled by his side. 'Normally, you would be examined at the infirmary. But there was fever on board the ships that arrived, so everyone has been quarantined. The doctor will give you a quick once-over here and then it will be straight to work.'

'What does quarantine mean?' William whispered.

'It's when you separate sick people so those who aren't—' Isaac began.

'Silence.' The man thundered towards them, his boots shaking the wooden walkway. He stood so close that William and Isaac could smell his stale breath as he drew the whip through his hand.

'When I say quiet, I mean quiet. That understood? This isn't some child's playground, and in case you have forgotten, you are all convicted criminals and here is where you start paying your dues.'

Isaac looked down at his feet, not wanting to meet the man's eyes, fearing he may use his whip if he did.

'Line up and follow me and no talking.' The man took a step back.

The doctor inspected each of them, an instruction to cough before he moved on. At his turn, Isaac coughed, a fleeting smile of acknowledgement from the doctor before he moved on.

Too frightened to speak, Isaac nodded at William as he and another boy were led away, disappearing from sight.

While the men were deep in conversation, Fraser moved closer, a dark look of vengeance on his face. 'Think you're the big man, do you? You caught me off guard once, but it won't happen again. When the time is right I'm coming for you and when I—'

'You.' The man raised his whip and pointed it at Fraser. 'Want the skin flayed from your back? This isn't like the place you came from where you get to run rings round old cons who are drunk half the time. Here you obey instructions and put your back into it, otherwise you are going to find your scraggy carcass striped. Got it? Now get over here, you scrawny excuse for a man.'

Fraser ambled towards where the man had pointed, some of his old swagger appearing to surface, as a second youth was sent to join him, then the pair were ushered away.

Unaware he had been holding his breath, Isaac let out a sigh of relief. He should have been more wary. Fraser had been humiliated after word got round about the fight. His bones and bruises healed, his threats may have been bravado, but he couldn't take any chances.

'Wait here,' the man said as he returned to talk to the other men.

The day still early, Isaac looked around, seeing the colony up close for the first time.

He could see now that one of the red-brick buildings was taller than the other. Its ground floor was windowless; lines of square windows laced with rusty iron bars filled the floors above. At its centre, a pair of wooden doors, bleached grey by the sun, seemed to be the only way in and out of the building. Separated by a barren square of scorched earth, the other building had shuttered windows, some open, the iron bars of the other building missing. It appeared to be the only other brick building on the colony.

'Right, you two come with me.' The man pointed his whip at Isaac and one of the remaining boys. 'The rest wait here.'

Steered away from the jetty in the opposite direction from a group of tents where only women seemed to be working, they walked through an assortment of ramshackle wooden buildings, their once whitewashed slats warped and split; what little thatch that remained was unlikely to keep out any rain. A cart rumbled by, piled high with rough-moulded bricks and pulled by four panting men.

They skirted a plot where a new building with a small paddock came into view, its fence twisted and neglected, a small set of stables at its edge. Scattered inside there were a few ponies, a bony colt of maybe two or three, some ageing workhorses, well past their best, and a grey hunter with a shaggy mane. Isaac felt sorry for the beasts as they nosed the parched ground in hope of finding a blade of grass. Their ribs were showing, and flies clouded around open sores on their backs and hindquarters. Standing apart from the rest, the grey hunter looked in better shape. She wasn't an old horse, maybe four or five judging by her size – still a filly. Clearly she belonged to someone important.

The rasp of saws rose from behind a thin palisade; a line of shackled convicts, their heads bent low, many barefooted, strained on a thick rope. Accompanied by a rugged-looking man, his sleeves rolled up, they hauled a colossal tree trunk, the whip in the man's hands finding the shoulders of those who slackened. The noise from the sawing and hammering fading, they reached a two-storey house, a fresh coat of whitewash making it stand out at the centre of a square green lawn. A dusty path edged with white stones led towards a wide veranda with steps at its centre, which rose to a pair of black-painted doors; marines stood to attention either side.

'Wait here,' the man instructed. 'And don't think of running otherwise you'll be taking the place of one of those men.' He nodded towards the snake of men who had made little progress with the heavy trunk.

The man grabbed the other boy and shoved him towards a squat church, a bell dangling from its stubby tower. Bemused, Isaac pondered on what work they planned to set him to. Where was George? The convicts he had seen so far looked half-starved, burnt brown, barely clothed. The work was heavy and without rest. What if...?

'Take this.' The man returned with a hoe in his hand and thrust it at Isaac.

He followed the man along a well-worn path that sloped upwards between trees and bushes, the shouts and bustle of the convicts at work replaced by the rustle of leaves and chirping of birds. His clothes stuck to him; the trees thinned. He saw rough-looking fields with men in a line jabbing at the ground.

'Know the difference between a weed and a plant?' Isaac nodded. 'Good, then get to work.'

The man shoved him roughly towards the field. 'Down there next to the old fellow, he'll croak soon and you'll be ready to take his place.'

Shocked by the man's callousness, he walked towards the line and fell in step behind the elderly convict. The man's skin was tinged with yellow; a thick gurgle came with each step he took, the hoe barely brushing the soil. Isaac knew the land was poor and unlikely to yield much. Back in the Brecks, the once cultivated sandy heath had begun to be given over to sheep, their wool and meat proving more profitable. This soil was no better. The few plants that had dared push up leaves were struggling against the creeping weeds, most only inches high, yellow tips showing they had little chance of blooming and ripening.

As the sun beat down on them, the stab of the hoes mixing with the coughs and sighs of the weary convicts and the ever-present threat of the overseer's whip, a halt was called. With a crust of rock-hard bread and a half cup of tepid water the only sustenance, Isaac joined the others at the edge of the field.

'Saw you arrive, lad,' the man next to him said, the lines around his eyes etched deep. 'Take a bit of advice; there are those that think this is an easy job, given the heavy work down in the colony. But the heat will sap the life out of you quicker than you can wring out a wet cloth. You'll get half a cup of water every two hours – make sure you don't waste it, and go as slow as you can. Word is that we are being moved further up to clear a new field soon; that means trees to be felled, roots hauled out and all the lumber taken down to the sawmill. The longer we can take here, the easier for everyone.'

Reminded of his days as a furrow boy, the long hours in the fields moving flints as the punches readied the fields for sowing, Isaac knew that it took months of backbreaking work to ready even the smallest of fields.

'Will there be horses to help?' Isaac wondered if maybe the horses he had seen were the old and sick ones. Maybe there were more somewhere he hadn't yet seen.

The man laughed, a rattling cough quickly silencing him. 'Oh yes, lad, not the sort you think, though. The ones they use in the fields come ten in line and only have two legs.'

Isaac was about to ask what the man meant when the overseer called for work to restart.

The jab, jab, jab of the hoes echoed across the hillside as the line of convicts plodded up and down. Pausing to wipe the sweat from his brow, Isaac looked to the side of the field where a pile of dirty rags lay, black birds with hooked beaks hopping ever closer. As one pecked at the ground, Isaac turned away, not wanting to watch, horrified that the prediction about the old convict had come true so quickly.

THIRTY-FOUR

Isaac was led through the door into the larger of the red-brick buildings and into a cavernous dormitory which heaved with restlessness. Everywhere the smell of unwashed bodies mingled with despair and defeat; the stench was overpowering in the sticky heat. Ready to drop, Isaac hunted in the shadowy light for an unoccupied bunk, with hardly space to walk between the endless rows. About to give up, Isaac saw a crumpled blanket that lay on top of an empty mattress.

'Would jump in quick – unless you fancy a night on the floor with rats nipping at you?'

Isaac shivered and looked up towards the voice. 'You sure it's free?'

'Normally a few spare,' the man said. 'The old fellow that bedded down there was crushed in the timber yard a couple of days back. Folks say his bones cracked like a fire spitting on bad wood when the trunks rolled over him. At least it was quick for the poor sod. So, I'd grab it before someone else does.'

Isaac pulled the blanket flat and lay down. Only last

night he had lain with his friends in the shelter. Now he was alone in a dead man's bunk. As he stared at the slats above, muttered conversations twisted with thick coughs and deep groans all around. He had to find George, but he couldn't just roam round the dormitory. What if he bumped into Fraser or Jeffrey? Despite the heat, he pulled the blanket over him, trying to hide. Maybe his best chance was to ask the other convicts, see if they knew where George might be, but there were hundreds of convicts and so many places to look. The work on the new field would begin soon and if the man was right the work would be heavy.

Unable to sleep, he heard the man from the bunk above land with a thump beside his head. 'Time to get up.'

'Is it day already?' Isaac asked.

'Sure is. When you hear the floor above start banging about, it means they have some light and it will soon be time to start work.'

A stream of men, weariness etched on their faces, dragged themselves from their bunks and made their way through the narrow doorway. Gulping down a watery portion of tepid porridge, Isaac headed towards the muster point he had been told to report to when they were dismissed last night, ready for the walk to the field. As the other convicts headed off to whatever work they were assigned to, he cut between two single-storey buildings, finding his way blocked by a man blacker than anyone he had ever seen. Taller than Isaac, the man wore a faded coat, unbuttoned to reveal a chest of black muscle that glistened in the sunlight. He had a small, squashed button nose, dark eyes that darted around, and the man's head was crowned with tight black curly hair. Close enough to breathe the man's musky odour, he moved to the side as the man strode past, a lumbering flat stride as his wide bare feet thudded the earth.

Agog at what he had seen, Isaac dashed to join the other men now waiting to set off for the field.

'You after being trussed up on one of those?' The man who had cautioned him against working too fast yesterday nodded towards a wooden trunk, taller than most men, placed upright in the middle of the muster ground. 'Twenty lashes the last guy who was late got. Ample to take the skin of his scrawny shoulders.'

Isaac shuddered. The sight and sound of the young man on the ship as he twisted against the grating came back to his mind.

The sun rose as they walked in silence up the path. Back at the field it looked even sparser than yesterday. Retrieving his hoe, he fell into line, traipsing up and down until a break was called.

He sat with some men at the edge of the field to shelter in what little shade there was. Isaac turned to the man next to him. 'How long have you been here?'

'If you mean on this field, a few weeks,' the man replied. 'If you mean at His Majesty's pleasure, about four summers and lucky to still be alive. Worked in the brick yard when I first came here. Now they have more need for food than bricks with all the new arrivals, so I got sent up here to clear the bushes and trees for new fields, not that they bear much. Locals don't farm – they get what they need from the bushes and the like. Savages they call them, but seems they have more sense than to waste time trying to get anything from this place.'

'I think I might have seen one this morning,' Isaac said.

'Here, or down at the colony?'

'Near the muster point.'

'That will be Yarran. They found him here on his own as a youngster. They are called Aboriginals and live in groups, like Red Indians.'

'Are there many of them?'

The man nodded at the dense wall of green that trimmed the field. 'Look carefully. Mostly they stay hidden and just watch, but the further up the hill we go, the more hostile they are becoming. The other day, about four or five of them – their bodies daubed with all this white stuff – slung rocks and threw these weird bent sticks that go back to them. The women and kids were as naked as the day they were born, baring their backsides at us and hollering and wailing.'

Isaac looked towards the bushes where the man had pointed.

'They see it as their land, and frankly they are welcome to it, but like as not they're not going to let us keep pushing them back without a fight.' The man fell silent.

Aware that the break would shortly end, Isaac plucked up his courage. 'I'm looking for my friend, George Thompson. Don't suppose you know him?'

'Could be anywhere. There is nigh on a thousand convicts here now, if you include those given their ticket of leave that have turned to working for His Majesty or can't buy their passage back. Most sleep in the dormitories. Those that work in the quarries and timber yards bed down under the stars, and any with trusted convict status can find their own place. Then there is the graveyard, of course.' The man chuckled. 'Could say those are the lucky ones.'

Summoned back to work, Isaac pondered the man's words. What if they had set George to work in the quarry? He'd never survive. Hoe in hand, he tried to drive the thought from his mind as he jabbed away. The searing heat all-consuming, Isaac tried to work out how he might locate George. As he leant on his hoe for a moment, the marines now gathered in the shade, Isaac noticed the overseer clutch his chest.

'Is he all right?'

'You mean is he crook, or is he one of us?' The man sighed and wiped the sweat from his eyes. 'Yes, to the first. No to the second. Take some advice, lad, never trust a convict turned guard. Most will do you in as soon as they can if they think it will help them get on.'

Not sure what the man meant, Isaac hacked along the row. Reaching the end, he paused before stepping over to begin the next line. At the far side of the field, the overseer leant against a tall tree; another man stood next to him, with his back to Isaac. The clothes were patched and tatty but there was something familiar. Too thin for the shirt that hung loosely from his shoulders, the man held out a green bottle which the overseer snatched from him, taking two long swigs before thrusting it back and waving the man away.

'That's the mixer with one of his remedies. If it was me, I'd poison the beggar,' the man said. 'Soon forget they were convicts once they get a bit of authority. Now, you going to look like you are doing some work?'

Isaac glanced back towards the overseer who now stood alone, whip in hand, his watchful eyes once more alert to anyone who dared to slacken off, the man who had provided the green bottle nowhere to be seen.

The sun finally relenting, they began the long trudge back. As he walked, Isaac couldn't get the man who had visited the overseer out of his mind. As a rut in the path made him stumble, he suddenly realised why the man had seemed familiar. How could he have been so foolish?

THIRTY-FIVE

Perched on the side of his bunk, Isaac took his head in his hands. Was it really George? He had only seen the outline of the man from the distant side of the field, but there was something about the way he stood, his poise. Tormented with anger at himself, he hardly dared hope that the gaunt figure he had seen with the overseer was George. The mixer, that is what the man had called him. George had told him how he created potions and remedies in his shop. Could it be that he had escaped the backbreaking work? It made sense if he was dispensing medicine. But how would he find him? If only he had recognised his friend. Helpless to hold back any longer, his chest heaved, the trickle of tears warm as they rushed down his face.

A bang nearby made him glance up to see the man from the top bunk standing in front of him. 'You going to carry on that noise all night?'

Isaac dried his face on a gritty sleeve and looked at the man. He had little hair, and his face was long and sallow; Isaac found it difficult to say how old the man might be.

'All right if I sit down?' The man smiled a lopsided smile, his face frozen down one side.

Isaac nodded cautiously. George had warned him that there were men in the colony that liked to befriend younger convicts, to do wicked things.

The man stooped and sat down on the bunk. 'It's rough, but you'll get used to it. Knack is to keep your head down and just get on with it. Do as little as you can and conserve your energy, but make sure they think you are grafting hard. No point sitting here all upset like.'

Isaac shifted awkwardly on the bunk.

'It's all right, lad, I'm not one of those unnatural fellows. Now you quit blubbing and get some sleep, then the work won't be as bad tomorrow.'

'It's not the work, it's just that, well, might you know where I could find the mixer?'

'The mixer. What you on about?' The man seemed puzzled.

'The mixer. The man who takes medicine to people in little glass bottles, do you know him? He's a friend, helped me out back home, and we were on the same fleet before they separated us. I think I saw him this afternoon, but I was too slow and then he was gone.'

'Well, if he is a medical man, the best place to try would be the infirmary.'

Isaac thought a moment. The infirmary. Hadn't the man said that it was out of bounds when he had arrived? There had been talk about fever aboard the last ships to arrive. Isaac looked at the man hopefully. 'Any idea who I might ask?'

'My advice would be to keep a watch out. If your friend isn't up at the quarry breaking rock or in one of the other outlying work camps, then I'm sure you'll spot him eventually.' The man smiled his lopsided grin. 'Feel better now?'

'Suppose so, and sorry about… well, you know.' Isaac suddenly felt guilty.

'Don't worry, lad. You are right to be wary, keep your wits about you.' The man stood up. 'Now get your head down and try to sleep.'

Isaac tossed and turned, the bunks around him now mostly silent apart from the occasional cry and the rhythmic snoring of those able to sleep.

The next day, Isaac asked the men working the field if they knew George, or how he might get to the infirmary. Met with the shake of heads and shrugs of bony shoulders, along with the fear that the overseer would use his ever-ready whip if he heard them talking, Isaac grew more and more despairing. Rumour had it they had completed felling the trees further up the hillside. Isaac knew this meant a longer trek each day, and if that happened, it could be ages before he found George. Panicked, Isaac contemplated approaching the overseer, now slouched in the shade, occasional threats to work faster shouted as he drew the strands of the whip through rough hands, but it was too risky. Maybe he could slip off and try the infirmary after rations? But if they found him where he shouldn't be…

Convinced the endless hoeing was futile – even the weeds no longer bothering to break the surface of the arid field – Isaac was glad when the call to stop came. With the sound of tired feet scraping the track all around him, Isaac wondered if he would ever see George, or any of his friends again.

Reaching the colony, Isaac saw a slightly built, pretty girl, wearing a stained apron, approach the guard. Called to a halt, he watched the girl say something to the marine who shook his head. Clearly not satisfied, the girl picked up her apron and walked towards the line. He studied her for a moment. Her face was kind and unblemished. She must have been a little older than him, but the way she carried herself suggested she wasn't a convict.

'Is one of you called Isaac Bone?' the girl said, her voice plain but light.

Confused, Isaac raised a hand. 'I'm Isaac Bone.'

'Come with me.'

Isaac, still unsure what was happening, glanced over at the marine who was growing impatient, but the marine gestured for him to go.

'Doctor Wheeler sent me to fetch you. He is over in the schoolhouse, but we need to hurry.'

Why would Doctor Wheeler send this girl to fetch him? Maybe the overseer had noticed him talking to the other men and reported him? But that made little sense. Why would Doctor Wheeler be the one wanting him?

'But I don't understand,' Isaac said.

'He'll explain. Now come on, we haven't got time to waste.'

Hardy able to keep up with the girl as her dainty shoeless feet tripped along the scorched ground, they made their way to a rough brick hut that was used as the schoolhouse for the children of the marines and officials.

'Wait here.' The girl disappeared through the door.

Expecting her to reappear, Isaac was surprised when the scarlet face of Doctor Wheeler appeared, his hands wet with blood. Wiping his hands on his already crimson apron, he looked down.

'You squeamish?'

'No, sir,' Isaac said as a wail that sliced the air grew from behind the doctor.

'Good. We have a young man here who was working at the saw pit, dividing up the timber into planks. Unfortunately, he slipped, and the saw has near severed his leg.' The doctor wiped his brow with the back of a bloodstained hand. 'I need to stem the bleeding and sew up the wound, but he won't let us. He's putting up a real fight. He kept pleading for you and I recalled you from the voyage.'

Isaac was even more perplexed. Why would someone from the sawpit ask for him?

'Think you can help steady him?'

'I can try, sir.'

'Good.' The doctor hesitated as another scream came from behind him. 'I've set up a makeshift operating table. He might seem groggy, but he is aware of what is going on. We have little in the way of medicine, so for now we have been pouring rum down him, trying to ease things a bit. I need you to reassure him, tell him everything will be all right. If not, I can't stitch the leg up, and we will lose him altogether. Ready?'

The doctor turned to enter the schoolroom.

'Sir.' Isaac struggled to steady himself, still unsure why they would seek him out. 'Could I ask who it is?'

'His name is William Tuck. Now, shall we get to it?'

THIRTY-SIX

Isaac stepped into the room, which was lit only by the yellow glow of an oil lamp that swung from a beam in the middle of the room. Below it, a narrow table constructed from an old door had been laid atop two trestles, the writhing shape of William threatening to collapse the makeshift table. Taking a step closer, Isaac could smell his friend's fear. 'William, it's me – Isaac.'

William raised his head for a moment and then sank back onto the table. 'Isaac.' William's voice was weak. 'You must help me. Don't let them take my leg. Promise you won't let them?'

Moving to take his friend's hand, Isaac tried not to look at the dark stain on the floor beneath the table. 'William, Doctor Wheeler is a good man. He needs you to lie still so he can help you. Do you understand?'

Eyes full of fear, William nodded.

'Franny,' the doctor said. 'Come closer and help me. Bone, stay where you are and talk to William. Thompson, give him what medicine we have now.'

It took Isaac a moment to register as a man stepped from the shadows. 'George?'

'Hello, Isaac.' George gave a tired smile. 'Good to see you.'

'I never thought I'd find you.'

The doctor cleared his throat. 'There will be time for all that later. Now, Thompson, if you don't mind.'

George took a green glass bottle from his pocket and gently raised William's head. William coughed and spluttered, and his face contorted as he swallowed the bitter contents. 'Give it a few moments and he should quieten down for a bit.'

Isaac felt William's grip lessen as the doctor moved towards the table, the glint of a short knife in his hand. Working quickly, the doctor cut away the sopping cloth that had once been William's breeches. Isaac could see a rope tied tightly around the top of William's leg, but the wound looked ghastly: a mass of glistening red flesh ripped away to reveal a length of white bone in the middle of the weeping gash.

Nearly slipping on the slimy floor, Isaac looked down at William. Worried for his friend, he tried to remain calm and to conceal his horror at the injury which had reunited him with his friend and George.

'Talk to him, Isaac,' George encouraged.

William's eyes fluttered as Isaac talked about the Brecks, the old plough horses, his time at the stables. Using a vicious hook with a trailing dark thread, the doctor's fingers worked at speed as he pulled back and forth through the raw flesh.

William writhed and bucked. 'Franny, Thompson, hold his leg steady,' the doctor commanded, a trickle of sweat running down his face.

William's eyes flashed open.

'Thompson, give him whatever you have left.'

George poured the last drops of liquid onto William's lips.

'Don't let them take my leg, Isaac. You promised me,' William gasped, his eyes wide and pleading.

The potion taking hold, the room fell silent as the doctor cut the thread and bandaged the wound with a grubby strip of material. 'Best I can do.' He looked up. 'If we can keep him still and without infection, he may stand a chance. He will have to stay here for now. George, I can't spare you. Franny, you can come back here and stay with him. And what about you, Bone? Be good if he had a familiar face around. I'll speak to the governor's clerk, see if I can get you reassigned here for a few days.'

'Thank you, sir.'

'Good, then that's settled. Franny, fetch me some warm water to my cabin and then clean up here the best you can. Bone, it's after curfew, so I'll get Franny to bring you back some food. George, I'll see you at the infirmary as soon as I've cleaned up. We've still work to do.' Pushing his sleeves up, the doctor picked up his coat and left, Franny close behind.

'Well, that's a turn-up.' George opened his arms.

Isaac rushed forward and grasped George, his head resting on his shoulder, taken aback at the skin and bones that George had become. Regaining his wits, Isaac smiled at George. 'It's good to see you. I thought I had missed my chance after the other day in the field.'

George looked puzzled. 'Not sure what you mean

about the field, but it will have to keep. The doctor wants me back at the infirmary. Franny will be back soon. Just watch William. He shouldn't stir for a while.'

Left alone, Isaac pulled a low stool from the corner and sat down next to William. The oil from the lamp running low, he listened to the rattling breath of his friend. Poor William. His misfortune had reunited him with George, but now his friend lay fighting for his life, his leg a mess of ripped flesh. Leaning forward, he took the pudgy hand, squeezing it gently, a lump in his throat. 'Come on, William,' he whispered. 'You can get through this.'

THIRTY-SEVEN

At the click of the latch being raised, Isaac turned to see Franny enter, her long hair scraped back. She walked across and laid a hand on William's brow.

'How is he?'

'Restless. Keeps mumbling and twitching,' Isaac said.

'Well, there is no sign of fever yet.' The girl inspected the bandage around William's leg, a stain of deep pink visible in the candlelight. 'Here, make yourself useful and light these.' Franny drew two more candles from her skirt pocket.

Candles lit, Franny fussed over William before dragging up a stool next to Isaac with a heavy sigh.

By the soft light Isaac could see her eyes were the truest blue, a wisp of fair hair loose beneath the grey scarf.

'I'm Isaac.' He extended a hand.

'I guessed that.' The girl smothered a giggle. 'I was the one who fetched you, remember?' She took the offered hand. 'Franny Oldfield.'

Isaac felt himself blush, her tiny hand grasping his with a grip that took him by surprise.

'Do you work for Doctor Wheeler?' Isaac enquired.

'Yes, as maid-cum-housekeeper. I'm not a convict.'

Uncertain what to say, they fell silent for a moment before Franny stood up and soaked a cloth in a bowl of water, squeezing it gently onto William's lips.

She sat down again. 'They accused my ma of stealing from this toff. He fancied his way with her, if you know what I mean. When she refused, he said she stole from him. She was convicted and sent here. Me with her.'

'Where is she now?'

'Somewhere at the bottom of the sea.' Franny looked down and smoothed her apron. 'She died of flux on the ship. Went over the side with all the other poor souls.'

'So, you live with the doctor?'

'What, me a convict's daughter from the gutter?' Franny grinned to reveal a set of near perfect white teeth. 'No, I live with the convict women in the tented camp on the other side of the stream. They assigned me to Doctor Wheeler on account of I don't have any convictions. He's decent, never tries it on and I get a bit of extra food now and then.'

Isaac yawned.

'You need to sleep. I'll keep a watch over him and wake you later. There's an old blanket in the corner, might not be too comfortable though.'

Isaac picked his way across the room and lay down. By the dancing candlelight, he watched Franny's outline as she wiped William's forehead and whispered, her voice soothing, as he fell into a heavy sleep.

A loud crash brought Isaac awake, the writhing outline of William face down on the floor a few feet away.

'What happened?' Isaac jumped to his feet.

'I don't know.' Franny's words had a hint of panic. 'One minute he was peaceful, the next he was thrashing about, and then the table gave way. Here, press down on his leg with this. I need to fetch Doctor Wheeler.'

Franny took off her apron and folded it. 'Try to keep him still. I'm worried the wound has opened again.'

Isaac took the apron and pushed down, causing William to groan. A pool of blood was now visible on the floor.

'Hold it there, I'll be as quick as I can.' Franny shot through the door.

Alone, Isaac tried to think of something to say. Groggy from the medicine George had given him, William's eyes flickered open, his lips moving. Isaac leant nearer.

'You promised.' Isaac saw the flicker of fear in William's eyes. 'Where are Tom and Edmund?'

'Tom and Edmund aren't…' Isaac checked himself, not wishing to upset him. 'William, you need to lie still. Franny will be back with the doctor in a minute.'

'Who's Franny? I feel so tired.' William's eyes drooped.

Isaac looked down; his hand was sticky from the blood-soaked apron. The candles, nearly burnt to a stump, flickered, giving the room a ghostly feel. William lay still, his head turned to one side as the sound of running footsteps outside drew nearer. *At last*, Isaac thought as the door opened and the doctor entered carrying a small swinging lantern, Franny a few steps behind.

'Here, take this.' The doctor passed Franny the lantern and inspected the now sodden bandage.

Isaac looked on in desperation. 'Please, Doctor, help him. Can't you do something?'

Gently, the doctor raised William's eyelids, his touch tender and caring, before he turned to Isaac and shook his head.

THIRTY-EIGHT

Isaac battled back the tears. If only he had stayed awake, an extra pair of eyes with Franny...

'It was my fault, wasn't it?'

'Don't be hard on yourself,' Doctor Wheeler said. 'He had already lost a lot of blood and there was no guarantee that infection wouldn't have set in. If we had fresh bandages and medicines maybe we could have helped him, but there was next to nothing on the last fleet. Couple of times I've taken George and Yarran out with me, tried to find some plants to make our own medicines. Yarran tries to converse with the locals, but they don't seem keen to help us. Best we get are vacant looks, the worst: rocks and exposed backsides, and the commandant won't allow us more than a couple of marines to protect us.'

'I know, but if I had just watched out for him, maybe...'

'The world is full of ifs and buts, Bone. Same for all of us.'

Isaac kicked at the hard earth, sending up a puff of dust. 'So, what happens now?'

'I've asked for you to remain here and help Franny clean up, then I'm afraid you will have to go back to the fields. Now, I need to get back to the infirmary – give the latest convicts a check-over before they are released.'

Isaac watched the doctor head off to the infirmary before fetching a bucket of water and a broom. Opening the door, his mind filled with the horror of the scene of the previous night. He hadn't known William long and never found out why he had been sent here, but it didn't matter now.

Slopping some water onto the blood-encrusted floor, he heard Franny enter.

'You all right?'

'What do you think?' Isaac said, instantly regretting it.

'People come and go here, that's how it is.'

'Maybe, but it seems so unfair. William never troubled anyone and now he's dead. Anyway, I've got to scrub this out.'

'I could help. I've finished my other duties. Here, give me that bucket.' She held out a hand.

Isaac passed the bucket to her, looking at the unblemished face, drawn in by the level-headed girl in front of him.

Quietly, they scoured at the stained floor and tabletop, Isaac trying to shake the vision from his mind of William lying on the floor. Everywhere scrubbed clean, they carried the table outside and left it to dry.

'I need to go get the doctor his lunch, not that he eats much. I'll be back soon.'

Isaac sat down and watched her walk away, the nimbleness in her step making him smile. His hands and tunic were caked in dried blood and dirt; he really needed to wash his clothes and himself. He would have to put them back on still wet, but it didn't matter; they would quickly dry.

Still stripped to the waist, he felt a tap on his shoulder.

'Here.' Franny reached into the pocket of her apron.

His face reddening, he pulled his tunic back on, aware of the glances from the blue eyes.

'Wow, cheese and bread!'

'Don't think you don't need to earn it,' Franny said, trying to stifle a smirk.

Despite the urge to scoff the food down, he took small bites, savouring the flavour of the ripe cheese.

'Doctor said to set the furniture back when it was clean. They are emptying the infirmary this afternoon so won't need this place now they have cleared out. We've been told to make room in the tents for more women, but at least it's dry at nights for now and I don't mind sleeping under the stars if I have too. One of the women is leaving to marry a freeman soon. She's probably married already, lots are, but the chaplain doesn't ask too much – all they want is some protection and a place to call their own. I hope the new women are better than the last lot. Riddled with pox some of them were. Should we go watch?

'Watch what?'

'Them coming out of the infirmary. I've seen it before. It's like mice coming out of a hole.' Franny giggled.

'Think I'll leave it.'

'Oh, come on.' Franny clutched his arm and dragged

him to his feet. 'I can pretend you are my fella, set them girls gossiping.'

Feeling awkward, Isaac let Franny lead him across the muster ground towards the infirmary. Settled by the wall opposite, they waited, the creak of the doors signalling the latest arrivals would soon be let out.

At first no one seemed to come through, but gradually the pale convicts – penned up for three weeks on top of the horrors of the long sea journey from England – emerged. Guarded by marines, the trickle became a steady line of squinting men and women, some grasping small children by their side, appearing into the fresh air. A lone straggler was the last to leave.

'Right, that's it. I'd best get back.' Franny looked at Isaac. 'Whatever is it?'

He tried to speak but the words wouldn't come to his lips, the urge to jump to his feet and sprint across the short distance prevented only by his legs, which suddenly felt as heavy as tree trunks.

'You're as white as a sheet,' Franny said. 'You look like you have seen a ghost.'

Isaac stared at solitary figure in disbelief. 'If only that was true,' he replied. 'If only that was true.'

THIRTY-NINE

Gone were the elegant clothes, the precisely cut hair, the fancy airs. But Isaac would have recognised him anywhere.

'Jack.' Isaac clambered to his feet.

'Who's Jack?'

Isaac felt Franny's hand on his arm 'Leave me alone.'

'But, Isaac…'

'I said leave me alone.' Isaac shrugged Franny away. He could see the figure more clearly now, the unmistakable glint of the red hair as he stood in the open.

'Have it your way,' Franny said, her voice betraying her hurt at Isaac's sharpness. 'I don't know who he is, but if you want me to go, I'll go. Just don't do anything daft.'

Isaac turned his back, incapable of replying. What was Jack doing here? All those nights in the gaol, on the ship, he had gone over and over what he would say and do if he ever met him again. The questions he would ask about that night: what happened to the horses? How he would make him pay for what he had done. Now he stood here looking at the person responsible for his arrest, his transportation to this place so far from home and family, all his plans seemed useless. He had to find George. He'd know what to do.

*

Aware they didn't have long before curfew, George had listened as Isaac convulsed in anger.

'You are certain it was him? I don't recall a Jack from the quarantine, but then there were so many from the ships and so many were sick.'

'Yes, I'm sure,' Isaac said, a hint of irritation in his voice. 'I'd recognise his face anywhere. He's not such a dandy now, but that fiery red thatch of his is unmistakable. When I get my—'

George raised a hand. 'Right, so let's say it is him. You can't just go up to him and beat him to a pulp. I know – from what you told me about Fraser – you have it in you if pushed, but you're not boys anymore. You'll be hanging off that whipping post, or worse. You must think, Isaac.'

Isaac knew George was right. He had to take his time, choose the place, then he could confront Jack.

George disturbed his thoughts. 'Did he see you?'

'I don't think so. He was looking the other way. If he saw me, he didn't show it.'

'You need to clear your head. From what you have told me, this Jack is trouble.'

Not able to think clearly, Isaac closed his eyes.

'And apologise to Franny, she's a good lass, but she

was upset and worried when she came back earlier. Hardly uttered a word the rest of the day.'

'I didn't mean to be sharp with her. It was just seeing Jack.'

'I know, but I'm on night watch at the infirmary, and you need to get to your dormitory before curfew. We can talk more another time. Go steady tomorrow up on the field. You are young and healthier than most, but this place will sap that out of you in a flash. And the field is still a sight better than some of the work. Promise me you won't do anything silly?'

*

Locked up for the night, he lay on the hard bunk, his mind turning over the day's events. He needed to find Franny and apologise. Then he had to work out how he could get Jack on his own without drawing attention. Jack probably didn't know he was here – that gave him an advantage – but like George had said: he needed to be careful. From tomorrow he would be working at the new field, even further up the track, maybe for weeks. 'Stay calm,' that was what George had said. He would need time to work out how to make Jack pay, and time was something he had plenty of, but he needed a plan. A plan that would make Jack tell him exactly what happened that night.

FORTY

A welcome breeze met them as they emerged out onto the hillside, the trunks of the newly felled trees scattered across the ground like matchsticks. Isaac knew how backbreaking the work was to ready a field even with plough horses. But unlike the soft sandy soil of the Brecks, the ground here was hard as stone, the roots of the fallen giants thicker than the pines, anchored as if in defiance of the convicts.

Having given them an assortment of scrapers and crude iron bars, the overseer divided the group. Cautioned against the impulse to run – the warning of the dog line further up the track, coupled with the threat the marines would shoot to kill – they sank to their knees and began to dig at the stubborn roots. Despite their efforts, there was little progress: the stumps held firm. His back aching, Isaac watched as a man marched towards the overseer, his stride and appearance that of someone who had authority.

'What do you think he wants?'

'How should I know? Perhaps he's come to say we can have the day off. Look lively, he's coming over.'

The man walked around the base of the stump where they had been hacking away all morning and kicked at the ground with a polished boot.

'It's not enough, the commandant wants this set. You need to dig harder, make more progress, or you will find yourselves on reduced rations. Colony only feeds those that work, not malingerers.' The man turned away and walked back towards the overseer.

Isaac rose to his feet. He could explain how difficult it was and that they needed horses and better tools.

'Don't.' Isaac felt a tug on his leg.

'I need to tell them it's hopeless to try to get this ready in time for sowing without horses and proper tools.'

'Sit down, you hothead, before you catch his attention.'

Squatting on his haunches, Isaac strained to hear the two men – snippets about men from the quarry, not being so lenient with the whip. Isaac shuddered. Everybody feared being sent there; the work was life-sapping and dangerous. Even those with the strongest resistance eventually met their end on the handle of a ringing sledgehammer.

The earth increasingly hot beneath them, they toiled on through the afternoon. Sporadically, small black children appeared from the undergrowth, dashing out to the edge of the field before turning and wiggling their exposed backsides, wails of laughter coming from deep in the bush.

The light fading, the overseer called a halt. 'Listen up. From tomorrow, you will live at the field till it's done. That way it will waste less time marching up and down.'

Isaac's spirit sank. When would he see George, be able to apologise to Franny, or find Jack? Not that he had any more of a plan than when he had seen him standing there like a devil outside the infirmary.

*

They had walked back in near darkness, a meagre supper of oats and flatbread all that was left. Curled up on the hard bunk amongst the usual commotion of the dormitory, Isaac thought sleeping out in the open would be a relief from all this. His mind refusing to allow his exhausted body to sleep, he fidgeted as he wondered how he could get Jack alone. With the prospect of weeks away from the main colony, it would be difficult. But he had to find a way, and when he did he was going to make him pay, although he knew he needed to be careful. Jack had tricked him before and if he went too far or got caught…

Isaac tried to shut out the thought of the pain of the whip on his naked back, the humiliation, the feel of the rough rope as they placed it around his neck. His skin cold with sweat, he tried to think. He didn't know which of the dormitories Jack might be in, and in the colony you were never alone. There were plenty happy to tell what they had seen if asked, and it would earn them extra rations or a bit of freedom.

When the night was over, Isaac gathered up his things, knowing he would have to look for another bunk when he returned, and traipsed the path back to the unfinished field. Oblivious to the usual grumbles of the others and filled with frustration, Isaac hacked and scraped, his anger directed at the stubborn roots.

A rhythmic rattle of metal began to float up the track. Most convicts were left unshackled, the only ways of escape blocked by turbulent seas, or by ravenous dogs who barred the way to the jagged peaks covered in thick forest and fearsome Aboriginals.

But the unmistakable rattle of chains was now ringing across the hillside, and two young marines appeared, with rifles pointed down the track. Haltingly they backed up the track until the first shuffling convicts appeared. The men looked pitiful, their grimy and torn clothes flapping around in the breeze, a grey pallor to their skin, ankles caked in scabs. Half a dozen men were now visible. The line jerked abruptly, with several convicts crashing to the ground; a bull-like roar came from further down the track. Rifles held high, the marines looked nervous, sharp orders coming from down the track as the chains rattled furiously. Restricted by their shackles, men struggled to their feet and began to move. The miserable state of them offered little hope of finishing the field quickly. Most of them were hardly able to walk let alone heave obstinate tree stumps from the ground.

Isaac was about to look away when a shadow was cast across the path as Jeffrey shuffled into sight. The man's face had hardly changed: there was the usual absence of any emotions. He looked a few pounds lighter, and his clothes were ripped and coated in dirt, but he still commanded an air of menace.

'He looks a wrong 'un.' A man nodded towards Jeffrey.

'He is,' Isaac said. 'I saw him flogged, never let out a murmur. Just stood there and took it like they were using strands of wool. And—'

'Stop talking and dig. I want this out before dark or there will be no rations for anybody.' The overseer let the coiled whip fall by his side, drawing it back through his clenched hand. For the rest of the day, he hovered over them, moving them aside every so often, wrapping ropes around the stumps and passing them to the chain of shackled men.

'One, two, three, heave.' The man cracked the whip, a sharp yelp coming from whoever had been deemed not to be pulling hard enough as it flicked across backs and shoulders leaving an angry-looking red line. Untouched by the whip, Jeffrey heaved, the men behind dragged along and the men in front scuttling forward as roots cracked and pulled. All afternoon they dug and hacked and hauled, but as daylight dwindled, Isaac looked at the patch of scrub and stumps. They had made little progress despite the labours of the day. It would take weeks even with extra men, many of whom would doubtless be dead long before the field was ready.

Work finished, he drew his blanket around his head to keep away the clouds of flies that descended at dusk and filed forward towards two figures sloshing liquid from a metal churn into outstretched bowls. At Jeffrey's turn, Isaac thought the churn was tipped more carefully – no splatters dotting the ground – and for longer, the bowl brimming with whatever came from the churn.

Head hunched, his stomach hollow, the dry biscuits

at midday the only food he had eaten since that morning, Isaac held out his bowl.

'Well, how about that? If it isn't the cock of the walk.'

Isaac looked up at the smirking face of Fraser.

'Just pour me some food.' He knew he couldn't let the thug see his fear; that if he tried anything, he was ready to fight back. He thrust out his bowl.

'Best you be careful what you say to me now your little band of friends are gone. You and me have a score to settle, and let's just say I've got a new friend.' Isaac saw Fraser's eyes flick towards Jeffrey with a slight tilt of the head.

Isaac looked at Jeffrey. What did Fraser mean by new friend?

Isaac lifted his bowl. 'Just pour,' he said.

'Certainly.' Fraser tipped the churn, a thin stream of liquid running over Isaac's upturned hands, leaving his bowl empty.

'You...' Isaac made to rise.

'Careful.' Fraser smiled. 'Wouldn't want to get into trouble now, would you?'

FORTY-ONE

Isaac wiped his brow, his raw hands smudging dirt across his nose. His back ached; the rags bandaged around his scabbed palms were little help. They had worked daybreak to sunset for days, the roots refusing to budge. Keeping his head low, keen to avoid the whip which the overseer used with increasing regularity, he fretted about Fraser and his warnings. He still appeared with the food from time to time, taking the opportunity to snarl threats under his breath, making out he was in league with Jeffrey, who looked on impassively. Men on the chain had crumpled, were released and carried off to die in the dirt, but still Jeffrey seemed undiminished.

The Aboriginals were appearing more and more frequently, their numbers growing as they taunted the convicts, showing their naked backsides followed by deep guttural grunts or piercing shrieks. More recently they had begun to creep nearer, shouting and waving, intermittently throwing rocks and curved sticks, one of which had struck one poor convict on his temple, leaving him dazed and bleeding.

Isaac's battered body yearned to feel cool water run over it; he wanted to take his fill and drink more than the daily ration of three cups. He arched his back and stood up, careful to keep the overseer in his sight.

The thud of a horse's hoofs approaching made him turn his head as the doctor rode into sight on the grey hunter; followed by George and four marines, Yarran at the rear.

Hand raised, the doctor beckoned the overseer. Beneath him the mare twisted, foaming white sweat on its flanks, its belly bloated.

Isaac presumed Doctor Wheeler was off on one of his expeditions George had told him about, to mingle with the Aboriginals, to try to learn about the plants they were rumoured to use as medicines. George must have bagged a spot as well, but something about the doctor's mount was amiss.

Isaac stood, trying to catch George's attention. The diggers around him mumbled for him to stop drawing attention to them, fearful of the whip. Leaving the doctor engaged in conversation, George walked across.

'Isaac, how are you bearing up?'

'My hands are shredded and my back aches, but at least I don't have to haul, just dig. So far I've managed to make it look like I am doing more than I am, keep the stripes from my back. Jeffrey is here though, over there on the chain, and remember I told you about Fraser? The two of them seem to have struck up some sort of partnership, goodness knows how.'

George brought his eyes to the men chained together. 'When did he appear?'

'Brought him up a few days ago, been quiet as a mouse. Don't know how he manages it, but he seems to be as strong as the first day we saw him.'

A whinny came from the mare, who strained on the bit as she dragged her hoof across the ground.

'Been out of sorts all day.' George tipped his head towards the uptight beast. 'Usually, she is as good as gold, but the doctor says today she is almost unmanageable – was trying to roll in the dirt this morning, suppose the flies are bothering her.'

Isaac studied the sweating horse, her eyes wide, ears pricked. 'George, it isn't the flies,' Isaac said. 'I've seen it before at the stables back in Newmarket. The doctor mustn't ride her any further. I should tell the doctor.'

'Isaac, will you never learn? You can't just walk over there and talk to the doctor. Let me speak to him.'

The horse was still bucking and twisting as Isaac watched George approach the doctor. Handing the reins to a marine, the doctor walked towards him.

'Bone. Thompson says you think there is something wrong with Lioness.'

'She is ill, sir. I've seen it before.'

'It's probably just the heat.'

'No, sir. When I worked with horses back in Newmarket, I used to help treat the sick ones. We had a special veterinary block, only one of its kind in town. She's sick, sir, I know it.'

'Well, there's no veterinary on the colony so I suppose you had better have a look, seeing as you seem to be so sure.'

Hand held out, Isaac made his way slowly towards the mare. 'Steady, girl, not going to hurt you.' The mare's ears pricked again as he rubbed her muzzle.

'Just going to have a listen down here.'

Still stroking the mare, he placed his head against the barrel of the animal; a conspicuous rumble came from deep inside. Her stomach was as hard as rock. He stepped back and the horse nearly yanked the marine's shoulder from its socket as she attempted to lie down.

Taking the reins from the marine, he gave a sharp tug, forcing the mare to dip her head. 'It's colic, Doctor. Do you know how long she has been like this?'

'I've been tied up the last few days so haven't been to see her. No one mentioned anything this morning when I asked for her to be saddled up. Colic, you say,' the doctor said. 'Do you know how to treat her?'

'Yes, sir. But it will be easier if we take her back down to the stables, and we might need some help.'

'Damn,' the doctor cursed. 'It was hard enough to persuade the commandant to spare me and a few marines for one day, and now this happens. Very well, Bone. I can't afford to lose her, so I'll inform the overseer you are coming with me.'

FORTY-TWO

A circle began to appear in the dust as Isaac walked the mare round and round, needing every ounce of his dwindling strength and skill to keep control. His legs heavy, he worried just working the mare wouldn't be enough, and that left only one other way if they were to save her. Back in Newmarket he had helped when a horse new to the yard had become sick, but what if he was wrong and it wasn't what he thought? He could make things worse, and he didn't have the narrow rails with gates secured at either end to steady the mare while they treated her.

Bringing the mare to a halt, Isaac looked across the rickety paddock rails to where the doctor plucked anxiously at his hat. Isaac tethered the sweating mare to a stout post and placed his hand on her belly, pressing gently. It was still as hard as a barrel. The mare scraped the ground, her mane flicking side to side, nostrils flaring as she tried to get loose.

'Is she any better? She still seems uncomfortable and has a fair lather.' Doctor Wheeler stood beside him.

'How many days since she produced any droppings?'

Isaac asked, running his hand down the mare's neck trying to soothe her.

'I'd have to ask Lewis, the convict who looks after the stables. Do you know what might have caused it?'

'Bad feed, usually.'

'Well, there's not much hay so she grazes on whatever is available. Do you think you can cure her?'

Isaac took a deep breath. 'I'd hoped lunging her would have shifted the blockage, but I'm fearful it's not going to be enough, and she seems to be getting more restless. There is something else we could try. I've watched the veterinary do it, but I've never done it myself.' Isaac hesitated. 'I think we have to try or we will lose her.'

'What do you need?'

'A tube long enough that we can feed it down into her gut and a purgative, if possible. I can tell you what we used, but not sure we would have the necessary ingredients so we will just have to make do. Suggest we take her someplace quiet. A couple of others who can help steady her would be useful.'

The doctor beckoned to one of the marines. 'Go to the infirmary and ask for Thompson. Tell him I need the big black bag with the gold clasp – he will know which one I mean. Then find Lewis, or if he isn't around, the commandant's gardener and the simple boy who works with him. Tell them I sent you and they are to come to the rear of the barracks nearest the square.'

The doctor's face was etched with worry as Isaac took the mare off her tether, the whites of her eyes darting in fear as she flung her head round.

'Remind me of her name, sir?' Isaac pulled the reluctant mare, starting towards the barracks.

'Lioness, on account of her shaggy mane. Suits her, don't you think? She was the last doctor's horse; I bought her off him when he left.'

George appeared carrying a battered black case. 'Everything all right? Where's the patient?'

'Lioness is the patient,' the doctor said. 'Leave the bag and then go back and prepare a purgative. Isaac can tell you what to put in it. A large jugful should be sufficient.'

George headed off, passing two people whom Isaac assumed were the gardener and his assistant who were now approaching. Isaac thought the old man looked used to hard work, the muscles in his arms solid from years of digging, but the lad, while stocky, had a vacant look in his green eyes.

'Beg your pardon, sir,' the gardener said. 'Wouldn't Lewis be better? I'm no horseman.'

'He's nowhere to be seen and we don't have time to wait. Isaac, what do you need doing?' the doctor said.

Isaac beckoned the young man over, manoeuvring the mare against the wall. Taking his hand, Isaac gently laid it on the mare's neck.

'Horse.' The lad's voice was deep and soft; Isaac knew Lioness would respond well to him.

'That's it.' Isaac smiled at the lad. 'Do you think you can hold her still for me, like this?' Isaac pulled down on the straps, demonstrating how to hold her head still.

'Horse.' A hand reached out, taking the reins.

The gardener put his shoulder to the horse's flank, ready to squeeze her against the wall.

'Doctor, do you have the tube, please?'

Doctor Wheeler took a coiled tube from the bag and handed it to Isaac.

'Everyone ready?' The mare snapped her head up, sensing something was about to happen, jerking the reins, but the young man held firm, the gardener pushing against her. Nostrils flaring, the mare twisted as Isaac brought the tube up towards her, the alarm in the struggling beast's eyes making him pause. Something was missing. Isaac stood back, casting his mind back to the days in the yard. Slipping off his tunic, Isaac placed it over the horse's head, covering the bulging eyes.

Brushing the sweat from his brow, the warm air cooling the sweat that trickled down his bare chest, he drew a deep breath and began to feed the tube into Lioness. Still resistant, but calmer, Isaac fed the tube through his fingers, careful not to push too hard, ready to stop at the feel of any blockage. Half the tube was now gone, as he took the jug from George, hoping he had gone far enough. A whiff of something sweet, a green aromatic liquid, flowed slowly down the tube. When the jug was empty, Isaac slowly withdrew the tube and removed his tunic from Lioness's eyes. Indicating the gardener and the boy could let go, he took the reins.

'Now what?' The doctor's face was anxious.

'Now we will have to wait. She needs as much water as we can get her to drink but absolutely no food. I'll keep her walking – help the mixture get into her system, then fingers crossed she will rid herself of the cause.'

'Take her back to the stables and remain with her,'

the doctor said. 'Do whatever you need and if anybody questions you, you send for me, understood?'

'Yes, sir.' Isaac led the mare over to the shabby wooden barn at the edge of the paddock.

'What you doing?' Isaac turned to see the man he guessed was Lewis step out of the barn, clearly only just having woken.

'She's unwell,' Isaac said. 'Doctor says I'm to stay with her.'

'Does he? Well, last time I heard, it was me who looked after the horses, not some young whippersnapper intent on making me look bad. I saw you walking her round and round. What good's that going to do?'

Isaac gripped Lioness tight and, despite his tiredness, pulled himself upright and stared at Lewis. 'Those are my orders. If you don't like it, best take it up with Doctor Wheeler.'

'Maybe I will. But you keep away from the other horses. He may have said you can look after this one, but this is a cushy job and I'm not about to give it up. Understood?'

'Sure, suits me.' Isaac gripped the reins and resumed walking.

FORTY-THREE

For the rest of the day, Isaac watched on as Lioness continued to sweat, scraping the ground as she paced the paddock. The doctor had sent Franny with some castor oil, which he had mixed with water, coaxing the reluctant mare to drink down as much as possible. As the sun clipped the horizon, he sat savouring a wedge of cheese and fresh bread leftover from the doctor's table. The spirit of the mare gradually appeared to calm. The last of the food gone, he raised himself to his feet and walked slowly across, pressing his head against her. Deep inside he thought he could detect a gentle wash, the barrel of the horse a little softer. That night, lit by a half-moon, he fought to stay awake, his chin dropping to his chest, as the mare became less restless.

The ding of the bell making him jump, he headed to rations. Wolfing down the food, he headed back to the stables just in time to see Lewis hold out a handful of dry grass towards the mare. Horrified, Isaac sprinted towards the pair, knocking the outstretched hand away.

'Stop. She mustn't eat anything, not yet.'

Lewis raised his hand towards the expectant mare. 'What do you know? She needs some food in her belly, just like we all do.'

'I said stop.' Isaac grabbed the convict's hand, feeling the dry, sagging skin twist in his grip.

'Bone. Lewis.' The doctor approached. 'You are supposed to be looking after her, not squabbling like children.'

'Sorry, sir. Lewis was trying to feed her and that's the last thing she needs. She was calmer this morning, but giving her food will just clog her up again. I was just trying to stop him.'

'That true, Lewis?'

Lewis remained silent.

'I'll take that as a yes. Recommend you get off and be doing something useful.'

As Lewis slunk away, the doctor turned to Isaac. 'So, you say she is calmer?'

'Yes, sir. If she produces some droppings, then she has a chance.'

'You seem to know a lot for one so young,' the doctor said. 'I recall, you were convicted of horse theft?'

'Yes, sir. I mean, I didn't steal any horses, just got the blame. Worked with horses back in the Brecks from the age of twelve and had just earned my papers to train as a jockey when—'

The doctor put his hand up. 'No need for explanations, every man here has a story. That first day at the docks you looked so young, you reminded me so much of...' Isaac noticed the doctor swallow, his eyes glistening, before clearing his throat. 'Bone, you have given Lioness a chance and seem to know what you are doing around horses. Lewis is good enough at mucking out and general duties, but with only a few horses in the colony we could do with someone who could look after them properly, and I'd be easier if I knew Lioness was being cared for.'

'I could do it,' Isaac said.

Isaac saw the doctor's face twitch. 'I'm sure you could, but I can't just march into the commandant's office and ask for you to be put in charge of the stables.' The doctor ran his hand down Lioness's mane, the mare snorting at his touch. 'She certainly seems more settled. Do you think you could you handle Lewis?'

Isaac hesitated. 'I think so. I could show him what to do, and I'd rather be here than in the fields.'

'Well, it makes sense, and maybe it's meant to be. Fate sent me here, just like it did you…' The doctor stopped mid-sentence again. 'When I've had the opportunity to speak to the commandant, I'll send word. Now, best I go and do my rounds.'

Giving Lioness a final pat, his blue coat flapping in the breeze, the doctor headed towards the infirmary. Alone, Isaac cast an eye over what passed for the stables. The single-storey barn was in a sorry state, its timbers warped and split. The few ponies that remained wandered listlessly around, ribs projecting through coats matted with sores, annoyed by the flies that flitted back and forth. What had the doctor meant when he said fate had sent him here? Isaac puzzled over it as he opened the door of a small lean-to at the side of the barn. Inside, a small pallet bed with a shelf above filled the space, which was lit by the gap in the dangling shutter. The only other items were a blurry, jagged-edged mirror hanging above a three-legged stool. Isaac assumed that someone must have lived here once, but judging by the thick coat of dust, it seemed they were long gone. Closing the door, Isaac sat down, still trying to work out what the doctor had meant.

Overpowered by tiredness, Isaac woke to find Lewis, still grumbling, watering the horses. When he was finished, Isaac tensed as Lewis walked towards him.

'Never meant any harm, you know. Just thought it might help if she ate something, get her strength up a bit.'

Isaac shook his head. 'Trouble is, when she is all clogged up it will make things worse.'

'Seems you know more about horses than me, so I'll take your word for it. Let's hope she is set right. The doctor is fond of her. All right if I sit down?'

Surprised at the change of mood, Isaac nodded.

'So where did you learn all this horse stuff?' Lewis asked.

'Grew up with them,' Isaac said. 'Sort of in my blood, I suppose. What about you?'

Lewis laughed. 'I once worked for six weeks at a coaching inn near Exeter – closest I ever came to looking after any horses. When I ended up in this godforsaken place, I found out the man who looked after the horses had died, so chanced my arm. Told them I could look after a stable. Better than the quarry or the like. Was all right…'

Lewis clutched his side, his face screwed up in pain.

'Shall I fetch the doctor?' Isaac made to stand.

Sweat beaded on his brow, his face ashen, Lewis pulled him back.

'It'll pass, just let me be a minute.'

Isaac sat down, feeling Lewis's clammy hand on his arm.

'The doctor is going to ask if I can take over here. Would you be all right with that?'

'Look, lad, I was wrong about feeding the horse, but if you could put in a word for me, I'd be grateful. My time's not long and this is easier than most of the work.'

Isaac hesitated a moment, a vision of his father's last days all those years ago coming to mind.

'Anyway.' Lewis nodded at Lioness as a few lumps of steaming dark brown muck peppered across the dust. 'Seems you know what you are doing after all.'

FORTY-FOUR

Isaac had spent the day tidying the stables with Lewis, making a note to ask if he could get some fresh timbers to make good the gaps. Using a salve, prepared from some thyme leaves ground with a little oil, he had covered the sores that bothered the horses and ponies.

Once Lewis had gone, he had emptied the modest space in the lean-to and swept the away the dust, rearranging the few bits of furniture and mending the shutter as best he could. Done, he sat astride the wooden stool, realising he had never had somewhere of his own, when a sharp knock on the door made him jump.

'I think the lord of the manor might be out, George.' Isaac heard Franny giggle. 'Too bad we don't have a calling card.'

Isaac rubbed his hands through his hair and sniffed his tunic before opening the door.

'Here.' Franny held out a bunch of wild flowers in one hand, a chipped mug in the other. 'Don't fret. George told me about Jack, no wonder you were speechless. Here, I brought these to lighten up your new home. Now, you going to stand there blocking the door or invite us in?'

'Not sure we will all fit.' Isaac smiled, beckoning them in.

Knees touching, they sat down. Isaac on the bed next to Franny, George on the stool.

'Well, Isaac, what's it like to have a place all to yourself?' George grinned.

'Sort of strange,' Isaac said. 'In addition to looking after the horses during the day I have to alert the sentries if I think anybody is trying to steal the horses, and that makes me nervous as I wasn't very good at it the first time.'

'That wasn't your fault.'

'Suppose so,' Isaac said. 'But with Jack around…'

Franny reached over and squeezed Isaac's hand. 'You've got me and George, and it seems the doctor has taken a shine to you. With him to look out for us we should be fine.'

'Seems so,' Isaac said. 'Do either of you know how the doctor ended up here? He said something strange the other day about fate. I assumed he had just signed on for the job.'

'Never talked about it,' Franny said. 'He's a private man, doesn't say much about his past. He treats me well enough – little bits of extra food, doesn't try it on – but sometimes seems melancholy, like he's lost something. Ever said anything to you, George?'

'I suppose we all have our troubles. Best not to ask. Now let's chat about happy things.'

They talked for a while until George stood up and stretched out his arms. Winking at Franny, he faked a yawn. 'Well, suspect an old man like me might be a bit of a crowd, I'll leave you two young lovebirds to it.'

'George,' Franny said, covering her mouth, her neck flushing red.

'Night.' George ducked through the door leaving them alone.

'Franny.' Isaac turned to face her. 'I'm sorry, Franny. I never meant to upset you.'

Crushed with shyness, he felt her hand cup his chin, lifting his face to look directly at her. His heart was pounding. He'd never known a girl so pretty, so perfect, as slowly she leant across and brushed her lips to his, lingering as she kissed him tenderly. When she stopped, Isaac realised his cheeks were wet, his whole body fluttering. How could such a good and beautiful girl exist in such a foul and terrible place?

'I know, Isaac. I understand now and it must have been a real shock seeing him standing there.'

Taking him in her arms, they lay down, her arms wrapped around him on the rickety cot until they fell asleep.

When he awoke, she had gone. A new lightness in his heart, he drew on his boots and stepped out to a new day. Encouraged that Lioness had freed herself some more, he made for rations, returning to devote the day to sorting out the saddles and bridles. Altogether there were three full sets of tack, the rest of the bridles, saddles and straps in a sorry state. He sent Lewis off to the tannery to see if they could be repaired, telling him to rest for the remainder of the day, having noticed him clutching his side throughout the morning.

Satisfied with the day's work, he went to wash, hoping Franny would come again. Able to make out his reflection in the glass on the shelf, Isaac tugged off his tunic, staring at his reflection. His arms and face were brown, and a mat of black hairs spread across his pale chest and down to his stomach. So much had changed, he hardly recognised himself. He had been a boy when he left the Brecks, but after all that he had been through, he had grown, learnt how to get through. Maybe there was the prospect of a better future.

After one last check on Lioness, Isaac returned to the shack as night settled. Disappointed Franny hadn't come, he closed his eyes and slept.

*

The following day, after repairing the sagging fence as best he could, he and Lewis had watched the horses. Already they seemed more at ease, Lewis applying new salve every few hours, the sores already beginning to scab over.

Isaac glanced across the paddock to where the gaunt figure of Jack leant on the rails, rubbing the blaze of one of the white and brown ponies. He was barefoot, his stained trousers hanging just above bony knees. His tunic dropping from narrow shoulders, Jack looked nothing like the dandy Isaac had first run into back in Newmarket.

'Seems they don't mind the smell,' Lewis said.

'What do you mean smell?'

'He carries the waste from the latrines up to the creek. Not the hardest job, but few last long, given all the disease and sickness in those buckets. They get a fair bit of freedom to move around the colony. He's been stopping here a few weeks now. Must be on the last ship that arrived. You know him?'

Half turning to avoid Jack seeing him, Isaac watched the figure pick up the sloshing bucket and head towards the creek. He had to find a way to get him alone, get him to explain what happened that night. If he could make Jack tell him where the horses went, then he could ask to see the commandant, explain what happened. Then they would have to release him.

Isaac took up the brush and ran it firmly down the pony's flank.

'You all right?' Lewis asked.

'Yes.' Isaac went on brushing.

He needed a plan. One where he could get Jack alone. Where they wouldn't be disturbed and he could force him to talk. The pony shifting, he patted her flanks, sending her off across the paddock, an idea began to form. He would need Franny's help, but maybe, just maybe it might work.

FORTY-FIVE

Isaac gripped the rough leather handle of the riding whip, shifting nervously as he waited. Franny had tried to talk him out of it, begging him to be careful. But in the end she had consented to Isaac's plan, knowing there would be no peace until he had confronted Jack.

Made to promise she would not tell George, Franny had waited by the rails, flirting with Jack as he went by on his way to the creek. Certain she had done enough, she invited him to meet her at the shack after curfew. An eager Jack had readily agreed, telling Franny how the grate at the rear of the barracks was loose, where some of the convicts crept out after dark.

Isaac heard the door to the shack open, a cool rush of the night air, followed by the disagreeable smell of the latrines wafting through the darkness of the shack. Keeping as still as he could, Isaac gripped the thin riding crop tighter, his shoulders tense as the shadowy figure of Jack whispered Franny's name.

Jack now so close that Isaac could feel his breath on his cheek, he leapt up, crashing into the blurry figure, sending him tumbling against the side of the shack. The tin mug rang out as Jack brought down the shelf, scattering the contents across the floor. Isaac thrashed the whip through the air; a howl from Jack made it clear it had hit its target. Filled with pent-up anger, Isaac continued to strike, his blows restricted by the small space but delivered with a force that had the cowering Jack yelping like a dog.

'Stop! I only did what you suggested. No need to thrash me half to death.'

Isaac grabbed a handful of Jack's clothing, surprised at how easily Jack jerked upwards, and dumped him onto the cot bed. Keeping a tight grip on the struggling figure, he listened to check no one had overheard the rumpus.

'Know who I am?'

'How the hell would I know? It's blacker than me mother's cauldron in here, but I'll hazard a guess you aren't that sweet maid of the doctor's. Haven't you got any light?'

Isaac let go and felt for the remains of the candle. In the trembling flicker of light, he scrunched up his nose in revulsion at the bag of bones, smelling of urine, who squirmed to sit upright.

'Jesus, feels like a swarm of bees has attacked me.' Jack rubbed at his arms and chest as a flicker of recognition crossed his face.

'You. You're that kid from Newmarket. What's your name? James... no, that's not it. Isaac?'

'Yes. Isaac.'

'Well, I didn't expect to see you here.'

'I'm here because of you. Because I got the blame for the horses you stole. Because I couldn't tell them where they were. Because…' Isaac raised the whip. 'Maybe I'll put an end to your pathetic being and be done with it.'

'Kill me and you'll be dancing on the end of the hangman's rope. What good will that do either of us?'

'Do you think I care? Look at you – stinking of people's waste, your clothes stained and in rags. You ripped me away from my family, the chance to be a jockey, got me labelled a criminal. Why me?'

Pulling the stool upright so that it blocked the door to the shack and laying the whip across his lap, Isaac leant forward. 'I want to know what happened. All of it, so you'd better start talking.'

'What do you want to know? I've nothing to hide now. To be honest it could have been anyone from that yard. We knew you and your pals would be in the inn that night, that you all had keys to the side gate. All we needed was to get one of you alone and then we were set.'

'How did you know we would be there? We rarely went to the inn.'

Jack shifted, the stripes on his arms angry and beginning to ooze. 'It's a long story, but the truth is, I needed to get away from someone, make some money, start again. He brought me to Newmarket, said he knew someone there and that we could make some money. I just went along with it.'

'He? Who was this fellow? Where did you meet?'

'Liverpool.'

'That's miles from Newmarket – what were you doing there?'

'Working.'

Isaac scoffed, remembering the fancy clothes and sweet scent. 'Doubt you have ever done a proper day's graft in your life. You're too soft, wouldn't want to get your hands dirty.'

'I'll give you that. See, I grew up in Ireland. One of five, two boys, three girls. It was my ma who had heard there was good money over the sea – working the docks, or as a navvy digging canals, or on the railways – so thought as the eldest I should try it.'

'Thought you said it was this man you were working for?'

Jack sat up. 'Told you it was a long story. You see Pa and our Connor, the eldest, scarpered after rubbing up some guys the wrong way down in Kilkenny one Friday night. With them gone we couldn't pay the rent, so the landlord kicked us out. We were sleeping under hedges, scavenging food, the girls were begging. I was the only boy left, so when Ma heard there was work over in Liverpool we gathered the few coins we had and she put me on a boat. Idea was I would find a job, send some of the money home.'

Isaac fell silent. That's what he had planned to do, send money home to his family, just like Jack. But he was nothing like Jack. He had worked hard to get his chances, and then Jack had turned up and ruined everything.

Frustrated, Isaac flicked the whip, making Jack cower back into the corner. 'Don't go making out you are some sort of saint. What you did to me cost me my future. Look where I ended up, all because of you. Hardly fair, is it?'

'Life isn't fair…'

Isaac brought the whip down, Jack wincing as it caught his shoulder.

'You're right, it isn't fair,' Isaac said. 'Keep talking.'

'Well, Ma was right. There were jobs aplenty and I soon got work on the docks, but labouring and dirt aren't my thing. When they found out I'd been selling some of the wood and bricks on the side, they gave me the shove. That was it. No one employs you if they know you are light-fingered. Soon I couldn't even raise the four pennies needed for the doss-house. That's when it all started.'

Isaac pulled the stool closer, ignoring the stench. 'I still don't understand how you ended up in Newmarket.'

'Put the whip down' – Jack rubbed at his arms – 'and I'll tell you the whole story.'

FORTY-SIX

Isaac leant forward. 'You mean you let men touch you, or...'

'Yes. I learnt to close my eyes with the big slobbering ones. Some were rough, others gentler, but it was good money and not twelve hours with a shovel or pick out in all weathers.'

'That's disgusting. George warned me about men who like young boys. George says they are sick.'

'I did what I had to. After I got turned off the docks I was sleeping in doorways, surviving on scraps. Then one day I met this lad – finely dressed, he was. Said he could get me work in a warm house, nice and safe, with good money, so I went with him. You should have seen it. Feasted like a lord that first night. Pheasant, rabbit, fruits I'd never heard of that burst in your mouth with this delicious sweetness. There were seven or eight other lads all about the same age, done up in snow-white blouses and breeches, black leather shoes with shiny buckles, all scrubbed clean and sweet-smelling. After dinner they sent me off to my room. I slept in a bed that was the biggest I'd ever seen, soft and cosy, had it all to myself – no sharing with the bairns like I did back in Ireland.

'The first time it happened I'd had a bit to drink. There was always plenty around – whisky, port, gin – and the landlord arrived with some other gentlemen, real toffs, not dockers or labourers. Tail coats and big black hats. Landlord drew me to one side and said that if I went to my room with one of them, just chatted and entertained him, I could earn two shillings or maybe more. Now two shillings for chatting sounded all right and I was feeling quite tipsy with the drink, so I went. When we got to the room, we chatted and drank some more, then he lit up this strange pipe – had this glass bulb filled with this liquid that bubbled when you placed a flame under, and it gave off this fragrant smoke. It was kind of weird but made you feel relaxed, like you were looking down on yourself.'

'A pipe doesn't do that to you,' Isaac said.

'This one did. Didn't know it then, but this stuff hooks you in real fast, makes you want more and more till you can't live without it. After a while he took off his coat and lay down on the bed. By now I was quite relaxed and a bit flushed, so when he suggested that I untie my cravat and undo my shirt, I was grateful. Next thing his hand was on my privates, telling me what a lovely youth I was, asked if I'd like to earn a little extra. Then before I knew it I'm half naked and he is playing with his member. Didn't last long, and then he got up and left. That's how it started.'

'Why didn't you leave?'

'Was decent money, even with the landlord taking a cut for board and lodging. Had to call some of them by a name, like Martha or Gertie. They'd call me their little flower or whatever they liked. I was seeing more and more men and I got good at it. They liked my pale skin and freckles, and the pipe made it all a blur. Then one day he turned up. He was a gambler, made his money on the racecourses, in the gambling dens, and – when his luck was down – by courting rich men's daughters. Course, he wasn't really into them, if you get my drift, but he'd make them believe he was going to marry them, take them away to his estates overseas. Handsome chap, tall, always very considerate, and paid well. Some of the other lads were envious, used to joke about his glass eye, but he turned into a regular, wanted me to pretend to be something he'd won in a bet.

'A few weeks after I first met him, he told me he had to leave Liverpool, and that he had booked a ticket on a boat bound for the continent via Harwich. Said if I would be his doxy, he would take me with him and that I could work with him around the racecourses as the bookies knew him and wouldn't take his bets. By this time, I was done with the molly-house so said yes and packed up. I was still giving him a bit of discreet attention, and the pipe had a firm grip on us both, but it was more of a partnership. We headed for Ipswich races, and there he met up with a couple of his old pals. I was still fronting for him and we were staying in respectable inns, sometimes grander places if the winnings were good. That's when he said he and his friends were on the lookout for some good horses to steal. They would sell them on to some blokes who would race them under false names. That's how we wound up in Newmarket. Seems he knew someone in town who would give him information. I would get a cut of the cash, and my cravings were costing me more and more.'

'I still don't understand, why me?'

'He told me to watch that yard, work out the routine. Pure chance that day when you ran into me you were from the same yard, but I mentioned it to him that evening and he had the biggest smile on his face, told me that he had a plan. All it took was some patience.'

'So you were waiting for us that night in the Wagon?'

'Sure was. Seems his friend had tipped him off. All I had to do was get one of you to have a little drink with me and we had a way into the yard. When I spotted you on your own, well…'

'So you drugged my drink?'

'Was worried I'd given you too much – it grabbed a quick hold on you. I helped you out and another acquaintance joined me. When we got to the gate, I took the key and let myself in and then waited till it was safe to open the main gates. When the others arrived, I kept lookout while they found the right horses and fitted wadded pads on their hoofs. Some of them were frisky, wouldn't stand still, but eventually they got them all on and led them off. I closed the gates behind them and left by the side entrance. You were out of it, slumped against the wall where I put you. I skirted the backstreets to the cemetery on the edge of town, where we handed the horses over. I got paid my money and told him I would meet him the next day. Then I walked down the high street until I was out of sight and doubled back and headed to Cambridge.'

'I don't understand how I woke up in the loft above the gates.'

'Suspect you came to at some point and found your way up there. You just don't remember it.'

Isaac tried to piece everything together, the revelations still making him confused. 'But they found out in the end you stole the horses and sent you here?'

Jack laughed. 'No. I got caught, but not for stealing the horses. Never knew what happened to the horses after we handed them over. Me, I took the wrong road in the dark, and after a few days wound up in Royston. Had myself a good time on the money, but it quickly ran out and so I thought I'd try London, as I was still using, and figured I could go back to my Liverpool trade if needed. I got arrested breaking into this house in a posh part of London to get whatever I could to sell on. I was desperate, living in miserable rooms with barely enough to eat, just wondering where to get my next trip to oblivion from.'

Isaac yawned and set down the whip, the faint light of daybreak sliding between the slats.

Jack sat up. 'Can I leave now?'

Unaware they had talked all night, Isaac felt a wave of exhaustion cover him. 'For now. I'll find you when I'm ready.'

Jack raised himself off the cot. 'I take it that little girl I was supposed to meet was in on your plan?'

Surprised at how protective he felt, Isaac summoned up the dregs of his strength. 'Yes, and she's mine so make sure you keep well clear.'

As Jack stood up, Isaac put his arm across the door. 'So how do you feed your cravings now?'

'I don't have any.' Jack grinned. 'Five months in prison and a long journey in a wooden hell gets you off the vapours. Now I need to get back.'

Isaac dropped his arm, shutting the door behind Jack. Still trying to put everything together, he slumped back on the cot. Since his arrest he had tried to work out what had happened, hating Jack for what he had done to him. Who was this man Jack was with? Who did he know in Newmarket? He wasn't done with Jack. Back then he had been a naïve country boy, but things had changed. Worn out, he lay back, closing his eyes, taking a few moments of rest before the day began.

FORTY-SEVEN

All day, Isaac went over the events of the previous night. He had all but given up hope of ever discovering the truth, never expecting to see Jack again, but since his arrival, there was a chance.

The mare twisted, catching his mood as Isaac ran the brush down her hindquarters.

'Did he show?' Isaac heard Franny's voice behind him. 'I barely slept last night. Nearly dropped the doctor's breakfast this morning worrying about you, and he is in a funny mood this morning.'

Isaac laid down the brush and patted the mare, sending her off across the paddock.

'What did he say? You didn't kill him, did you?'

'No, I didn't kill him, although I wanted to. Just a few stripes with the whip.' Isaac studied Franny, noticing the look of relief on her face. 'You didn't say anything to George, did you?'

'No, Isaac, I promised I wouldn't. Is it finished between you and Jack now?'

'If I'm honest, I don't know. I think I know a little more, but there are…'

Looking up, Isaac saw the doctor striding towards them 'Best we get on.'

'I'll see you later.' Franny hitched up her skirt and pecked Isaac on the cheek.

'Bone,' the doctor said without any greeting. 'Saddle Lioness up. I'm going out. I just need to check on something first.'

Isaac nodded, sensing the doctor was not in the mood for talking, and walked over to where Lioness was standing contentedly by the rail. Once she was saddled up, Doctor Wheeler returned and, grabbing the reins, led Lioness towards the gate. Without speaking, he swung up into the saddle and signalled for Isaac to clear the way, heading off with no acknowledgement.

His head full of Jack and troubled by the doctor's mood, Isaac worked through the morning, telling Lewis to rest in the stables, whatever it was that ailed him clearly worse. At the sound of the bell for midday rations, Isaac spotted George in the queue.

'You all right? 'Look like you haven't slept for days. That little girl of yours keeping you busy?' George winked.

Isaac forced his face into a grin, hating the fact that he hadn't told George about Jack.

'The doctor didn't look in a good mood this morning.' Isaac changed the subject.

'Have you seen him? He didn't show up at the infirmary.'

'Last I saw him he was riding off on his own towards the peak.'

'Darn fool. The doctor knows the orders about not

going out alone, how unsafe it is. The commandant will have a fit if he finds out.'

'Did he say when he would be back?'

'No and I didn't ask. Was clear he was out of sorts and I didn't want to upset him.

George turned. 'Think I'd best head back. Perhaps I can cover for the doctor until he shows up, but he knows it's not safe to go out there alone. A few weeks back, a party of marines had a close call when they ventured up to the caves beyond the dog line. Aboriginals came out shouting, torsos painted in white and orange stripes, started throwing rocks and spears at them. Let's hope he'll see sense and come back soon. I'll tell people he is out if they come looking. See you later.'

*

Isaac was left alone to complete the daily tasks, Lewis fit for little more than a few menial chores. Isaac kept a watch on the trail towards the peak in hope of seeing the doctor return. Lioness was surefooted, but any unexpected root or dip in the track could make her stumble. He didn't want to raise the alarm, fearful of what the commandant would do, but as the daylight faded he was worried something terrible might have happened to the doctor. The stables shut up for the night, he headed for the infirmary to find George. Using the side entrance, he lifted the iron latch and opened the door. Not sure where to go, he cast his eyes up and down the rows of cots containing curled-up figures arranged down each side of the vast room, the smell of sickness and despair heavy in the air as he looked for George. Maybe he should go back to the stables? The doctor would probably be back by now, and had just forgotten the time, like Franny said he often did, turning up late for supper.

About to leave, Isaac heard a screech as George emerged from a small door in the corner.

'Isaac, is he back?'

'No sign and I didn't know what to do. It's nearly dark and I'm worried.'

George frowned. 'Damn fool; let's hope he's just lost. I'll come with you, see if he is back, but if he isn't I'm afraid we must tell the authorities. I can't cover for him any longer and like as not he will be expected for dinner at the commandant's house.'

There was no sign of him at the stables, or the doctor's house, Franny shaking her head when she answered the door. The three of them agreed they couldn't wait any longer; George smoothed down his hair and buttoned up his jacket. 'The commandant is not going to be best pleased when he hears about this, but I don't think we have any choice. You two try and get some sleep, nothing more you can do. I'll let you know how things go.'

FORTY-EIGHT

A thumping at the door of the cramped shack threatened to shake the rickety timber from its rusting hinges.

'Isaac, wake up. We need to report to the commandant.'

Isaac opened the door, still tugging on his shirt.

'George, what's all the commotion? Why does the commandant want to see us?'

'I went to his house last night, as we agreed, and an aide took the message. Turns out the commandant had retired for the night and the aide left it until this morning to inform him. The commandant wasn't best pleased when he was told the doctor was missing.'

'Blimey,' Isaac said, 'let's hope he has calmed down a bit by the time we get there.'

Isaac followed George, ascending the steps to the white-painted door to the colony's administrative building. Ushered in by the aide George had spoken to, they found themselves inside the commandant's office. The aide sat sheepishly at a small table piled high with parchments and papers, while the commandant, hands clasped behind his back, stood behind a dark desk, staring out of the window.

'Bone, tell me what Doctor Wheeler said when you last saw him.' The commandant turned and seated himself in a green studded chair and glowered at them.

Isaac fidgeted and repeated what he had told George, careful to keep his eyes lowered. The commandant, his hands held in front of him as if he was praying, sat and listened without comment.

When Isaac had finished talking, the commandant banged the desk, making them all jump. 'He's the only doctor in this godforsaken place and he runs off on one of his foraging trips, expecting the Aboriginals to help him. He knows it is against the rules to go off.' His face thunderous, he turned towards the aide. 'Tell the captain of the marines to ready a search party. Yarran is to go with them – his native tongue and tracking skills might come in useful. Thompson, I'm sending you as well. It will leave the infirmary without medical expertise, but if the choice is between him and a few convicts, then so be it. If he's had an accident, do what you can. And you, Bone, get your things.'

Isaac stood stunned.

'Doctor Wheeler keeps telling me how you cured his horse, so you had better be part of the party in case the beast has come to grief. Draw some rations from the kitchen on my orders and report to the search party by mid-morning bell. My aide here will square everything off.'

Dismissed, they turned and followed the aide from the room out into the spreading heat of the day. Spying

Franny standing by the doctor's house, he ran towards her.

'I can't be long. Commandant's not best pleased about the doctor going off on his own. He's sending a search a party of marines out, with Yarran as scout and me and George to look after him and Lioness if either of them need it.'

Franny let out a gasp. 'Be careful, Isaac. It's bad enough the doctor is missing. I couldn't bear to lose you and George, especially you.'

Isaac wiped away the single tear rolling down her cheek.

'Be back before you know it,' Isaac said, embracing Franny. 'You can't get rid of me that easy.'

Back at the stables, Isaac collected his blanket, eating utensils and jacket, giving instructions to Lewis, telling him he didn't know how long he might be gone, and raced to where grumbling marines stood, rifles and packs by their side, ready to set off. Crouched at the foot of the trail, Yarran rubbed at the soil, sniffing the air like a bloodhound. George stood to one side.

'Listen up,' the marine captain said. 'Our orders are to find Doctor Wheeler. Yarran will take the lead once we are beyond the boundary of the colony. If we meet any Aboriginals, we stay calm and let Yarran do the talking. Don't raise your rifles or fire unless I tell you to. We've got a few hours of daylight, so the sooner we are out, the better chance we have.'

The marines shouldered their packs, picked up their rifles and fell in behind Yarran who was already heading up the path, seemingly untroubled by the heat or terrain. The path led relentlessly upwards, passing the fields Isaac had worked on, and towards the line of dogs that guarded the boundary of the colony. Ahead, Yarran paused occasionally, the red-coated marines cursing when he set off again after just a few moments, their thick uniforms and heavy packs unsuitable in the humid air.

The bushes and trees were pushing in from the sides and Isaac could hear the barking of the dogs long before they arrived at the boundary of the colony. Forced into single file, the path meandered on, emerging into a small clearing, where a line of solid mastiffs barred the way, straining against a heavy chain, teeth showing and slobbering.

Hushed with a kick and a sharp command, the mastiffs quietened as a man who had been sheltering in the shade approached the captain. Grateful for the rest, the search party slumped to the ground, sipping cautiously at their water flasks.

Conversation over, the captain walked across.

'Says the doctor went through yesterday about midday, never came back. We will rest here briefly, then carry on up the track as far as we can before either we find the doctor or it gets dark.'

Isaac wiped his forehead, the rag already sopping. 'The doctor is probably miles away, given he was riding; that's unless something happened to him or Lioness.'

'Let's hope he has just got lost,' George said. 'I can't bear to think of the alternatives.'

Their jowls covered in slobber, the mastiffs were hauled, growling and barking, to one side to allow the party to continue.

Isaac held his breath as he passed, in no doubt any convicts wanting to escape were not going to do it via the peak.

Glad to be past, the sound of the dogs faded, replaced by the slim, silvery forest which was crowded with birds, their cry like chalk dragged across a school slate.

The marines halted, and Yarran walked a few paces before kneeling and tracing his fingers across the soft trail, studying the leaves and branches on each side, before sniffing the air. Animated, Yarran beckoned the marine captain, pointing up the trail, a few words exchanged between the two.

The captain turned. 'Reckons he can smell horse, so looks like the doctor was here. Says there were others here as well, maybe six or eight. We need to be on our guard, so I want two men at the rear looking down from where we have come; the rest of you divide into pairs and keep a lookout on each side. You two convicts stay in the middle. Ready up.'

FORTY-NINE

Rifles levelled, the cautious procession wound their way through the rustling green passage, the impenetrable foliage alive with the cracks and crashes of invisible creatures, no one certain if it was man or beast. With bodies sapped of strength by the never-ending climb, coupled with the continuous vigilance for fear of attack, the captain hailed a halt for the night. A patch of low bushes was cleared to make camp. People nibbled at sparse rations in silence. For fear of attracting attention, there was no fire to keep away the swarm of black flies, so everyone drew their tunics tight around them to try to block the constant irritation.

Watch set, they settled for the night. Despite Yarran pausing and stooping along the track before lumbering on, there had been no sign of the doctor or Lioness all day.

Huddled next to George, Isaac spoke in a whisper. 'Do you know why the doctor went off on his own?'

'Not really. He's been a bit out of sorts. There weren't as many medicines on the last ships as he had hoped for, and we have next to nothing left in the infirmary. Thinks we ought to take more notice of the locals, that they know these lands better than us and have ways that might be helpful to us.'

'Maybe that's why he has gone off,' Isaac said. 'To talk to the locals.'

'Could be. Still, he would have done better to have spoken to the commandant first, taken Yarran with him. Maybe he was thinking about the new settlement.'

'What new settlement?'

'The commandant is planning to build a whole town. With so many getting their ticket of leave, and talk of free settlers bringing their families, there will be a need for more houses. There will still be plenty of convict labour to build it all. Just think, one day, me and you might be free, have a nice little place in town, start a little business.'

Isaac's shoulders slumped. 'We might end up living next door to Jeffrey or Jack, and I don't want to see or speak to either of them again.'

'You've spoken to Jack, then?'

Isaac hesitated.

'I hope you didn't do anything stupid.'

'No. I wanted to, but apart from a whipping that he will soon get over, he is all right.'

'When?'

'A couple of nights ago. Franny helped me trick him into coming to the stables. He talked freely enough. I'm sorry, George. I wanted to tell you, but I knew you would try to stop me.'

'What happened?'

Isaac recounted the events of the night, while George remained silent. 'So, is that it?'

'Franny asked me the same, but I can't get my head straight. I hate him for his sweet-talking and the way he stole the horses and left me to take the blame. As for the things he has done with men for money, that disgusts me. I don't think I'll ever be able to forgive him. He needs to pay for what he did to me, but I can't figure out how.'

'Keep clear, that's my advice. You know most of what happened and you can't change that. If you don't let it go, it will eat you up. You are doing well, and if you keep your slate clean, leave Jack alone, then you will get your ticket of leave. Plus, you've got a sweet girl in Franny. Jack's not worth risking all that for.'

The forest alive with snapping and strange cries and screeches, Isaac pondered what George had said, but he had lost everything. And the prison, then the hulk, and the long sea journey, and time in the boy's prison, had hardened him. The world had turned against him back in Newmarket; he wasn't ready to give up yet. He still needed answers from Jack, but that would have to wait. First, they had to find the doctor.

FIFTY

Feeling thankful as light slunk through the leafy wall, the song of birds taking over the ceaseless rustle of the passing night, Isaac packed up his kit. The marines were ready, and Yarran grunted, raising his hand towards the dense forest; there was the slightest of movements as a group of Aboriginals emerged.

'Reckon they've been there long?'

George fumbled with the buttons on his jacket. 'Possibly a while. Best we keep our wits about us until we know if they are friendly or not.'

The marines shuffled, rifles by their sides, observing the order not to shoot as the captain moved towards Yarran.

Isaac could see the men lined up along the tree line had painted white ribbons across their cheeks and near-naked torsos, giving their already lean bodies a fearsome appearance. With big staves carried at their sides, they advanced towards them, their faces without expression adding to the menace of their unheralded arrival.

His words sharp and guttural, Yarran spoke to the group. Unable to understand, everyone waited. The man at the centre of the group was throwing his arms around, his feet stamping at the earth as his voice filled the woods. His words a torrent, the native to his side launched a fist-sized rock, which slammed into the shoulder of a marine. The marine let out a cry of pain as he dropped his weapon, the remaining raising their rifles in a flash, fingers hooked around triggers.

The captain approached the marines, his face troubled. 'Yarran told us they want us to leave. That this is their sacred land and we shouldn't be here. I'll get Yarran to reason with them, see if they have seen the doctor. But stay calm; there may be others hidden in the trees.'

Words rushed back and forth between Yarran and the man, neither of the groups moving from where they stood as the men by the forest shook their fists, ready to throw more rocks and curved wooden sticks at the marines.

Careful not to startle the Aboriginals, the captain returned and spoke to Yarran again, who relayed his words, a shake of the head from the man who led the Aboriginals.

'They said that no one has come past here, and we should go,' the captain said. 'Given there is no sign of the doctor or his horse, he could have strayed off the path further back. Nothing is to be gained by getting into a fight – we can leave that for another day. On my command, pick up your kit and retreat. We can look for signs as we retrace our steps.'

The men in the trees whooped and hollered, sensing victory. Waving their arms, they crouched before leaping into the air, their celebrations causing the greenery to twitch and rustle as if full of snakes.

Isaac crouched to collect his things, one eye on the men, their decorated black bodies giving them a ghoulish appearance. He was ready to move out when a flicker of red caught his eye, where the man on the edge of the group was dancing wildly.

'George, don't stare, but I think that man is wearing the doctor's scarf.'

George turned his gaze towards the group. 'You sure it's the doctor's?'

'As sure as I can be. He was tying it when he told me to saddle Lioness.'

'Best you tell the captain, and sharp, before it's too late.'

'Captain,' – Isaac approached him cautiously – 'I think the man on the right is wearing the scarf the doctor was wearing when he rode out of camp.'

'Can you be positive it's his?' The captain frowned.

'The doctor was knotting a red scarf when he ordered me to ready Lioness, so I'm pretty sure.'

'All right. We'll retreat as planned, make them think we are leaving, then we can think when we are out of sight.'

The captain issued the order to withdraw and they retraced their steps down the path, the triumphant cheers and whoops of the Aboriginals fading. When the notes of the forest were the only ones to be heard, the captain stopped and raised his hand.

'The convict reckons he saw one of the men with a red scarf, possibly the same one the doctor was wearing when he took off from the colony. They claim they haven't seen him, but Yarran was certain he could smell his horse. That means that either the convict is mistaken, the Aboriginals found something red lying around, or they are not telling the truth when they say they haven't seen the doctor. We have two choices. We can believe what the Aboriginals say and return to the colony, or we can take it they are lying and that the doctor is someplace beyond the point that we clashed with them. Everything points to the doctor coming this way. There was no sign of him on the way up to here and no alternative trails.'

'We should shoot the damn savages and be done,' muttered a marine with a pock-marked face. 'No better than animals.'

'Quiet,' the captain rebuked the man. 'They may still be tracking us. We are a big group and stand out in these red uniforms. Yarran, you sure you smelt the doctor's horse?'

Yarran nodded, choosing as he often did not to speak.

'Right, Private Jenkins, strip down your uniform, pick up your rifle and water bottle. You too.' The captain pointed at Isaac. 'I want the two of you to go with Yarran and scout ahead – you are both small and should make less noise – we will follow at a safe distance. Private, you are only to shoot if you need to. Your orders are to see if you can spot the doctor and then report back. You are not to approach. If you haven't found him by nightfall, return anyway. Understand?'

'Yes, sir,' the private snapped back with a smart salute.

'Good. We will wait a short while, make sure we are alone, then we start.'

FIFTY-ONE

His back turned, Yarran said nothing as he set off back up the track. Near the place where they had camped the preceding night, he waved for Isaac and Jenkins to conceal themselves in the bushes while he inched towards the trees where the Aboriginals had gathered and taunted them.

'Can't say I'm keen on this. One convict who looks after horses, one of them' – Jenkins nodded towards Yarran – 'and a single rifle doesn't add up to very much if they set on us.'

Isaac took in Jenkins, the flies nipping at his exposed skin, and wondered how old he was. 'Was a bit of a surprise when the captain ordered me to come,' Isaac said. 'Suspect the captain thinks that losing two marines might be one too many, and a convict is dispensable. Anyhow, I can look after myself. The doctor has been decent to me, and Lioness is a good horse. If I can help, I will.'

'Brave words, young 'un. Let's see if you are so brave when they crack your head open like a melon, or one of those curved sticks catches you.'

Before Isaac could reply, Yarran reappeared, putting his finger to his lips and pointing up the track. 'Guess he's found something,' Jenkins said.

Isaac climbed to his feet, feeling Jenkins tug his sleeve. 'Let me lead – at least with a rifle pointing at them, they might think twice about attacking us.'

Leaving the track, Yarran cut to the left, moving through the dark green undergrowth and slipping through invisible gaps in the dense foliage. Jenkins, with only his cotton shirt to protect him, tried to duck the vicious barbed vines that hung everywhere, his arms a lace of red lines where they slashed at the thin skin. Isaac flinched as another branch flicked back at him, quickly raising his arm to protect his face. Every so often they would stop while Yarran disappeared, returning a few moments later to wave them on. Waiting again, Isaac took out a rag from his pocket and wiped his arms and legs before offering it to Jenkins. 'What's your name?'

'Jenkins.'

'No, your first name. I'm Isaac.'

'Hugh, but no one has called me that since I took the Queen's shilling and became Jenkins, 45367, Royal Marines. That was three years ago. Never dreamed I'd end up in this pit of gloom at the bottom of the world. Thought I was signing on to fight for my country, not guard a load of crooks and murderers.'

Isaac held out his hand. 'No one could ever have imagined they would end up here. I sometimes wish they had just thrown me in jail. At least I wouldn't be stuck here, six months from home and never likely to see any of my family again.'

Jenkins hesitated before taking the outstretched hand. 'I'd say pleased to meet you, Isaac, if it wasn't for the situation, but guess we are stuck with each other for the moment.'

Causing them to jump, Yarran glided out of the lush veil unheard. 'Doctor.'

'You found him?'

'Tied to tree. Horse there too.'

'Is he all right?'

Yarran turned his foot, making his leg an unnatural shape.

'Any sign of the men we encountered?' Hugh asked.

Yarran shook his head. 'No men. We go back, get captain.'

'Suits me.'

'Wait,' Isaac said. 'By the time we get the others, the Aboriginals could have come back. If we go now, we could be in and out before they return. I could lead Lioness – she trusts me. If you free the doctor, you can help me get him onto her back.'

'No. My orders are to report back if we find anything, and I'd like to avoid a court martial.'

'Those are your orders, not mine.' Isaac wrung his hands. 'If Yarran can lead me to the doctor, he can help me, and we can meet you at the camp we used last night. You can say that we got separated.'

'I'll still catch it for letting you out of my sight, and goodness knows what they will do to you. You seem a decent lad, but it would be best if we both went back as ordered.'

'I can't. You go if you choose, I'll take my chances. I owe it to the doctor.'

'I can't give you my rifle, you understand that? If they set upon you, you and Yarran are on your own.'

Isaac nodded. 'Yarran. I go with you, which way?'

Leaving Hugh behind, Isaac picked his way through the trampled undergrowth, Yarran leading the way. Focused on finding the doctor, Isaac hardly noticed the scratch of the briars and bites of the insects as he struggled to keep close – Yarran was likely to disappear into the green blanket if he didn't.

Colliding with Yarran's taut frame, Isaac took fright, but peering through a parting in the foliage, he saw not the band of Aboriginals but the familiar shape of Lioness tethered to a fallen trunk, beside her the motionless figure of the doctor, head on his chest, the white of a shattered bone in his ankle poking out through a bloody gash.

There were no signs of movement as Isaac edged towards the doctor, but Lioness shifted and flared her nostrils in acknowledgement as he drew closer.

'Doctor, can you hear me?' Isaac worked at the green vine holding the sagging figure. 'Doctor Wheeler, wake up. We need to go.'

The doctor stirred, his head rising.

'Doctor, we need to go. Can you stand on your good leg? Yarran, help him while I free Lioness.'

The doctor looked first at Isaac and then at Yarran's blank face, a weak smile on his face. 'Seems I got myself into a bit of a mess.'

'Don't worry about that now, we just need to get a move on before the Aboriginals come back.'

The doctor screwed up his face as he hauled himself up, leaning on Yarran, his injured leg dragging behind him.

Fingers working on the horse's tether, Isaac heard a snap behind him. Uneasily, he turned to see the man who had thrown the rock yesterday, and three others, fresh paint smeared across their chests, slip from the bushes. At a grunt from Yarran, Isaac glanced behind him: the rest of the men now barred the way back down the track. Trapped between the two groups of Aboriginals, Isaac waited, his fingers still, the forest around them holding its breath. For a heartbeat, nobody shifted, carved sticks and grey rocks visible in the Aboriginals' hands. Outnumbered and unarmed, Isaac cursed. Why hadn't he listened to Hugh?

FIFTY-TWO

The Aboriginals stood like granite sculptures, their stillness adding to the menace as the forest around moved restlessly in the breeze. A grunt from the leader saw a young man spring high into the air, launching a rock at them, hitting Yarran high on his temple. The doctor still in his grasp, Yarran lifted his hand and wiped a trickle of blood away. As the men surrounding them moved closer, Lioness twisted on her rope, ears pricked. His arm drawn back, an Aboriginal loosed one of the carved sticks, striking the doctor just above the knee of his injured leg, causing him to jerk free of Yarran's grip.

With a fleetness of foot Isaac had never seen before, the normally plodding Yarran launched himself at the group of Aboriginals blocking the path, lashing out with deep roars. Alongside them, Yarran was taller and broader than their attackers, his clenched hand landing like a hammer as Isaac heard the crack of a jaw. Blow after blow, eyes wild, he struck out, but eventually he was overwhelmed and the encircling group fell upon him, rocks smashing into the now kneeling defender, and a constant thud of blows falling like a drumbeat on the stricken Yarran.

Isaac felt a sharp blow on his arm, followed by a searing pain as one of the curved sticks landed at his feet. Their dark bodies glistening with sweat, the natives advanced, rows of yellow teeth gritted in a display of power.

His arm pulsing, he felt the draught of a stout stick swinging passed his head. Ready for another blow, a loud crack filled his ears as the stick fell to the ground, along with its lifeless owner. More shots rang out, and the red-coated marine captain sprinted past, his bayonet fixed, lunging into the belly of the nearest attacker. All around, rifle smoke rose through the trees, cries and screams shrouded in its cloaks, as more red coats filled the clearing. Vulnerable without a weapon, Isaac edged away, the marines overwhelming the native's rocks and stones with bullets and bayonets. The onslaught subsiding, the natives fled into the trees, dragging the limp bodies of their wounded with them.

The smoke clearing, George dashed forward. 'You all right? What were you thinking, Isaac? The captain was furious when Jenkins showed up on his own.'

'Just a knock to my arm. Where's Yarran? He took such a beating.'

'He's behind you. I'll see to the doctor, you get Lioness.'

Ignoring the pain in his arm, Isaac untied Lioness and led her round to where the captain and another marine were helping the doctor. Yarran, his face hanging to one side, swollen almost beyond recognition, lay completely still, his eyes staring upwards.

Fearful the blows had killed Yarran, Isaac steadied Lioness as Doctor Wheeler was helped into the saddle. 'Captain, Lioness could take Yarran as well.'

The captain turned, his eyes bulging with rage. 'If you had obeyed my orders, convict, then we could have avoided this. I'll be reporting back to the commandant and it will be for him to decide, but if you were one of mine, you would be on the frame tomorrow, the skin peeling off your back.'

Isaac winced but said nothing, not wanting to infuriate the captain further.

Yarran was half supported, half dragged by the marines; they moved quickly, the heat forcing every drop of moisture from their bruised and tired bodies. The doctor's ankle, bound and twisted, sat astride Lioness, each jolt showing on his face as the mare picked her way down towards the track.

Isaac watched his feet as he walked, fearing each step brought him closer to a flogging or maybe worse. Why hadn't he listened? George was always telling him to think before he acted. But how could he have left the doctor? Maybe if it was only a dozen lashes, he could withstand it, but what if it was more? Two dozen, five dozen? Their pace quickened by the downward slope, everyone fearing another ambush, Isaac felt a hand on his shoulder.

'Should be back by nightfall.' Hugh fell into step beside him.

'Not sure I want to get back.'

'Listen, lad. You did a brave thing up there. Without you, they might have moved the doctor, or worse. We have the doctor, and no one in our group was killed, but the commandant is going to want to know what happened out there. The captain is a military man, sees things black and white, that's how he will tell it. The commandant will have his own thoughts on what happens to us, so best get your story straight and stick to it. I'll not say anything other than we got separated.'

'Thanks, Hugh,' Isaac said, the sound of snarling dogs in the distance announcing the boundary to the colony was close. Then, who knew what awaited him?

FIFTY-THREE

Standing in the near darkness, Isaac knocked on the door of the doctor's cottage. The door flew open to reveal a worn-looking Franny. 'Isaac.'

He squealed out in pain as she hugged him to her, his injured arm crushed between them.

'Isaac, are you all right? Where is the doctor – is he alive? What about George, is he with you? It's been terrible here. I kept thinking: what will I do if none of you come back? You are all I have.'

'They are all fine. Well, not fine. The doctor has a badly broken ankle and Yarran took a dreadful beating, but they are both alive. George has gone off to the infirmary to set the doctor's leg properly and do what he can for Yarran. I took a blow to my arm.' Isaac grabbed at the door frame.

'Gracious, Isaac, let's get you inside.'

Franny helped Isaac inside, where a few sticks of furniture were arranged around a hearth, and a shelf of neatly arranged books sat above a small writing desk.

Gently unbuttoning the cuff, Franny rolled back the sleeve, running her fingers over the grazed skin where the stick had struck. 'I can't feel any movement in the bone, so it's probably not broken. It will be sore for a few days but should heal.'

'Just in time for my flogging.'

'Flogging? You brought the doctor back, and Lioness; why would they flog you?'

Isaac put his finger to Franny's lips. 'Tomorrow. I need to sleep.'

Snug under a blanket, Franny still holding his hand, he felt himself drift away.

*

When he woke, light showed through the window.

'Morning, sleepyhead.' Franny stopped what she was doing and walked across, kissing him lightly on the cheek.

Isaac stood. How long had he slept? His arm was a purple mass, his joints stiff and resistant.

'I'd better get to the stables. I'm in enough trouble already.'

'What on earth happened? You found the doctor, but you talked about a flogging.'

'I'll tell you later. It's not all it seems, and I think I may be in trouble, real trouble, but I'll explain this evening, promise.'

'Want me to walk back to the stables with you? Then I'll head over to the infirmary, see if there is any news.'

Careful of his arm, he hugged Franny. 'That would be nice.'

Franny left him at the shack with a tender kiss, and Isaac called for Lewis.

His face drawn and tinted with yellow, Lewis appeared from the stables, his shoulders slumped.

'Heard you had a bit of an adventure – everyone is talking about it.'

'Well, I don't want to,' Isaac said. 'Have the horses been fed and watered?'

Lewis took the hint, asking no more questions as he carried on with the daily routine.

Isaac walked to where Lioness stood. 'Steady, girl, just going to look you over.' He patted the side of the mare's neck. He slowly checked her out, but she seemed none the worse for her experience. Satisfied, Isaac found Lewis, his face greyer than ever, sitting in the shade.

'Everything all right?

Lewis nodded. 'I've done my best, but not feeling too good.'

'Maybe you should go to the infirmary.'

'Nought they can do.'

'Your choice, I've got enough to worry about. I'm going to wash, shouldn't be long.'

Isaac collected the small jug from the shack and walked towards the stream. Stripped down to his breeches, Isaac washed in the warm water, feeling the ordeal of the last few days ease slightly as the dirt flowed away. Dipping his shirt in the water, he tried to make it clean, scared to scrub too hard in case the threadbare cloth ripped. Wringing it out, he headed towards the paddock, draping the shirt to dry on the rails.

'Isaac. Lewis said you were here. How are you feeling? That arm giving you much pain?'

'I'm all right, George. How's the doctor and Yarran?'

'I've splinted his leg, just need to keep him from moving about too much, see how it heals. Yarran is in a bad way, though. He took some heavy blows to the head, just keeps gibbering away in his own tongue. Franny is with the doctor; will probably suggest they go back to his cabin. Franny can look after him there. You heard anything from the commandant yet?'

'Not yet.' Isaac shuddered. 'Suspect the captain will write his report and then the commandant will decide. Think I'm in big trouble this time, I dread to think of what they might do to me.'

'We will just have to hope the commandant will see you were trying to help the doctor. With a bit of luck, you may just get a talking-to.'

'But what if they flog me, George? I'll never be able to take it.'

'Well, hopefully it won't come to that. Try to stay positive.'

'It's all such a mess. The captain will report I didn't obey orders, Yarran is half dead and it might make the natives more hostile. I'm scared, George.'

'Well, there is nothing you can do now but wait. You did what I thought was right and I'm sure the doctor...'

Two marines approached. As they drew nearer, Isaac relaxed a little as he recognised Hugh and one of the other marines from the search party.

'Sorry, Isaac, you are to come with us.'

'Does the commandant want to see me? Just let me wash my hands and put my shirt back on.'

'Not the commandant, at least not yet. The captain has handed in his report and my orders are to escort you to the cells. For the moment, you are under arrest.'

FIFTY-FOUR

With his legs drawn up in the tiny space, and separated from the outside world, time crawled for Isaac. Although the day outside was hot, he was barefoot and without his tunic, and the chill of the cell added to his discomfort.

Shifting to try to gain some warmth from the sliver of light that slanted across the floor, his bruised arm scraped the wall, making him smart; he imagined the pain of what might be to come would be unbearable. Jeffrey had barely flinched as the lashes landed, but the young man had twisted and screamed through the wooden bit. Worse, Franny and George would have to watch. Every time he tried to help, it seemed to go badly. All he had done was to rescue the doctor, but the commandant was obviously furious, and those in authority viewed the world differently to the likes of him.

A small hatch at the base of the door opened, making him jump, and a grimy hand offering a bowl of thin yellow soup appeared. As Isaac reached to take the food, the holder plucked it away, its contents splashing onto the floor.

'Seems you are for it, you little turd.'

Isaac sat up, recognising the roll of Fraser's voice.

'Word is you are going to be trussed up and flayed like a goat. Must say, me and Jeffrey are looking forward to it.'

'What is it with you and Jeffrey?'

From the other side of the door Isaac heard Fraser laugh.

'Me and Jeffrey? Let's just say I'm his right-hand man, looking after his stash for him. Nice little pile we have. Add to it when we can, and if anybody tries to interfere, I tell Jeffrey, and sooner or later…'

'Sooner or later what? You'll run bleating to Jeffrey like the coward you are. Jeffrey isn't a threat anymore. I've seen him chained up, watched every moment. He's up at the fields right now, and then he will return to the quarry.'

'Is that right? Shows what you know. I'm on my way up and Jeffrey is keeping my back, so I suggest you watch yours. That's if you have any skin left on it after they have finished with you.'

Isaac heard Fraser draw up the contents of his throat before the bowl reappeared through the space in the door. 'Enjoy your food, sir.' The hatch slammed shut as the bowl tipped, its contents spreading across the dirty floor.

The light turned pale, then black, then back to pale again, until Isaac lost count of the number of days he had spent in the cell. Each day the hatch opened, and a damper and a small beaker of water were delivered in silence, no sign of Fraser. At some point an oversized ragged coat had been pushed through, making the cold more bearable, although the smell of the overflowing bucket was none too pleasant. Unable to find any comfort, he lay awake, shifting and turning, more and more certain of his fate.

The sound of footsteps, the door swung open, and two marines stood in the passageway.

'Put these on.' One of the marines held out a rough shirt and pair of boots. 'The commandant wants to see you.'

The warmth of the clothing breathed new energy into his numb body as Isaac followed the marines. Back in the same room where just a few days ago the commandant had ordered him to join the search, he tried to read the face of the man who sat impassively waiting. A pale Doctor Wheeler, his leg raised on a wooden box, was seated where the commandant's aide had sat.

'Bone, I have studied the captain's report. What you did was both disobedient and foolish. The whole business is an utter disaster, and now I have angry Aboriginals on my hands and the prospect that they will resist us advancing further up the peak. My orders are to govern this place and maintain law and order. That, and to generate goods and trade for the benefit of England. How am I supposed to do that when you and your foolishness start a war with the savages?'

Hands clasped tight, Isaac looked at the floor, trying not to show the panic he felt.

'Look at me, Bone.' The tone was sharp. 'I'm inclined to see how you respond to the whip, or put you to work in the quarry, or both.'

The doctor shifted uneasily in his seat as the commandant wrinkled his forehead, pausing before continuing.

'The captain tells me his explicit orders were for you and Jenkins to return to the main search party if you located the doctor, and not to engage with the Aboriginals. Jenkins' story is that he became separated from you and Yarran. Is that correct?'

'Yes, sir,' Isaac said hoping he sounded convincing.

'Doctor Wheeler has put it to me that your actions were out of concern for him, and if wasn't for you and Yarran finding him when you did, he may well not have survived another night out on the mountain. However, you seem to keep coming to my attention, and I need to maintain authority and discipline.'

Isaac shuffled on the spot. How many lashes? The whip would rip him to shreds in just a few strokes. The quarry. Nobody ever survived long there. Better they hang him and be done with it.

The commandant paused and looked at Doctor Wheeler, then back at Isaac.

Isaac stood in silence and tried not to fidget. So many times, he had tried to tell his side of the story, but no one ever listened.

The commandant cleared his throat. 'If the doctor hadn't ignored my orders, none of this would have happened in the first place and he has argued that you acted out of concern for him rather than disobedience. But I must maintain my authority. I am aware that you have been in the cells for over a week and that during that time you have been on basic rations. Given your age and that the doctor has pleaded your case, I have decided that no further punishment is required. However…' the commandant paused, his face set hard, '… if you come to my attention again, I promise you there will not be a shred of skin left on your back. Do you understand?'

Relief flooding through him, Isaac looked first at the doctor then at the commandant.

'Do you understand?' the commandant said sharply.

'Yes, sir,' Isaac said, struggling for breath.

'Get out of my sight and back to work. I need to speak with the doctor.'

The sweat making his shirt cling to his back, Isaac ducked his head and hurried from the room, his lungs dragging in the fresh air as he stood shaking against the wooden veranda. Happy to be back in the relative sanctuary of the stables, he crossed to where Lioness stood. Wrapping his arms around the warm mare, she nudged her head against him with a gentle snort, oblivious to the lucky escape he had just had.

FIFTY-FIVE

Keen not to get into any more trouble, Isaac busied himself, a wary eye out for Fraser. He had been lucky to keep his job at the stables, but everything felt different, as if one stumble would be his end. His mood was low and even Franny and George had been unable to lift his spirits.

Around him, the colony continued to grow; convicts finished their sentences, settling on the edge in crudely built huts, many returning to their old trades or working for others. Rumours that a new fleet carrying fresh supplies would arrive drew both hope of news and medicines as well as the dread of more mouths to feed, disease, and who knew what else.

The daily rub-down of the horses finished, Isaac and Lewis leant against the wooden shack. 'Ever thought about breeding some of these?' Lewis said, his chest heaving as he struggled to speak. 'Goodness knows when the next fleet will arrive and even though we are getting more traders, they aren't interested in horses. Given the number of folks settling and the push to expand the colony, there would be a good market for them.'

Surprised at the suggestion from the usually reserved Lewis, Isaac looked around. He guessed the young colt must be nearly old enough; he certainly had been more interested in the mares lately, and Isaac had begun to think about separating him from them. 'I don't know. It's difficult enough to feed the ones we do have, and I wouldn't know what to do if something went wrong. Back in the Brecks we lost a mare when the foal was the wrong way round and they couldn't get it out.'

'You could ask for more feed, try to get a couple fattened up. Got to be worth a go, and if there is money in it, then the commandant is likely to be interested,' Lewis said.

Isaac shuddered. 'The commandant made it clear he didn't want to see me again after the matter with the Aboriginals.'

'Don't blame him.' A voice came from behind.

The voice was immediately familiar. Isaac leapt to his feet. 'Tom! When did you…'

'Steady on, you'll crush me if you're not careful.'

Isaac released Tom. 'Where's Edmund?'

'Will be another year before he is old enough to be transferred here. Feels funny with him not around; that's why I figured out I'd best find you and William.'

The mention of William's name prompted the swell of guilt Isaac still felt at the death of their friend. 'He didn't make it. Had an accident in the timber yard and, well, it's a long story.'

Tom's face fell. 'Poor William. I'd just assumed we would meet up again, the old gang back together.'

'What's that?' Isaac nodded at the folded parchment Tom held in his hand.

'Oh, nearly forgot about that.' Tom grinned his old mischievous smile. 'They have assigned me to the colony admin – delivering messages, running errands, that kind of thing. Suppose they thought I was too puny for the hard stuff. I'd best get on. You in the big dormitory? I looked around for you but couldn't find you, then someone thought they remembered you and suggested I ask here.'

'I live here.' Isaac pointed to the lean-to. 'Isn't much.'

'Isn't much? Seems like a palace to me. At least it is snug and has a door,' Tom said. 'I'll try and come later, so we can catch up properly.'

Tom scurried away, Isaac feeling his spirit lift at his unexpected arrival.

'Friend of yours?' Lewis asked.

'We were in the boys' prison together.'

'Seems a lively one. Bet you two…' Bent double, Lewis clutched his side, screwing his eyes shut.

'You still not been to the infirmary?'

'No point. I know what's coming and I can sort it by myself. One day you'll get your papers and be out of here. I've got three years left but will be in the ground long before then.'

Isaac pondered. 'Three years left?'

'Seven years, in case you were wondering, done four. Set fire to the cottage where I lived after the landlord turfed me out – needed a younger man, said I wasn't up to the work anymore. Probably right, but I was determined if I couldn't have it, no one would. Didn't help me the landlord's brother was the judge.'

Isaac studied the dust between his feet. 'Go see George, he might at least be able to ease the pain.'

Lewis clapped Isaac on the back. 'I will. Now cheer up. Why don't you go see that little lass of yours? I can shut up here.'

'Maybe I should. I've shut her out a bit since the debacle up the peak. I'll see you in the morning, and I'll give the breeding some thought. Maybe ask George if he thinks we could sound out the doctor, see if he might let us use Lioness.'

Isaac mulled over the idea of foaling the mares as he made his way to the doctor's cabin. Lewis was right: if they were going to expand, then they were going to need more horses to move folk around as well as goods.

Hair held back in a yellow scarf, bucket in hand, Franny stood at the door.

Isaac waved, giving a nervous smile.

'Feeling better?' she asked.

'A bit.' Isaac wondered at her calmness, how she never expressed any anger at her lot.

'Let's forget about it. Shall we go for a walk?' Franny slid her arm into Isaac's.

As they strolled arm in arm, Franny settled her head against Isaac's shoulder.

'Just think, the sun rises and sets every day in London and the Brecks and everywhere, just like it does here. Sometimes I think this feels more home than anywhere.'

'I think of the Brecks all the time,' Isaac said. 'I can see the heath clear as day, the yellow gorse and scampering rabbits. Don't expect I'll ever see it again or my mother and sisters. Did you have any brothers or sisters?'

'Not that I know of. Was just me and mother when we left England, she never mentioned anyone else.'

'You didn't know your father?'

Franny turned and kissed Isaac. 'No one left for me, so reckon we will both have to put up with each other. What you say?'

Isaac nodded. 'Could be worse I suppose.'

'Careful,' Franny smiled giving Isaac a friendly punch. 'Otherwise, you might just regret it.'

FIFTY-SIX

As they neared the stables, Isaac noticed the door was slightly ajar.

'Damn Lewis, he couldn't have secured the door properly. Best I go check.'

Franny tapped Isaac on the shoulder. 'The horses are still out. Shouldn't they have been taken in for the night?'

Isaac felt his breath catch, sensing something was wrong. 'You stay here, I'll go look.'

Hand on the door, Isaac saw the shadow first, then the lifeless frame of Lewis hanging from the beam, a brown leather strap round his neck, his blue tongue lolling from the side of his mouth.

'Fetch help!' Isaac called to Franny.

'What is it?'

'Don't come in, just go get some help – George, the doctor, anyone, but be quick.'

Isaac wrapped his arms around Lewis, feeling the faint warmth of the man's legs, and tried to hold him up, aware he was probably too late.

Breathless, Isaac found himself pushed aside as two overseers barged through the door.

'Best you go outside, we will see to it from here,' the older of the two said.

Isaac let go of the dangling legs and skirted past the men, one now holding a knife in his hand. As he stood beside Franny, Isaac heard the thud as Lewis fell to the floor.

'I was only with him an hour ago. It was him that suggested I come and find you. He must have planned it.'

The strap was still around his neck as the two men dragged Lewis's limp body from the stable, a small trickle of dried blood where the buckle had cut in.

'First this week, all the same, one for the pit.' Seeing Isaac's face, the overseer went on. 'Against the law, you see, and the commandant don't want anyone thinking they can escape from here by doing themselves in. He needs the labour.'

'He was sick though.'

'Sick or not, they'll not bury him in consecrated ground. He's sinned against the Lord, although many think He has abandoned them anyhow.'

'Doesn't anybody say a few words?' Isaac remembered the parson at his father's funeral. 'I never asked him if he went to church before he came here, but surely someone says something?'

'Once they have marked him off, into the pit he goes. One less mouth to feed, one less convict to guard. What did you say his name was?'

'Lewis.' Isaac realised he had never known his first name.

By now, a small crowd had gathered, feasting on a break from the monotony of colony life. Pushing his way through, a marine sergeant looked at the pale corpse before ordering the overseers to find something to cover the body.

Aware Franny was trembling, Isaac put his arm round her. 'I knew he was sick but I didn't think he would do this. I told him to go to the infirmary, but guess he thought it wouldn't help. Maybe I can find out where they bury him, and then we can say a few words. Maybe you could do a posy of wild flowers?'

'Sure, I can find some. Walk me back, will you?' Franny said.

No more to be done, Isaac led Franny away. Numb from the shock of discovering Lewis's lifeless body, they walked in silence, hands entwined.

'Shame about your mate.' Fraser stepped in front of them. 'Must have been working with you that drove him to do it. But at least his end was swift, unlike yours will be. One day me and the big fellow will get an opportunity, and when we do…' He let the threat hang. 'But in the meantime, maybe we might have some fun with this pretty little lass of yours. What do you think?'

Isaac pushed Franny behind him.

'Nah, maybe not tonight, be sweeter if I leave you both to sweat. Anyway, be a shame for Jeffrey to miss the fun.' Fraser dipped his head at Franny in a mock bow, pausing for a moment. 'Be watching you.'

'I'll be ready, Fraser, and this time I won't stop at a beating.' Isaac took a step forward but Fraser just sneered.

'Like to see you take on Jeffrey. Remember what he did to your friend on the ship?'

'How did you know about that?'

'Told you me and Jeffrey were pals. Best you watch yourself; have a good day.'

Fraser sauntered away. 'Don't worry, they won't hurt you.' Isaac took Franny's hand. 'I can handle Fraser – I've done it before.'

'But what about Jeffrey? You can't take him on. Don't go back to the stables tonight, I'd feel better if you were elsewhere. There's a space under the veranda at the back of the doctor's house, sure he won't mind.'

'Sounds like a good idea. I don't really want to go back to the stables. How is the doctor? I never asked.'

'He's managing. Walks with a stick but will always have a limp. Says he is going back to England at the first opportunity.'

'Think he will?'

'If he can get passage, and who can blame him? If we had a choice, would we stay? Have you heard how Yarran is?'

'Much the same. George says the beating has taken his wits. He calls out in his own tongue, so no one really knows what he is saying, sits and rocks all day. Doesn't think he'll recover.'

'Poor Yarran. He always struck me as lonely. Never knew why he stayed,' Franny sighed.

'Like us, probably never had a choice,' Isaac said. 'The natives wouldn't have trusted him.'

'Wonder what will happen to him now? This place

doesn't have much time for you if you can't earn your keep. Anyway, time to get some rest.' Franny handed Isaac a blanket and kissed him lightly on the cheek.

It was nearly dark as Isaac lay down to sleep, the blanket wrapped around his shoulders. Exhausted, he tried not to imagine Franny trying to fight off Fraser and Jeffrey. He needed to protect her, and there was still his unfinished business with Jack. Nothing was easy in this place, not like it was back in the Brecks. Here you had enemies all around and who knew what they might do to him, or even worse, those you cared for. Isaac closed his eyes and tried to remember the rolling warren and happier times, but try as he might, all he could see was the swollen face of Lewis.

FIFTY-SEVEN

The night ending, Isaac folded the blanket and, leaving it on the veranda, made his way to the stables. Hesitant to enter the box where Lewis had ended his days, he checked the paddock, noting the horses that needed some balm on weeping sores, before scooping up the manure. By mid-morning he could avoid entering the stable no longer. With the door open as far as it would go, Isaac stared at the remains of the strap wrapped around the beam. It was too high to reach, so he made to fetch the stool from the shack when he caught sight of two figures, one leaning heavily on the other, heading towards him. Unable to make out who they were at first, Isaac recognised Jack, half hauling, half carrying Tom.

'I found him at the back of the kitchen. Someone's given him a right pasting. He kept asking for you.'

Tom's blood-covered face drooped towards the floor, his arm limp by his side, as Jack struggled to keep hold.

'Tom, can you hear me?' Isaac looked in to his friend's face. 'Put him down here. I'll fetch some water and a cloth.'

Isaac wiped the red clots from Tom's face, before holding a beaker to his swollen lips.

'Tom, who did this to you?' Isaac put his ear close to his friend's lips.

'Fraser.'

'Fraser?'

'He was waiting for me, him and the giant man.' Tom gulped, his voice quivering. 'It hurts, Isaac. It hurts so much, and I can't see out of my eye.' Tears flowed, a wet line forming down the blood-covered cheek.

'There was no one around when I found him, might have been there a while, hard to tell,' Jack offered.

Isaac ignored him and continued to dab at Tom's face, causing him to wince.

'We need to get you to the infirmary – I can't do anything for you here. Do you think you can walk?'

Tom shook his head.

Jack stepped forward. 'Need a hand?'

'I'll take care of him,' Isaac said, wondering how best to get Tom to the infirmary without hurting him; he was still slumped, his face turning purple, the eye closed tight, blood caking his face. Isaac turned to Jack. 'All right, but don't think this makes us even.'

Jack held up his hands. 'Never.'

Isaac brushed the matted hair from across Tom's brow. 'We are going to take you to my friend George, remember I told you about him?'

'I couldn't stop them, Isaac.' Tom sobbed. 'That big fella held my arms while Fraser punched and kicked me – he just kept going. I thought I was going to die.'

'Shush, plenty of time for all that later.'

Careful not to hurt him, they helped Tom to his feet, the slightest jolt making him cry out. Taking it slowly, they cradled the broken boy across the paddock to the infirmary. People stopped to stare, but kept their distance, making their own assumptions about what had gone on.

They paused inside the door to the infirmary, as Isaac tried to spot George or Doctor Wheeler, but they were nowhere to be seen. Tom, barely conscious, gave out a whimper as they laid him on an empty bed.

Isaac turned to Jack. 'You'd better leave. Only the sick and those assigned can be in here.' He turned back to Tom. 'I'm going to go find George.'

Isaac turned away again and weaved his way between the beds towards the door George had emerged from the night the doctor had gone missing.

'Isaac, what are you doing here?' George entered the infirmary, the light snuffed out as he closed the door behind him.

'It's Tom. Fraser and Jeffrey got to him.'

Isaac led the way and stood back as George unbuttoned Tom's shirt, revealing a mass of crimson and mauve skin. Putting his thumb on Tom's eyelid, George raised it gently, his fingers working lightly across the bloated face. He moved his fingers down across Tom's shoulder; a scream rang out as he pressed against his chest. 'He has at least three broken ribs, and I think his cheekbone might be cracked, but his arm worries me the most. Leave him here. I'll see to him.'

'I want to stay.'

'Isaac, you can't be here, you know that. I'll look after him and come and find you later. Now go, before we all end up in trouble.'

Isaac picked up Tom's hand. 'George will take care of you. Just lie still and do as he says. He'll soon have you all fixed up.'

'Isaac, go.' George turned back to Tom and began to examine his arm more closely.

Reluctant to leave his friend, Isaac left the infirmary. Outside, Jack stood waiting.

'What is it with this man and Fraser?' Jack fell into step beside Isaac. 'Why did he want to do that to some kid with nothing of worth?'

'Never you mind. I'll sort it.'

Jack smiled. 'You have spirit, I'll give you that, but likely you'll find yourself in the same place as your mate, or worse, if you try to take those two on.'

'That's what everyone keeps telling me.' Isaac rounded on Jack. 'Jeffrey stole the only thing of value I had, and Fraser, well he's a coward, just like you. Tom didn't deserve that beating – no one deserves that. Although I'd like to give you what you deserve for what you did.'

Jack picked at his dirt-encrusted nails. 'Finished? Do you think I'm any different to the rest of you? Everyone needs to survive as best they can, and sometimes that means doing things that aren't that pleasant. You and I are the same in their eyes, the lords and the landowners. We are cheap labour to be bought and used as they want, and if they think we might upset their nice little life, then we are replaceable, just like an old pair of shoes. If you think you can take on this Fraser and his minder, feel free. I'll come and throw a handful of dirt on the box when they put you six feet under. There are many ways to get even with a fella, believe me I know, but have it your way. I'll see you around.'

FIFTY-EIGHT

Wary of the shadows, Isaac knocked on the door and waited. He was about to leave when the door opened, Doctor Wheeler leaning heavily on a stout stick filling the frame.

'Bone, you looking for Franny? She's not here. Went off a while ago on an errand for me. Would you like to come in and wait?'

Isaac hesitated. 'I can come back later.'

'Come in. I could do with some company.'

The doctor beckoned Isaac inside the small cottage, closing the door behind them, and hobbled towards the table. 'Bit of a pastime of mine.'

Isaac looked to where a large book lay open, with finely drawn sketches of plants and trees, their colours so bright they could almost have been real.

'Many of these will be unknown back in England, probably the rest of the world. Everywhere I go I find new plants, new insects and new creatures. You like them?'

'Yes, sir,' Isaac said, unable to take his eyes off the leaves and flowers that filled the pages.

'Come and sit down. Franny shouldn't be long.'

Perched on the offered stool, Isaac grasped his hands on his lap.

'I've never thanked you for what you did for me when I got myself in that mess a while back. Brave thing you did trying to get me away from those Aboriginals. Dashed unlucky they came back when they did. The commandant thinks I'm a fool, and I'm sorry I got you and Yarran, poor soul, into trouble.' The doctor shuffled in his chair. 'How's Lioness?'

'She's well, sir, misses you. Maybe you could come and visit her?'

'Maybe I should.' The doctor looked at him, a pained expression on his face. 'You look so much like him.'

'Like who, sir?'

'My son.'

Isaac tried not to show his surprise. George had said the doctor never spoke of any family.

'You have a son, sir?'

'Had a son, Bone – or can I call you Isaac? He would have been about your age now. High-spirited, always in some sort of scrape, but not in a bad way, just childish things like scrumping apples and knocking on doors. The village children were always quicker witted than him, though, and he was generally the one left to take the blame.'

'What happened?'

'He loved his pony, would go out riding on the moor for hours, worried his mother senseless. One day he was out riding – no one realised he was there – and he must have startled a grouse. Gamekeeper pulled the trigger just as he emerged from the clough, took him clean off the saddle. His mother never forgave me, said I should have kept him at his lessons, and maybe I should have done, but he was a free spirit, not one for books. Much like you I suspect.'

'I'm sorry, sir.'

The doctor cleared his throat. 'You came from Newmarket, I recall?'

'Well, the Brecks really. I went to Newmarket to try out to become a jockey. Had just got my apprentice papers, and then all this happened.'

'I read your conviction notice; seems you were the only one apprehended. Might have stood a better chance if there had been others caught.'

'I didn't do it, sir, not how they say anyhow, but no one would listen.' Isaac wondered if he should tell the doctor about Jack. Maybe they would question him, get him to tell them Isaac wasn't responsible. But then he still had questions for Jack and he wasn't going anywhere.

The doctor leant across. 'That first day I examined you on the quay, you were shaking. I wasn't certain if it was from cold or fear, but like so many others mixed among the villains and criminals, your fate was already sealed. Guilty or otherwise. I noticed your similarity to my son that day, and for some reason our paths keep crossing.' The doctor paused, shifting his leg, his discomfort showing, despite his best efforts. 'How much longer have you to serve?'

Isaac thought. 'I'm not sure. I was in the boys' prison

for a time, then the colony for two, and before we set sail I was on the hulks at Millbank.'

'What will you do?'

'Remain here, I expect. I don't have the money to buy the passage home, and I'm no sailor so can't work my way back. Maybe one of the new settlers will take me on.'

'You're a resourceful young man. Once you have your trusted convict status I'm sure you'll do well. Many take up their old trades once they finish their sentences, and I've seen how you are around horses. With the roads reaching further and further out, and land being given to settlers and those freed to establish on their own, moving around and transporting goods is going to be essential.'

'Sir.' Isaac hesitated. 'Do you think the commandant might consider letting me set one of the mares to foal? Maybe Lioness, if you were inclined.'

'It's a sound idea, Isaac, but I'm not sure you or I will get any favours from the commandant right now. As for Lioness, I'm sure she would make a suitable mother, and when I'm gone…'

'Are you really leaving, sir?'

'This leg of mine will never be the same and I'm no longer a young man. When the next ship arrives, I will go wherever it's heading, try to find a way back home and see if I can make things right with my wife. I intend to get these illustrations published, maybe tour the institutions and societies. George can hold the fort until a new doctor arrives. May even be one on the way for all we know.'

'Sir,' Isaac began just as the door flew open, and a flustered Franny entered, wiping her brow.

'Isaac, what you doing here, troubling the doctor?' she said, casting a stern look at Isaac. 'I'm sorry, Doctor Wheeler. Is he bothering you?'

'No damage done, Franny. In fact, I'm quite enjoying our talk. In fact, I'd quite like it if you would visit again, Isaac.'

'Yes, sir, of course.'

Franny smiled. 'Best you are off now, Isaac, so the doctor can get some rest.'

Isaac stood up, feeling himself blush. 'Good day, Doctor.'

'Good day, Isaac. I promise I won't keep her too long.' The doctor winked as he spoke.

This time it was Franny's turn to blush.

FIFTY-NINE

They hadn't assigned a replacement for Lewis. Although the man had had a reputation for idleness, Isaac missed his company. The endless grooming, feeding, watering, repairs and mucking out left him exhausted at the end of each day. Nearly finished for the day, Isaac saw Jack leaning on the rail. Determined to ignore him, he led the last of the horses into the stables as the gathering clouds overhead threatened rain.

'How's that friend that got beaten up?' Jack stood by the stable door as Isaac fumbled with the latch.

'None of your business.' Isaac kept his back to Jack.

'Just asking. He seemed a decent lad, not much more than a boy. I saw Jeffrey earlier, his little sidekick scurrying along like a dog. Together, those two are a right pair.'

Isaac turned. 'George thinks Tom's ribs will mend and his eye is opening, but he will probably be unable to use his arm again.'

Jack took a step closer, the stench of the latrines ever present. 'I'm sorry to hear that.'

Isaac clenched his hands. 'The bigger they are, the harder they fall.'

Jack laughed.

Isaac sat down by the fence. 'I'll work out a way. You don't need to get involved.'

'Maybe not, but I could have left your friend where I found him, so I'm involved anyhow.'

Isaac wrinkled his nose. It was true he had helped Tom, bringing him to the stables when he could have walked by, but he'd never trust him.

'I'll sit here if that is all right with you?' Jack lowered himself to the ground. 'I know I smell, but there is no way to get rid of it. The others in the barracks said if I died in the night, the stench wouldn't be as bad if they left me there a week. Doesn't make you feel great when people think you stink worse alive than a mouldering corpse.'

'Why you so interested? Like you said, most keep clear of other folk's troubles. You must think there is something in it for you, just like you always do.'

'Well, if there was, I wouldn't say no, but I certainly wouldn't go searching for a fight with those two. You mentioned Jeffrey stole something from you?'

'Took the only thing I ever had of my father's, not worth much, just an old horse brass, but to me it was precious. Stamped on poor old George to make me hand it over.'

'I heard he likes to take things. He must have quite a stash. Be hard to keep things hidden round here.' Jack fell silent a moment. 'You realise, Isaac, there are many ways to get even. Sometimes you need to bide your time, work out what would hit the hardest. Find the weak spot.'

'You would know,' Isaac said. 'It's what you did to me.'

Jack raised his eyebrows and continued. 'Maybe there's a way to get back at both Fraser and Jeffrey. If there is a stash around, I wager Fraser knows where it is. Jeffrey takes the stuff, Fraser stashes it. In return he gets protection from Jeffrey to do what he wants. What we need is a way to get Fraser to spill the beans about where the stuff is hidden.'

'We? What do you mean we? I told you: this is nothing to do with you.'

Jack stood up. 'Fair enough, but I've met my fair share of their types. Violence will only get you so far. You need to use your head, outwit them. Folk like Jeffrey rely on brute force to get by, and snakes like Fraser hide behind the bigger man picking up the crumbs.'

Isaac watched as Jack walked away, the stained clothes so different to that first day back in Newmarket. Why wouldn't he just leave him alone? He had caused nothing but trouble and now he was tormenting him again, like a bad spirit. Troubled, Isaac made his way into the shack and took off his tunic ready to wash up. Half-finished, he heard a light tap on the door.

'Tom.' Isaac drew out the small wooden stool. 'Here, let me help you.'

Tom sat down. 'How are you?' Isaac put a hand gently on Tom's shoulder.

'Not bad, George reckons I must stay bound up for a few more weeks and not try juggling.' A smile spread across Tom's face.

'Good to see you haven't lost your sense of humour.'

'Nah, still hurts when I move though. George says he is under orders to get everyone who can walk out of the infirmary and back to work. The commandant is demanding every man, woman and child – convict, marine or settler – is working for His Majesty, building roads, producing food, sending stuff back home.'

'What sort of stuff? The soil's so wretched the colony can barely produce sufficient for next season's seed, let alone to send back. Plus, where are the ships to take it? Folks get next to nothing to eat as it is.'

'Maybe we should trap some of those roos again.'

'Wish we could, but you don't see many around here. I can still savour those we caught, the smell of them roasting on the forge. It was a miracle we never got caught.'

Tom exhaled. 'I'm set to go back to running errands day after tomorrow. George said he would put a word in for me, tell them I can't lift or walk far, see if they will let me remain in the infirmary a few more days, but I suspect there isn't much hope of that.'

'What about working here at the stables? They haven't replaced Lewis yet and I'm hoping to breed one or two of the mares. Lewis told me he exaggerated about his working with horses, maybe you could do the same. Imagine you and me back together.'

Tom's face beamed. 'Worth a shot, otherwise I'll finish up assigned to a settler. You think we could persuade them?' He pointed at his arm. 'A one-armed stable hand.'

'Doubt I can, but George might.'

'Talking of George, I'd better get back. He thought a

bit of a walk would do me good. And I need to thank that lad who brought me here. Do you know where I can find him?'

'Don't you know who it was?' Isaac could barely hide his surprise.

'No, I asked George, and he said it was best to ask you.'

'It was Jack.'

'The Jack you told us about? The one that stole the horses?'

'Yes, that Jack.'

'Well, blow me down, no wonder George didn't want to tell me. You told me he was here but of course I'd never seen him so didn't know what he looked like.'

'Well, now you do and if you want my advice, keep clear. He's a slippery one and me and him still have business to settle.'

SIXTY

Tom's ribs had healed, but his arm refused to straighten, the bone crushed. For a while he had returned to running errands, but attempts to get him transferred to the stables had floundered, with neither George nor the doctor ready to approach the authorities. In the end he broke the news to Isaac that he was assigned to an elderly watch-mender half a day's walk away. Unsure when he would see his friend again, Isaac felt a renewed sense of loss.

From time to time a whaler or clipper, crewed with hardened, foul-mouthed sailors, would call at the colony seeking to trade barrels of whale oil, exotic fruits and intricately carved white whales' teeth. The doctor had attempted to gain passage, but none would take him, or were headed in a different direction. The seasons had turned full circle, nearly a year since the last fleet had arrived. Rations were stretched to the point it was hard to find anything of worth in the endless bowls of soup-like liquid. His lean frame had lost its strength but Isaac was happy to be among the horses, spared the hard labour of the ever-growing number of fields that still yielded barely enough to keep the colony from open rebellion. Every day he worked from dawn till dusk, his pace slower than before, still aware that Fraser and Jeffrey were around, but finding comfort in spending the evenings with Franny, the doctor turning a blind eye to her absence.

With the unending battle to keep the fence that surrounded the paddock in good order, Isaac began his daily inspection, stamping the ground around the swaying posts. Sure that the corner post would need replacing soon, he noticed Jack and Fraser leaning against the infirmary wall, deep in conversation, Jack's arm draped around Fraser's shoulder. With a mix of anger and curiosity, Isaac watched, wondering what business the two of them could have. Whatever it was, he was sure it would only benefit the pair of them.

Lioness gave a loud whinny, and Isaac looked away from Jack and Fraser to see the doctor limping towards him, a stout stick in hand. 'Good morning. I thought I'd visit Lioness.'

'I'll fetch her over for you.' Isaac glanced across to the spot where Jack and Fraser had stood, now empty, as he led the mare across.

The doctor ran his hand down the mare's neck, her head dipping at the familiar touch. 'She looks well, a little thin, but I can see you have been taking good care of her.'

'Thank you, Doctor Wheeler. She's happy to see you. They miss people, you know, just like we do.'

The doctor stood stroking the mare. 'Isaac, I have

something to tell you.' The doctor rubbed his leg. 'Maybe I could have a seat?'

Isaac fetched the stool from the shack and placed it in the shade.

'I'm afraid Yarran has gone. Ever since he suffered that beating, he has been a lost soul. The commandant has ruled out searching for him, says his wits are gone and he is no good to us anymore.'

'But he saved your life,' Isaac began. 'And he was the only one who could fully understand what the Aboriginals were saying.' Isaac kicked at the dirt, sending up a cloud of fine dust. 'His own kind are hardly going to welcome him after he sided with us, and what if he stumbles into the dog line or falls off the rocks along the coast?'

Isaac felt the doctor's touch on his arm. 'Yarran's gone, Isaac. Even though his wounds healed, his mind was still broken. He's not spoken since the attack – you know that – and if it wasn't for a few kind souls, he'd have starved long ago. No heroics, promise me. You only just escaped the whip last time, and the commandant has a long memory.'

Lioness's reins still gripped tightly in his hands, Isaac sat down beside the doctor.

'You look tired,' the doctor said. 'Are you still here on your own?'

Isaac nodded. 'I had hoped my friend Tom might join me, but he was assigned elsewhere.'

'That's a shame, but I have other news that might cheer you up. I had supper with the commandant last night. He was in a pleasant humour, so I raised the idea of breeding some mares, just as you proposed. At first he held out, but little by little I managed to persuade him, and eventually he saw the sense in trying to give the colony the means to move around more quickly now it is expanding. I offered to let Lioness be the first, and he has agreed.'

'Are you sure you want to risk Lioness? She would need feeding up a bit.' Isaac rubbed her flank, earning a playful nudge.

'She is a fine animal and I have every faith you would look after her and see it through.' The doctor reached out, the mare lowering her nose, snorting loudly into the outstretched palm.

'I've sounded out some of those with smallholdings outside the colony. They have little hay to spare but said they will trade what they can with me in return for me treating them and their families for as long as I remain here.'

'Well, I'm sure the colt is ready – he's been paying the mares more attention recently and he'll smell Lioness's scent when she is ready, although she might resist at first.' Isaac cleared his throat, feeling his neck flush.

'Oh, Isaac.' The doctor laughed. 'Don't trouble yourself explaining, I understand. Now I should let you get on. Are you seeing Franny later?'

'I don't want her getting into trouble.'

The doctor struggled to his feet, a grin on his face. 'It's fine.' He tapped his free hand on the side of his nose. 'But if you ask me, it's about time you made an honest woman of her.'

SIXTY-ONE

The breeze was refreshing after the heat of the day, as George and Franny listened patiently while Isaac told them about the plan to breed Lioness.

'How long till a foal is born?' Franny asked.

'Near on a year,' Isaac said. 'You can feel it kicking after about six months if it's strong. But it's risky. Lioness needs enough food to build her up and keep her and the foal healthy while it's growing inside her, and then there's the birth. I asked around, and from what I gather they have tried in the past but neither the mares nor the foals lasted long. It's going to be…' Isaac paused as men scurried by, pointing towards the horizon where three ships had sailed into view.

George rose. 'Doesn't look like whalers or trade ships. I'd say they are from home with another cargo of poor souls.'

Isaac felt Franny's hand tighten around his. 'I've been dreading a fleet from home, I expect the doctor will leave now,' Franny said. 'I will need to find work elsewhere – perhaps one of the new settlers will take me on.'

'Won't they assign you, like they did Tom?' Isaac asked.

'Not likely. You forget I'm not a convict, so they can't send me anywhere. I'll need to make a living somehow, but the doctor has been so good to me, it will be difficult to find someone like him.'

Isaac could feel Franny was near to tears as she leant against him.

'You never know, the new doctor might need someone,' George said. 'And I'm sure Doctor Wheeler would recommend you. Now I best go and check the infirmary; count how many beds we have empty. Bound to be some on the new ships that will call for one. Let's hope there's no need for quarantine, though. Last time the infirmary was cramped enough, and we had to find space elsewhere for those we needed to move.'

George pulled on his coat and headed off.

Isaac took Franny's other hand, turning to face her. 'Do you really think you might have to move outside the colony? I couldn't bear for you to go.'

'If the doctor leaves, I won't have much choice. He mentioned once he asked his wife to come with him, but she refused. If the message got back and a new doctor is on these ships, like as not he'll bring his family with him.'

Isaac could hardly bear the thought that Franny would have to leave. If the doctor made good his intention to leave and with Tom no longer close, it would just be him and George. 'Franny.' Isaac took a breath.

Isaac's heart raced, words tripping over each other in his head as he tried to form what he would say next.

Dropping to one knee, he looked up at the tear-streaked face. 'Franny Oldfield, will you become my wife? I've not much to offer, but…'

Franny pulled Isaac gently to his feet. 'Well, you took your time. Of course I'll marry you, Isaac Bone.'

'Thank you, Franny. I will look after you and make as good a life as I can for us both. I promise.'

'I know you will, Isaac, and I will look after you too.' Isaac looked deep into Franny's blue eyes before tenderly pressing his lips to hers, everything else forgotten. 'George is going to be so excited when we tell him,' Franny said. 'Will they allow him to be a witness?'

'I hope so.' Isaac drew Franny closer to him. 'Mrs Franny Bone, sounds nice.'

'It sure does but it will have to wait for now as I need to check Doctor Wheeler doesn't need anything. I'll come back later if I can.'

After a final kiss, Isaac watched Franny skip away, her steps so light she seemed to float until she disappeared between the buildings. Alone, he wanted to burst with joy. Him married, what would his mother and sisters say? Maybe one day he would return to the Brecks with Franny, introduce her to his family. Lying on the cot, he waited eagerly for Franny to come back. The door creaking, he felt her warmth against him as she slipped in beside him, her arm around his waist, as they drifted away.

*

The morning bell bringing them both awake, Isaac grabbed his bowl and Franny headed back to get the breakfast ready for the doctor. As he shuffled down the queue, he tried to imagine the surprise on George's face when they told him they were to be married. He was sure George would be pleased and they would need to tell Doctor Wheeler as well. Happier than he had been in a long while, Isaac glanced at the ships still moored off the colony and looked around, hoping to spot George.

'How are you?' A freckled hand offered a strip of damper.

Taken aback, Isaac stared at Jack, the hand still outstretched. 'Don't you want it?'

'What are you doing here?'

'Got myself reassigned, good behaviour. Looks like I am going up in the world. Next stop commandant.' Jack smiled. 'Don't stare,' Jack taunted Isaac. 'I smell sweeter now, don't I? Although I suspect it might take me a while to be totally rid of my latrine perfume.'

'Get a shift on,' a voice complained from behind Isaac. 'There's hungry folk here.'

Isaac took the offered food and shuffled along, holding out his bowl for the watery porridge that made up breakfast each day. How had Jack managed to wrangle a job in the kitchen? Maybe it had something to do with Fraser. That's what they must have been talking about, he thought as he stirred the grey, lumpy liquid, slopping it over the side of the bowl. Goodness knows what the two of them would be capable of. Jack was devious, Fraser a thug and somehow he and Jeffrey were connected. Then there were the threats Fraser had made against Franny. Isaac shuddered. He had seen what they were capable of when they had beaten up Tom.

His bowl empty, he wandered back to the stables, picked up the brush and ran it down Lioness's flank. Now he and Franny were to wed, they would need to find somewhere to live but if the doctor left, she would have to find work and that might be anywhere. Maybe that would keep her safe from Fraser but while he was still a convict he couldn't leave the colony and he couldn't bear to think of them apart. Lioness turning, he rubbed her forehead. He still needed to get Jack alone again, but how could he do that with Fraser around? '

Sensing his unease, Lioness nuzzled against him. 'Guess I need to be prepared,' Isaac whispered. He knew he would be able to do little to defend himself or Franny against Jeffrey if the time came.

SIXTY-TWO

The ships had remained offshore, the customary small boat rowing out and returning with a blue-uniformed officer, clasping a black leather pouch, who had headed towards the commandant's residence.

Reminded how he had felt that first day, his legs too wobbly to walk properly after the long voyage, Isaac watched the first ship unload itself of the usual assortment of men, women and children. Chained and dishevelled, looks of apprehension on their faces, the uninterrupted line of convicts filed down the gangway and onto solid ground. They were led away, and Isaac waited as the next ship edged against the dock. This time the men and women stepped off freely, their faces and clothes suitable for Sunday service, children with looks of excitement close behind. They were greeted by the commandant's aide. Isaac presumed they must be settlers, tempted by free passage, the grant of land and the promise of convict labour.

'You'll be in trouble if they catch you skiving.'

'George.' Isaac clutched his chest. 'You made me jump.'

'Sorry, Isaac. Any of those look like a doctor?'

'Hard to tell, why?'

'Doctor Wheeler told me the commandant's office has confirmed his replacement was on board one of the ships.'

'Does that mean Doctor Wheeler will leave?'

'Expect so, he was just waiting for a ship.'

'Did they say whether the new doctor brought anybody with him?'

'Rumour is he did. Franny may be right in her fears.'

'George, I have some news. Me and Franny, well, we are getting wed.'

George broke into a broad smile, slapping Isaac on the back. 'Well, when did that happen? Have you told anyone else yet?'

'No one to tell – oh Tom, I suppose, and the doctor. Maybe I'll write home if I can. We will have to get permission from the commandant. Do you think we will have to wait long?'

'You in a rush? Is Franny…?'

'No, George, she is not.'

'Sorry, Isaac. I didn't mean to suggest…' George sputtered, and it was Isaac's turn to grin. 'The commandant is all about making the colony appear respectable, give the impression all the convicts here have reformed and are working hard for the old country.'

'That's not likely.' Isaac stared at the ships. 'Do you know if there were any horses?'

'Not that I've heard. How you getting on with putting Lioness into foal?'

'It's tricky, George. All the horses are so underfed.

Even with the extra feed the doctor has arranged, she might not be strong enough to come into season. Then there is the colt, of course. He will have the instinct, but it doesn't always follow that when they couple it is successful.'

'Nature will take its course when it is ready, just be patient and don't worry. I'll see you later.'

*

Over the next few weeks, Isaac had brought Lioness and the colt together but the colt had taken no interest, walking away, his tail swishing in the air. Two of the three ships had already left the colony. One taking settlers further down the coast to a new township, still unreachable by road, the other to trade wherever they could for much-needed food and medicines, the fields barely producing enough seed to plant the following season to supply grain for the growing colony. The third lay at the dock, with the sound of hammering and sawing while repairs were completed. Soon it would sail for England and the doctor with it.

The light spreading, Isaac turned Lioness out of her box, letting her pass the colt, his head appearing over the half-opened door. The colt sniffed the air, his nostrils flaring, the bang of a hoof against the wooden door as she passed.

'Looks like he is up for some fun.' Isaac turned to find Jack leaning on the rails.

'What would you know?' Isaac didn't hide his irritation.

Jack gave out a loud sigh. 'Don't you ever tire of hating me?'

'No, if you really want to know.'

'Suit yourself. But I can't change anything and neither can you. Best let it go, otherwise you'll end up all twisted inside with no one to call a friend.'

'Rather no friends than friends like you and Fraser. He'd as soon as rob you, not that you are much different.'

'Maybe not. But the way I figure it is, no one is rushing to hand you anything, so best you get it for yourself. Me and Fraser, we have an arrangement. Fraser's sharp, already worked out who is worth anything among the new arrivals and him and Jeffrey are quietly filling their coffers. Why shouldn't I have a bit of that as well?'

'Perhaps I should tell the commandant.' Isaac turned his back on Jack. 'See what he has to say.'

'From what I hear the commandant isn't a friend of yours, but feel free if you think you can prove anything. Oh, and congratulations, I heard you and that little girl of yours are getting married.'

Isaac swung round, his irritation now replaced by anger. 'How did you find out? You keep away from her, and that goes for Fraser too.'

The colt kicked the box again, this time making the wood crack at the force.

'Think I'd better leave you to it, and don't worry, nothing will happen to either of you, I promise you. Fraser is too busy scampering around, lining his pockets, with Jeffrey as his minder,' Jack said as he turned and ambled away.

The colt straining to be let out, Isaac raised the latch, quickly moving to one side as a streak of black bolted across the paddock, dust rising from beneath thumping hoofs, to where Lioness stood. Isaac watched anxiously, mindful that even if she was ready, she wouldn't make it easy, as the aroused colt worked his way round her flanks. Teeth bared, Lioness made to bite the colt, her hind legs keeping him at bay. The colt, undeterred, drew nearer Lioness, and she was suddenly still as the colt reared on his back legs and covered the now passive mare. The two horses joined, a small crowd looking on. Isaac forgot Jack and the rest of the world as the two locked, moving together. Finally spent, the colt dismounted and trotted off to the far side of the paddock shaking his mane. No idea what the outcome would be, Isaac picked up the fork and made to clear out the stables.

*

'No way of telling,' Isaac told Franny as they lay together that night. 'Be a couple of months before there will be any signs. I might have to let them together a few more times.'

'Seems like we will have to be patient.' Franny snuggled closer. 'Isaac, is there something else? You seem tense.'

'Jack was hanging around this morning, shooting his mouth off as usual.' Isaac told Franny about the conversation with Jack. 'Do you think I should tell someone?'

'I would leave well alone. He is doubtless all talk, and you can't risk being caught up in whatever he and those other two have going on. Anyhow, it is your word against his.'

'Suppose you are right.'

'Suppose I'm right. You know I am, Isaac Bone.' Franny sat up. 'Better get used to it if we are getting wed.'

'If? You mean you have changed your mind?'

Franny took out a piece of paper from her pocket. 'If you don't get this filled in, I might.'

'What is it?'

'An application for us to get married and best we do it soon. The new doctor has brought his wife and a maid with him – seems I'm no longer needed. I'll stay on till Doctor Wheeler leaves, but then who knows where I will end up. But it might be easier if we are married. You know, respectable like.'

Isaac looked at the square of paper, many of the words making no sense. 'We will get George to help us.' He reached out, pulling her close to him. 'Come here, Franny Oldfield.' Isaac pushed back a strand of hair from her face. 'Despite everything, at this moment, I think I'm the happiest man alive and I can't wait to marry you.'

SIXTY-THREE

'Why do we have to wait three weeks?' Isaac asked.

'Because the rules say the banns have to be read out for three Sundays, so we will just have to be patient.' Franny took Isaac's hand. 'It will soon pass. Not as if we can go anywhere.'

'More's the pity. Any news on finding a new position?'

'There is the laundry. But I don't fancy it much, all that steam and dampness in your lungs, not to mention what it does to your hands. I'm sure something will turn up, so quit brooding and get to it.'

Kissing Franny goodbye, Isaac picked up an assortment of tack and headed towards the workshop, hopeful that the newly arrived ships may have brought buckles and leather to repair the dwindling number of useful bridles, harnesses and reins. Arms aching, Isaac paused and set the load on the ground. The new tannery, built using the felled trees from the cleared fields, had replaced the old canvas shelter that was once used for a workshop. It had been erected on the outskirts of the colony, where a brick church was being built, alongside new marine quarters and an asylum. The convict crews were endlessly hauling, digging and lifting as the structures rose, the original colony growing rapidly.

Ready to move on, Isaac saw Fraser and Jack appear from the kitchen, a battered churn swinging between them, and head in the same direction he was planning to go. With half a mind to turn back to the stables, Isaac waited until they disappeared before continuing. All along the path, splotches of wet suggested the churn would be empty long before it reached its destination, and ravenous men would be disappointed. Haltingly, with no desire to run into both Jack and Fraser on their way back, Isaac saw the workshop come into view. The frames of the buildings had lifted higher since the last time Isaac had seen them, and groups of men, now at rest for rations, were using the towering timbers for shade, Jack and Fraser moving slowly among them.

Everyone eating in silence, a thunderous roar ripped through the calm, followed rapidly by the crash of shackles as Isaac saw Jeffrey knock away the men around him and head towards a startled-looking Fraser. Jeffrey bellowed like a bull, his face set hard, his enormous hands bunched as he thumped across the ground. Jack now stood to one side, a petrified-looking Fraser standing aghast, the spilt churn by his side, a space rapidly clearing around him. Standing face to face, Jeffrey towered over Fraser, who seemed unable to move. 'Dare to double-cross me, you little cockroach?' Jeffrey growled before swinging his shackled wrists round, a sicking crunch as they slammed in to Fraser's head.

Isaac winced as Jeffrey grasped the dazed Fraser by his neck, hauling him on to his knees.

'Where have you put them? Tell me now, before I beat you to a pulp.'

Fraser, blood pouring down his face, recoiled in fear, pleading to know what he had done.

'You dare ask?' Jeffrey lifted his foot, with the clank of metal as the shackles tightened, before stamping down hard.

Fraser let out a scream as his leg buckled, writhing in agony as Jeffrey raised his foot again, bringing his bulk with full force against Fraser's hip.

A rush of marines arrived with half a dozen rifles levelled at Jeffrey. Isaac heard the command to stand away.

Whether Jeffrey heard or ignored the command, he seemed in no mind to comply until a volley of shots rang out, causing Isaac to close his eyes and duck as the echo danced around the colony, momentarily drowning out Fraser's screaming.

When he opened his eyes, Jeffrey still stood tall beside a cowering Fraser. Bayonets fixed, a line of red advanced cautiously towards Jeffrey who took two defiant steps towards them.

'Get down on the ground.' The marines took a few steps forward.

'I said get down on the ground or I'll order my men to charge.'

Jeffrey remained standing, those around watching intently, uncertain what would happen next.

Jeffrey stood defiantly, the whisper of the breeze the only sound to break the tension.

When the order came, the onslaught of red-coated marines blurred as they covered the few yards towards Jeffrey. Polished bayonets flashed in the sunlight, bloody patches appearing around the rips in Jeffrey's clothing, who still refused to submit. Transfixed, Isaac watched a marine, a thick wooden club clutched tightly, step behind Jeffrey and bring the club with full force, halfway down the rooted legs of the giant, who dropped to his knees; a second blow, to the back of his head delivered full force, finally toppled Jeffrey face down onto the ground.

Seizing the moment, the marines piled in, pinning Jeffrey down, a rope bound around his wrists, a second rope securing his arms tightly against his side.

'Seems Fraser and Jeffrey's little enterprise might be at an end.'

Isaac heard Jack standing behind him. 'What do you know about it?'

'Plenty,' Jack said. 'But not here.'

'Why?'

'Like I said, not here.'

Isaac itched to tell Jack to leave him be. But part of him was curious. How would Jack know anything about what had just happened?

'Just you, not Fraser.'

'Don't think he will be in a fit state any time soon.'

Isaac looked across to where the overseer directed a group of convicts to carry Fraser to the infirmary, a piercing scream as they lifted him from the ground.

'See you later,' Jack said.

Isaac watched as Jack made his way to where the abandoned churn lay, picking it up by one handle, shaking his head at the expectant bowls held out towards him.

Stunned Isaac wondered what had caused Jeffrey to attack Fraser. Jack had said they were in league, but something had caused Jeffrey to turn on him. After the brutality of the beating, Isaac wondered if Fraser would survive, and Jeffrey… the marines had bayoneted him over and over. The hammering and sawing already back in full swing, Isaac continued to the workshop, life on the colony resuming its routine as if nothing had happened.

*

'He's coming here tonight? What were you thinking, Isaac?' Franny pursed her lips. 'He's nothing but trouble. Me and George have told you that enough times.'

Isaac was about to explain when a sharp tap on the door caused them both to jump.

'Too late now,' Isaac said as he stood and pulled the door open.

The day fading behind him, Jack stood with his hands in his pockets.

Pressed against the wall, Isaac waved Jack in, pointing at the stool, taking his place beside Franny, reaching for her hand.

Jack looked around. 'Nice place. Don't suppose you've got any rum?'

Isaac glared at Jack, who seemed not to notice.

'Thought not. So, you two are getting married?'

'You said you knew something about Jeffrey and Fraser?' Isaac interrupted.

'See we aren't bothering with pleasantries.' Jack pulled the stool closer. 'Now, where shall I start?' He rubbed his chin, obviously trying to rile Isaac.

'Get on with it.' Isaac felt Franny squeeze his hand.

Jack cleared his throat. 'Got a swig of water?'

Franny stood and poured water from the jug, handing the cup to the outstretched hand.

Jack took a sip, winking at Franny. 'Thanks.'

Isaac struggled to remain seated, enraged by the nerve of the smirking Jack.

'Remember I told you that sometimes knocking the hell out of someone isn't the only way to get even?' Jack took another sip from the cup, before placing the cup on the shelf. 'I figured out there must be a way to get closer, find out what they were up to, but with Jeffrey at his back, most kept well clear of Fraser. There was no way I was going to get anything out of Jeffrey, so I used a plug of bacca I lifted to get the overseer to reassign me to the kitchens. Reckoned Fraser would be an easier touch. He was wary at first, but you know old Jack, a bit of flattery and some kind words and soon he was singing like a bird. Seems Fraser worked out something was going on not long after he transferred here and beat it out of some poor wretch who Jeffrey had in his grasp since the hulks. Between them they relieved people of everything of worth and stashed it as best they could. Jeffrey was always being moved around and watched, so the other guy buried the stash, adding to it whenever they could. Fraser planted the seed in Jeffrey's head that his assistant was about to give him up to the commandant, said he had overheard him bragging he was going to sail away from here a free man.'

Isaac fidgeted on the cot, clutching Franny's hand tightly as Jack picked up the cup, draining the rest of the water before wiping his mouth with the back of his hand.

'Shall I go on, or you know the rest of it?'

Isaac bit his lip, nodding for Jack to continue.

'Fraser saw off the sidekick by telling him Jeffrey was suspicious someone was helping themselves to the bounty and the finger was pointing at him. First chance he got, he was gone, leaving the door open for Fraser to worm his way in. Don't know why, but Jeffrey seemed to trust Fraser and they carried on as before, lifting a bit here and there, adding to the pile. Deal was that when they got released they would divide it up and go their separate ways.'

Isaac jumped up. 'Why are you here, Jack? What's all this got to do with me? I don't care what Fraser and Jeffrey had going on, they deserved each other.'

'Sit down will you, or should I leave?'

Isaac felt Franny pull on his arm. 'Let's hear him out, then maybe we can forget all this.'

'Seems your girl has brains and beauty.' Jack gave a smile.

Isaac made to grab Jack, wanting him out of the shack.

'If you throw me out you'll never know the truth, but I'll go if you want me to.'

Isaac sat down. 'Get on with it.'

'Well, I said I wanted in. At first Fraser said no, but I palmed a few bright things and offered them to him. Then he began to talk about him being free before Jeffrey and how me and him could take the hoard and get away, pay a whaler to take us somewhere where they wouldn't find us, and that played right into my hand.'

SIXTY-FOUR

Franny gripped Isaac's hand. 'Go on.'

'It was child's play. After a few weeks I asked Fraser where he hid everything, told him I could put my bits and pieces there, save him the trouble. I didn't push it, then one night we were alone in the kitchen, finishing up after supper. I was doing the old pals act, making out I knew people who would see us right when we got back to England, talking sweet about how we would live like gentlemen. Then he showed me, right there under our very feet. He lifted the bricks – the kitchen is one of the few places with a brick floor – and then the planks, and there it was. First time I saw it I could hardly believe my eyes. There were gold pieces, coins, chains, all mixed in with rings, stones like the colours of the rainbow. There was so much there he could barely close the lid. I told him how clever it was – you should have seen him puff his chest out. Then two nights ago I crept in and moved the lot. Next day I gave him this little brooch I'd taken from the bottom of the tin, and he said he would put it with the others later that night. You should have seen the state he was in when he came back to bunk down for the night, sweating and shaking. Course, I acted all shocked, told Fraser I'd help him identify the culprit and that he should tell Jeffrey.'

'So, you stole the lot then, just what I would expect of you,' Isaac said.

'I just moved it, don't know what to do with it if I'm honest, but I took a leaf out of Fraser's book and whispered to Jeffrey at first bell that Fraser had told me he was planning to cut free. Made out I knew where he had moved it to. Said how I'd retrieve it for a share. Jeffrey must have festered all morning, but when me and Fraser went to take the lunch, that's when he erupted.'

'So that's why Jeffrey was so angry.'

'Yep, couldn't have hoped for it to have gone better. Fraser's out of action, Jeffrey will probably swing, you and this lass are rid of them both and I haven't done too bad either.'

'Typical of you to come out on top.'

Jack sat back. 'Like I said, I'm not sure what to do with it all now. I can hardly set up shop, and, given that few have a farthing to their name let alone a guinea, it's doubtful I would sell much. And I'm not keen on hanging on the frame while they flay the skin from me or stretch my neck.' Jack went quiet.

Isaac looked at Franny, then back at Jack. 'I still don't see what all this has to do with me.'

'Thought you'd be pleased. With those two out of the picture you won't have the chance to do something daft.'

'At least that is something,' Franny said.

'So it might be, but he's still not paid for what he did to me, just lined his pockets and thinks he can walk away again.' Isaac stared at Jack. 'Who was this man who you stole the horses for – how did he know we would be in the pub that night?'

'If I'm honest I don't know what his real name was – he used so many: Captain Henry Cavell, Albert Franklin, Right Honourable Frederick Herbert, although he was anything but honourable. I knew him as Henry. The one thing I can tell you is that he used this woman he'd once courted. I only met her once, thank goodness, sharp as a knife and no looker. He made her believe that he would come back for her, elope to France, when the dust had settled. Doubt he did though. She's probably still waiting – left high and dry like all the others he's left in his wake.

'I'm sorry, Isaac, I really am. You're not a bad person. Anyone can see that. Maybe back then you were wet behind the ears, but few deserve to finish up in a place like this. I'm no saint and have done things I'm ashamed of, but I was just getting by.' Jack stood up, fishing in his pocket. 'There is something else. I believe this belongs to you.'

Isaac stared at the tatty cloth, hesitating. His hands trembling, Isaac looked at Jack's, his fight gone, before taking the small package. At the hardness of the small item concealed in the cloth, Isaac held his breath, feeling the familiar bumps and holes of the most precious thing he had ever owned. A lonely tear ran down his cheek as he peeled back the ragged cloth, a glint of yellow metal winking out at him.

As his fingers ran over the cold brass, the nightmare of the last few years flowed from his body, his shoulders slumping as the sobs rose from deep within him. Unable to speak, he leant against Franny, the images of his father, of the Brecks, the try-out on the heath, the night on the ship crowding his head. Spent, he sat up.

'May I hold it?' Franny asked.

Isaac passed the brass across, placing it in the dainty palm.

'It's beautiful, Isaac, so beautiful.'

'I never thought I would see it again. Seems silly I know, but…'

Jack held out a hand. 'I wish you luck, Isaac, I mean that.'

Nudged in the ribs by Franny, Isaac shook the freckled hand. 'This woman, the one the man knew, what was her name?'

'As I say, I only met her once, but that was enough. Her name was Stokes, married to the man who ran the yard.'

Isaac leapt to his feet, knocking the shelf from the wall, its contents crashing to the floor. He shook the bemused-looking Jack.

'Mrs Stokes, Colonel Stokes' wife?'

'That's her. You know her?'

The blood pumping though his head, he pulled Jack close. 'That woman had it in for me since I was a boy back in the Brecks. You're telling me she was behind all this?'

'Isaac, let him go.'

Franny's hand on his shoulder, he dropped Jack back to the stool.

'Well, you know more than I do.'

Jack smoothed down his tunic. 'Henry, or whatever his name was, had a charm about him, reeling well-off women in with stories about how he lost his eye. Of course, it helped him cover up his fancy for slim young men but he and Mrs Stokes had met before, so he said. She not being a beauty, he flattered her, used her to fund his gambling, then her father found out her allowance was disappearing and stepped in and stopped them meeting.'

Isaac held his head in his hands. That day in Newmarket when he had run the errand to the butcher's, he had seen Mrs Stokes with a man, his eye just as Jack described. Surely it couldn't be the same one?

'Henry knew she had been married off and moved to Newmarket, so he just renewed his acquaintance with her, discreetly of course.'

Head still bowed, Isaac scrunched his brow, trying to make the pounding stop.

'You still don't get it, do you?' Jack reached out and rested his hand on Isaac's shoulder. 'You were a scapegoat, pure and simple. The day you ran into me, I mentioned to Henry that you were from Palace Stables. He must have planned it with Mrs Stokes as it was her who told us you and your friends would be in the inn that night. One of you would be blamed for the theft, leaving her and Henry in the clear till they could run off. Or that's what she thought. I was watching for my chance, and when your pals left... well, you know what happened.'

Isaac looked up, his whole body rigid with anger. 'I want you to leave. One day I'll find this Henry, but you,

I never want to see you again. Get out,' Isaac shouted, flinging open the door. 'Out, and don't even think of coming near me or Franny again.'

Jack stood and smiled. 'Sure, I've done my bit, told you all I know. Time for me to move on I reckon.'

The door shut behind him. Franny held out the brass, which filled her dainty hand.

Isaac took it and gripped it tight. For so long he had wondered what had happened, who was behind the theft of the horses. This morning he had only known part of what had happened back in Newmarket, fearful that Fraser would carry out his threats to hurt him and Franny. Now Fraser and Jeffrey were finished and Jack had told him everything. Suddenly he felt empty, the anger that had eaten away at him all this time replaced by an understanding that he would never return, never be able to clear his name, never see his beloved Brecks again. George and Franny were his family now and when the time came and he got his papers then he needed to make a new life here as best he could.

SIXTY-FIVE

Sitting with Franny, Isaac almost felt sorry for Jeffrey, his head bowed, a heavy yoke lashed to his outstretched arms, a wide iron rod stretching his ankle cuffs making him walk like a crab. Everybody had assumed he would hang, but instead he had been banished to Norfolk Island. It sounded curious that somewhere so far from home should have the same name as the county of his cherished Brecks, but everyone knew the brutality of the place, its location hundreds of miles from the colony ensuring that no convict committed there had ever escaped or returned.

'I never expected I'd see him like that,' Isaac said. 'He was a savage man, and his strength never seemed to fail him, but looks like they have finally broken him.'

The ship bobbed restlessly at the jetty, ready to depart as Jeffrey was led up the gangplank. What remained of his clothes were ragged and bloodstained; old gashes and wounds were surrounded by fresh mauve bruises; scabs covered his face. Out of sight for weeks, many of the colony had been pleased to forget about the man. Now, he was starved, bound and beaten, his public parade testimony that the authorities always win out.

'I'm glad he is going,' Franny said. 'It unnerved me just to look at him. I've never known a man like that before and hope I never will again. What about Fraser? Have you heard anything?'

'His leg and hip are shattered; he'll never walk again.'

Franny shuddered. 'Not much use for someone who can't work; he'll need to rely on others and I suspect he doesn't have many friends after his association with Jeffrey. So, is it over?'

'I hope so,' Isaac said. 'Seems like I've been watching over my shoulder for so long, a bit of peace would be welcome.'

They watched the ship edge away from the dock, its sails unfurled, eager to be free. When she was a mere speck on the horizon, they stood and made their way back to the stables.

'Mind if I stick around?' Franny asked. 'The doctor has given up the cottage to his replacement and moved into a room in the commandant's residence till he leaves. The new doctor brought his wife and a maid so there's not much for me to do these days.'

'Be nice,' Isaac smiled putting an arm around Franny's waist.

'Do you think she is with foal, Isaac?' Franny nodded towards Lioness. 'I was minded to think that she was rounder about the belly.'

'It's possible. We let the colt have his way a few times, and with the extra food the doctor traded she's as strong as she can be, although I'm still worried that when the time comes she won't have enough strength. Time will tell if it was a foolish idea.'

'So, you ready for tomorrow then?' Franny wrapped her arm around Isaac's waist.

'I wish we had somewhere to live other than the shack – it's so small. I promise, one day you will have somewhere better.'

'We will have each other, that's all that matters.'

They were interrupted by a hammering sound from across the parade ground: a notice being pinned to the post at the centre of the square.

'Probably informing us they are cutting rations, or some miserable soul is for a flogging, or worse, no doubt,' Isaac said.

'Shall we go and have look?'

'Let's go later – there's a crowd there already – we can get closer then.'

Franny busied herself cleaning the inside of the shack as Isaac brushed the dust from the horses' coats. The shack felt cosier now with Franny there all the time, and the endless dirt and dust that penetrated the gaps in the side certainly didn't get the chance to settle.

'Morning, Isaac.'

'Doctor Wheeler. Sorry, is it Franny you want? I could fetch her for you.'

'No, Isaac, I just came to see how Lioness was. Do you think she is carrying?'

'Franny has a notion she is swelling round the middle. It's possible, but another few weeks and we'll know for sure.'

'Fingers crossed.' The doctor leant on his stick. 'Isaac, have you looked at the notice?'

'Not yet. There was a crowd earlier and it will only be bad news.'

'Not everything is bad news,' the doctor said. 'Best you go have a look. Now if you will forgive me, I have some loose ends to tidy up before I leave.'

Curious, Isaac set the brush back in the box and clambered over the fence, forgetting about Franny. The corner held in his fingers, he read the summons. Those listed were ordered to report to the commandant's house when the end-of-work bell rang. Andrews, Apsley... Isaac traced his finger down the list. Bone – his own name stared back at him. What on earth could it mean? Norris, Nugent... surely he wasn't being sent to the new settlement or, worse, another colony. Separated from Franny? The doctor said it was nothing to worry about, but it must be something. Thompson, George was on the list. Surely they couldn't send him away from the infirmary, but then the new settlement would need someone who could treat the ills and ailments of its people, and there would be only one doctor after Doctor Wheeler had left.

How long till the bell would sound? Maybe he should tell Franny, but he didn't want to spoil the girl's happiness, and maybe if they were already married then she could come with them.

Franny emerged from the shack and Isaac waved, holding up the bucket and pointing to the stream. He could tell her later, make something up if it was bad news so they could still get wed tomorrow.

At the ding of the bell, Isaac joined the small group already gathered, all of them as bemused as he was. There was still no sign of George. He dragged his foot back and forth in the grainy soil as gradually a ragtag of fellow men and a few women arrived.

'Listen up.' The commandant's aide appeared on the veranda. 'When I say your name, I need you to line up in that order. No talking.'

Taking his time, the clerk's eyes flicked back and forth to the list as he called out the names, waiting for people to take their place in the line. There were half a dozen in front of Isaac. He glanced around to see George standing waiting. The final name called, the aide walked along the line, counting out loud.

'You will each pass in front of the commandant. Say nothing unless asked and listen to what he says carefully.' With that, he marched through the door, the name of the first convict bellowed from inside as the procession began.

SIXTY-SIX

Hands trembling, Isaac knew he hadn't got long to wait as the first two men stepped through the door. Summoned, he walked forward, the room now familiar to him.

'Name.'

'Isaac Bone, sir.'

The commandant held a sheet of paper in his hand. 'Age twenty. Sentenced to seven years for horse theft.'

'Yes, sir.' Isaac kept his head down, longing to get whatever it was they had summoned him for over with.

'Bone.' The commandant spoke in the same sharp way as the magistrates and judge had all those years ago.

The commandant peered at Isaac. 'Taking into account your time on the hulks, the boy's prison and the main colony you have now served over four years of your sentence. I see you have kept out of trouble since that episode with the Aboriginals and worked hard at the stables. Accordingly, you have been granted a Ticket of Leave. Do you understand?'

'Not really, sir.'

Isaac watched the commandant put down the piece of paper.

'You are a free man, but on condition that you continue to work in the colony until your full sentence has been served.'

'Free, sir?' As he had so many times in his life, he struggled to work out what was happening. Did that mean he wasn't a convict anymore?

'Bone, I understand you have worked hard in the stables, and it has been reported to me there has been a big improvement in the health of the horses and that we may soon have a new arrival. I would like to propose you continue those duties in return for a small government wage, and I have ordered a grant of two pounds for work already completed.'

Isaac could hardly believe what he was hearing. Two pounds. That was more money than he had ever had in his life. He could buy Franny a new dress, and George…

The commandant cut off his thoughts. 'You are free to leave.'

Ushered out through a side door, Isaac strode into the warmth, its touch like a velvet glove as it greeted his face. It could only have been a few minutes since he entered the commandant's office, but it felt as if he had emerged into a new world. A free man. He had to find Franny, tell her the news, but she was nowhere to be seen. All day he had waited, eager to break the news, but as the sky melted red across the horizon, there was still no sign of Franny. Thinking he would go to the doctor's, he heard a familiar voice call his name.

'Tom?' Isaac crushed his friend to him. 'What you doing here?'

'If you let me breathe, I'll tell you.'

Overjoyed to see Tom, Isaac blurted out his news. 'I'm a free man, Tom.'

'Me too. They sent word about a month ago, but the old boy I was assigned to was sick, and he was good to me, had no one else so I stayed. He passed away about a week ago, so I tidied up and thought I'd come and find you, hear what scrapes you had got yourself into.'

'Well, actually, me and Franny are getting wed.'

'Wed!' Tom seized Isaac's hand. 'That's wonderful news. When?'

'Tomorrow. Although I can't find her, or George, at the moment.'

'Best get a couple of cups then.' Tom pulled a bottle of liquor from his pocket. 'No use to the watch-mender, was it? Now we can use it to celebrate.'

'Make that three cups.'

'George, are you…?'

'Yes, Isaac, I'm a free man, just like you. Tom, nice to see you. How have you been?'

'I'm free as well. Looks like we have a lot to celebrate. Now, where's those cups?'

'I wish Franny was here,' Isaac said, 'I can't wait to tell her the news.'

'Afraid you will have to wait,' George said. 'She asked me to tell you she would see you tomorrow, some superstition about seeing the groom before the wedding.'

'Damn. Do you know where she is, George?'

'More than my life's worth. Now let's toast our freedom and the man of the moment.'

Drinks poured, Isaac and George took a large gulp. Throats burning and eyes stinging, they turned to Tom who was bent over with laughter.

'Sorry. They make this out of potatoes and anything else they can throw in. Wicked stuff, but you get used to it. Want some more?'

'Not sure,' Isaac said.

'One more won't hurt.' Tom topped up the cups.

'Not for me,' George said. 'These old bones need a lie-down, and that first glass sent everything spinning.'

Isaac and Tom drank till the bottle was empty, falling asleep against the shack, the moon bright and silvery in a cloudless sky. No longer convicts, the future was still likely to be tough, but at least now they were closer to choosing their own path.

SIXTY-SEVEN

Isaac's skull was pounding with the force of a blacksmith's hammer as he dunked his head in the bowl, trying to clear his thoughts. Outside the shack Tom lightly snored as Isaac tugged on the shirt Franny had washed and darned, threatening to do unmentionable things to him if she caught him mucking out the horses in it.

'Tom.' Isaac shook his friend, waiting until Tom came awake. 'We need to get a move on. Here, use the rest of the water to flatten your hair and tidy yourself up.'

'My brain hurts.' Tom held his head in his hands.

'Mine too.' Isaac vowed never to touch liquor again as he hauled Tom to his feet.

For a moment Tom looked bemused. 'Oh yes, someone's getting married.' He shook his head. 'Wonder who that is?'

'Not me if we don't get to the church double-quick.'

Tom and Isaac hastened across the colony to where the new church, with its towering spire, stood grandly against the hillside. Still no sign of Franny. Isaac felt Tom's elbow in his side.

'Maybe she's changed her mind. I'll take a peek inside.'

Tom disappeared as Isaac inhaled hard, struggling not to be sick.

'You look rough, Isaac.'

'Thanks, George. Do you know where Franny is?'

'Lady's prerogative to be late.'

Isaac turned to see Franny, her hair woven with a band of yellow flowers, a shawl of blue around her shoulders, walking towards him.

'Shall we go in?' Franny linked her arm through his and walked towards the door.

'You look… you look beautiful.'

A smile on her face, Franny looked at Isaac. 'And you look like you and Tom have been up all night. George warned me.'

'Sorry, I'm just not used to it.'

The door flew open, Tom beckoning them in. As they stood together, Isaac held Franny's hand, the words tumbling from the parson.

'Names.'

'Isaac Bone and Franny Oldfield.'

Satisfied, the parson took up the book, the words read so rapidly Isaac and Franny barely knew when to reply.

'I pronounce you man and wife.'

Isaac leant over and kissed Franny, the parson clearing his throat noisily before directing them to the small table. Astonished, Isaac watched Franny step forward and sign with a flourish.

'I thought you couldn't write. You said you couldn't.'

'Mine and George's secret, he's been teaching me my letters and how to write.'

Outside, George wrapped his arms around them both. 'Mr and Mrs Bone, don't you make a lovely couple. Nothing could make me happier than to see you wed.'

'Can I kiss your wife?' Tom darted forward, pecking Franny on the cheek. 'Have you told her yet? Tell her, go on, tell her now.'

Isaac looked at George and then back at Tom. 'You mean you haven't told her?'

'Not our place to,' George said.

'Told me what? Why are you talking in riddles?' Franny asked.

'I'm a free man. So are Tom and George. We are all free.'

'When did you find out?'

'Yesterday, but I couldn't find you.'

'I was on board ship, helping Doctor Wheeler get unpacked ready to sail. Then I went to the women's camp.'

'So, the doctor is really going? He's already on board?'

'Ah, but you can get off a ship,' a warm voice said from behind.

Still holding hands, they turned to see Doctor Wheeler, holding a stout new cane, the top shiny with silver.

'So you are leaving?'

'I am, but before I go, I need to talk to you. Shall we all sit down? I find it troublesome to stand for too long. Your friend too.'

Finding a spot away from the heat, they settled, the doctor perched on a discarded barrel.

'As you know, I am returning to England, and to my wife to start over. This place is done with me and I with it, but I believe there is good here and that those with the right ways will succeed. Isaac, I once told you of my son and how you reminded me of him. From the first day when I met you, I felt you had a good heart and nothing has altered that. You saved Lioness, and I will forever be grateful for your and Yarran's courage in rescuing me. Franny, you have looked after me and kept house for many years. You have always gone about your work without complaint, and your smile and cheery ways have made everything a little more bearable. George, you have helped me in the infirmary, and your knowledge of herbs and remedies has saved many an ailing soul. You recognise the Aboriginals' ways and have been a loyal and able assistant.'

Isaac went to speak but the doctor held up his hand.

'As you know, Franny was helping me yesterday to get my belongings ferried and stored in my cabin as the ship sails within the week. The only thing I can't take is Lioness. That's why I have decided that I am giving her to you.' The doctor looked at Isaac.

'You mean to look after?'

'No, I am giving her to you, she is yours.'

He could hardly believe it. He cherished Lioness, but to think that she was his was beyond his wildest dreams. All these years he had cared for horses that belonged to others, but now he had his own.

'How will I pay for her keep though?'

Isaac watched George look at the doctor, a knowing smile giving away a secret between them.

'I know that you and George are free men, and I assume this young fellow is as well.'

'Doctor,' Franny said. 'Isaac and I don't even have anywhere to live, and Tom needs a job, and it's very kind, but we don't have the means to keep Lioness.'

'That is all taken care of. One of my fellow passengers is a man who has, or should I say had, a small parcel of land close by with a two-room cottage on it. He is returning to England, having made enough for his fare, and I have acquired it from him. It now belongs to you and Isaac; consider it a wedding present. There is enough space for Lioness if you carry on working at the stables, and with the two pounds you have, you should get by.'

'I don't know what to say. Doctor Wheeler, how can I ever repay you?'

'It is I who am repaying you, Isaac – I and Lioness. Look after her, and you all look after each other. Now I must leave you as I have a few more things to do and I am expected to dine with the commandant tonight.'

Tipping his hat, the doctor pushed on his cane, standing upright.

'It comforts me to know Lioness is in good hands and that there is hope for the future for us all. I shall think of you all often, as I hope you will think of me. Farewell, my friends.'

EPILOGUE

September 1844

'Isaac, where are you?'

Isaac laughed to himself, rubbing the neck of the grazing Lioness. 'I was just checking on the foal. He's a fine, strong young thing, soon be old enough to think about breaking him in.'

'Quit your babbling and grab hold of this. I need to get the laundry out.'

Isaac took the end of the cord from Franny, looping it around the post. The little patch of earth had proved better than they could have wished for. Enriched with manure from Lioness and the foal, plus a supply of water from the nearby stream, tender shoots had risen and blossomed, more than sufficient to feed them all. Tom had decided not to go back to the new settlement and readily agreed to join Isaac at the stables. The joy in his eyes when Edmund had turned up a few days after the wedding had moved them all to tears.

When they had left the shack at the stables, Franny had insisted that Isaac and the two brothers clear their new home until it was thoroughly clean, before directing them to rearrange the furniture that remained until she was satisfied.

'Stop daydreaming, Isaac, and stretch it tight otherwise the clothes will drag in the dirt.' Franny put her hands on her hips and frowned.

George had continued at the infirmary, the new doctor taking charge when Doctor Wheeler had left, but somehow it wasn't the same. His advancing years had started to tell, the discomfort on his face when he went to stand, the slowness of his movements, all beginning to show. Worried, Franny and Isaac had persuaded him to join them, to resume his old line of work. With a modest addition to the cottage, George set up a consulting room where he mixed and dispensed potions and medicine to the ever-developing colony. Unable to walk long distances, George had shown Edmund pictures from a dogeared booklet, and the boy showed a keen interest, bringing back the leaves, roots and bark George needed. Before long, Edmund was mastering how to mix the potions, proposing they clear a small patch to cultivate their own plants to keep up with demand from the continuous stream of callers.

'Is he awake?'

'No, Isaac, he's sleeping.' Franny wagged a finger at Isaac. 'Don't you dare go rousing him – took me an age to settle him down.'

'Just a little look. I won't wake him, I promise.'

As he crept into the room and peeped into the cot, the tiny hands clenched as a dream caused the baby to wriggle.

Franny had delivered their son just over nine months into their marriage, a surprise for everyone but a sheer delight. Tenderly, he reached down and smoothed the wild black hair, breathing in the smell of the sleeping baby.

As he felt in his pocket, the curves of the brass brushed his fingers – memories of his family, the Brecks, happy times at the hall and at the stables. Images so clear he could barely credit so many years had passed. He wondered what happened to Jack after he had returned it to him. Just as promised, he had never troubled them again, disappearing without a trace. George thought it likely he had bought his freedom with Jeffrey's stash and sailed away on a whaler or the like. Wherever he was, Isaac was sure he would survive.

Wary not to wake his son, Isaac reached out and slid the brass under the pillow, a sense of someone standing behind him. A soft breeze of refreshing air against his neck, he stood up, the room tranquil and empty around him. As he tiptoed to the door, he wondered what the world held next for him, his family and friends, in this strange new place. Content, he took one more look at the sleeping infant, now the most precious thing in his life, and pulled the door closed behind him.